SEP - - 2014

P9-DEU-482

WITHDRAWN

CIRCLE
OF
FIRE

WITHDRAWN

 ALSO BY
MICHELLE ZINK:

Prophecy of the Sisters

Guardian of the Gate

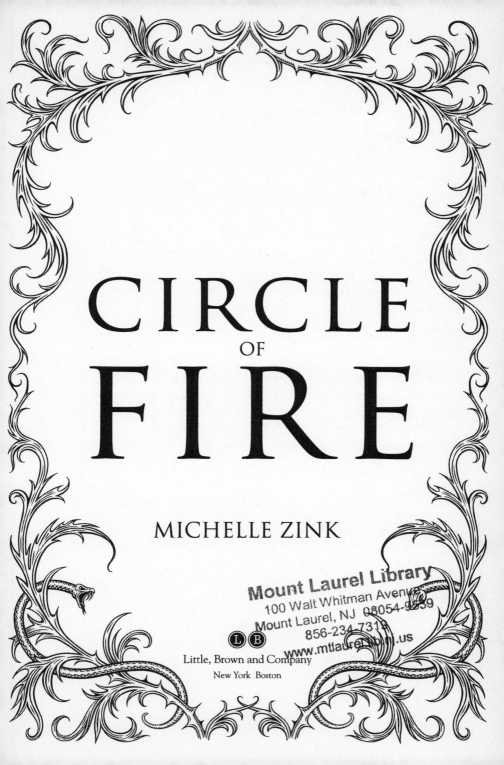

CIRCLE
OF
FIRE

MICHELLE ZINK

Mount Laurel Library
100 Walt Whitman Avenue
Mount Laurel, NJ 08054-9539
856-234-7319
www.mtlaurel.lib.nj.us

LB
Little, Brown and Company
New York Boston

This book is a work of fiction. Names, characters, places, and incidents are the product of the author's imagination or are used fictitiously. Any resemblance to actual events, locales, or persons, living or dead, is coincidental.

Copyright © 2011 by Michelle Zink
Hand-lettering and interior ornamentation by Leah Palmer Preiss

All rights reserved. In accordance with the U.S. Copyright Act of 1976, the scanning, uploading, and electronic sharing of any part of this book without the permission of the publisher is unlawful piracy and theft of the author's intellectual property. If you would like to use material from the book (other than for review purposes), prior written permission must be obtained by contacting the publisher at permissions@hbgusa.com. Thank you for your support of the author's rights.

Little, Brown and Company

Hachette Book Group
237 Park Avenue, New York, NY 10017
Visit our website at www.lb-teens.com

Little, Brown and Company is a division of Hachette Book Group, Inc.
The Little, Brown name and logo are trademarks of Hachette Book Group, Inc.

The publisher is not responsible for websites (or their content) that are not owned by the publisher.

First Paperback Edition: July 2012
First published in hardcover in August 2011 by Little, Brown and Company

Library of Congress Cataloging-in-Publication Data

Zink, Michelle.
  Circle of fire / Michelle Zink. — 1st ed.
    p. cm.
  Sequel to: Guardian of the Gate.
  Summary: With time dwindling but her will to end the prophecy stronger than ever, Lia sets out on a journey to find the remaining keys, locate the missing pages of the prophecy, and convince her twin sister Alice to help — or risk her life trying.
  ISBN 978-0-316-02737-3 (hc) / ISBN 978-0-316-03446-3 (pb)
  [1. Supernatural—Fiction. 2. Sisters—Fiction. 3. Twins—Fiction. 4. Magic—Fiction. 5. Good and evil—Fiction.] I. Title.
PZ7.Z652Ci 2011
[Fic]—dc22

                                                                                          2010038305

10 9 8 7 6 5 4 3 2 1

Book design by Alison Impey

RRD-C

Printed in the United States of America

To my father,
Michael St. James,
for all the lovely darkness

1

The gowns are heavy in my arms as I leave my chamber. There are no windows to gather light, and I make my way carefully down the richly papered hallway by the light of the sconces flickering along the wall. Milthorpe Manor has been in my family for generations, but it is still not as familiar as Birchwood, the home in New York where I was born and raised.

Even still, this house does not harbor the ghosts of the past. Here, I do not have to remember my younger brother, Henry, as he was before his death. I do not have to wonder if I will hear my twin sister, Alice, whispering from the Dark Room as she conjures frightful, forbidden things. If I will see her, prowling the halls, at any hour of the day or night.

Not in the flesh, in any case.

It is Aunt Virginia's idea that I should seek advice from Sonia and Luisa regarding which gown to wear to tonight's

Masquerade. I know my aunt is trying to help, but it is a testament to the changed nature of my friendship with both girls that I now must brace myself to be in their presence. Or, more accurately, in the presence of Sonia. Although she and Luisa returned from Altus weeks ago, the tension felt in the early days of their return has not abated. In fact, it seems to grow with each passing day. I have tried to forgive Sonia her betrayal in the wood leading to Altus. Am *still* trying to forgive it. But every time I look into the chill blue of her eyes, I remember.

I remember waking, Sonia's kind face above me, her warm hands pressing the hated medallion to the soft skin at the underside of my wrist. I remember her voice, familiar from many months of shared confidences, feverishly whispering the words of the Souls who would use me as their Gate to bring forth Samael.

I remember it all and feel my heart harden just a little more.

The Society's Masquerade is one of the year's most celebrated events. Sonia, Luisa, and I have been anticipating the event since they returned from Altus, but while they quickly settled on costumes, I have remained indecisive.

My mask, chosen and created long ago, was not difficult. I knew immediately what it would look like, though I have never attended a Masquerade and make no claim of creativity in matters of fashion. Nevertheless, it came to me as easily and clearly as if I had seen it in a store window. I commissioned it shortly thereafter by describing it to the seamstress and watching her sketch it on a thin piece of parchment until it looked just as I imagined it.

But while I set upon the idea for a mask quite easily, my indecisiveness forced me to give up the possibility of having a gown made. Instead, I chose two from those already hanging in my wardrobe. As Aunt Virginia suggested, I will ask Sonia and Luisa for assistance in deciding, but while it was once a ritual of friendship I would have relished, now I only dread it. Now I will have to look into Sonia's eyes.

And I will have to lie and lie and lie.

Arriving at the door of Luisa's room, I lift my hand to knock but hesitate when I hear the raised voices coming from within. I place one of them as Sonia's and hear my name spoken in frustration. Leaning in, I do not even pretend that I'm not going to listen.

"*There is nothing more I can do. I have apologized over and over. I have submitted without complaint to the rites of the Sisters on Altus. Lia will not forgive me, whatever I do. And I'm beginning to believe that she never will,*" Sonia says.

The rustle of fabric is followed by the thud of wardrobe doors before I hear Luisa respond. "*Nonsense. Perhaps you might try to spend time alone with her. Have you asked her to ride with you at Whitney Grove?*"

"*More than once, but she always has an excuse. We haven't been since before you arrived from New York. Before Altus. Before . . . everything.*"

I cannot tell if Sonia is angry or only sad, and I feel a moment's guilt as I think of the many times she has asked me to Whitney Grove. I have denied her even as I have gone alone to practice with my bow.

"You simply must give her time, that's all." Luisa is matter-of-fact. *"She bears the weight of the medallion now—in addition to the burden of decoding the final page of the prophecy."*

I look down at my wrist, peeking out from the yards of silk and lace. The strip of black velvet taunts me from beneath the sleeve of my gown. It is Sonia's fault that I must bear the medallion alone. Her fault that I must worry it will make its way to the mark of the Jorgumand, the snake eating its own tail with a "C" in its center, on my other wrist.

No matter how many excuses Luisa makes for Sonia, these things will always be true.

My inability to forgive brings with it a powerful blend of resentment and despair.

"Well, I'm getting tired of pandering to her better nature. We are partners in the prophecy. All of us. She is not the only one who feels its burden." The indignation in Sonia's voice stokes the fire of my anger. As if *she* has any right to feel indignant. As if forgiving her should be that easy.

Luisa sighs so loudly that I hear it from the hall. *"Let's try to enjoy the Masquerade, shall we? Helene will arrive in two days. This is our last night to be friends as we once were."*

"I am not the problem," Sonia mutters from within the room. A rush of blood heats my cheeks, and I attempt to check my temper before raising my hand to knock on the large wooden door.

"It's me," I call, trying to smooth the tremor in my voice.

The door swings open and Luisa stands in its frame, her

4

dark hair lit with burgundy from the lamplight and fire in the room.

"There you are!" Her cheerfulness sounds forced, and I imagine her trying to push aside the conversation she has just had with Sonia. For one irrational moment, I feel that she is complicit in Sonia's betrayal. Then I remember Luisa's loyalty and the pain she must feel standing between Sonia and me. My petulance dissipates, and all at once I am surprised to find that it is not so difficult to smile.

"Here I am. And I've brought two gowns for inspection."

Luisa's eyes drop to the armful of fabric in my hands. "I can already see why you cannot make up your mind. They're both beautiful! Come." She steps back, allowing me entrance.

Sonia's eyes meet mine as I enter the room. "Good morning, Lia."

"Good morning." I try to feel the smile I give her as I cross to the carved mahogany bed at the center of the room. The shyness around my dearest friend is new, for once we spoke of everything and nothing. Once, it was Sonia and I together in London while Luisa remained in New York with Aunt Virginia and Edmund, our family driver and trusted friend. Recalling the many days Sonia and I spent riding at Whitney Grove, speaking of our hoped-for futures and laughing over the too-proper girls of London society, is one of the many ways I try to remember my love for her. "I come bearing dresses!"

She approaches the bed as I lay the gowns across the coverlet. "They're gorgeous!"

5

I stand back, eyeing the two dresses critically. One is crimson, a daring choice for any young lady, but the other, a deep emerald, would set my eyes off nicely. It is impossible not to think of Dimitri when I imagine myself in either of them.

As if reading my mind, Luisa says, "Dimitri will not be able to take his eyes off you, Lia, whichever gown you choose."

My spirits lift ever so slightly as I think of Dimitri's eyes, dark with desire. "Yes, well, that *is* the idea, I suppose."

Sonia leans over, fingering the fabric, and for the next thirty minutes we speak of nothing but dresses and masks until I finally decide upon the scarlet silk. For the next thirty minutes we pretend that all is as it used to be and that the workings of the prophecy do not stand between us. We pretend because it will do no good to say aloud the thing we all know — that nothing will ever be the same again.

I sit at the dressing table in my room, clad only in a chemise and stockings as I prepare for the Masquerade.

It is with some scandal among the household staff that I have shirked the use of corsets and maids since my return from Altus nearly three months ago. It was not my intention to shun the trappings of modern fashion. For a time, I allowed a maid to help me dress for formal occasions, as is proper for a young lady of my stature. I stood silent and resentful as I was bound and laced into a corset, my feet shoved into elaborate shoes that pinched until I had to fight the urge to throw them across the room.

But it was no use.

I could think only of Altus silk, a whisper against my bare skin, and the luxurious freedom of bare feet or sandals.

Finally, after a particularly long night socializing with the spiritualists, Druids, and psychics of the Society, I came home to Milthorpe Manor and announced my intention to dress myself from that moment forward. There were only token protests. Everyone had already noted the changes in me. Nothing I did came as a surprise, and the staff seemed resigned to having an eccentric mistress.

I reach for a pot of powder, gazing into the mirror as I sweep the fine particles across my forehead, my cheeks, my chin. The young woman staring back at me is hardly recognizable as the girl who first came to London. The girl who fled her home, her sister, the man she loved.

And yet, it is this new person who seems most familiar. Her emerald eyes flash like those of my dead mother, the angular cheekbones pronounced as if to remind me of the sacrifices I have made on behalf of the prophecy.

It is no wonder the round-faced girl who first came to London is nothing but a memory.

The dull sheen of Aunt Abigail's adder stone catches my eye in the mirror. I reach up, closing my fingers around the rock and wondering if it is my imagination that it is only warm.

It has become a daily ritual — testing the temperature of the powerful stone given to me by Aunt Abigail — for even as my own strength has grown, I remain convinced that little else stands between the Souls and me. Aunt Abigail gave her life

for my protection, imbuing the stone with every ounce of her remaining power as Lady of Altus. When the stone's heat is finally gone, any protection received from it will be gone as well.

And it grows colder by the day.

I turn away from the mirror. There is no point thinking about the things over which I have no control. Instead, I pace the room as I contemplate the mystery of the prophecy's final page. The page itself, found in the sacred cavern at Chartres, is gone forever, burned to ensure it never falls into the hands of Samael or his Lost Souls. Even still, the words inscribed on it are a mantra I never forget. A reminder that there is still the possibility of a future in which the prophecy does not stalk my hopes and dreams.

I remember it almost without consciousness, reciting the words in my mind as I ponder their meaning.

Yet from chaos and madness One will rise,
To lead the Ancient and release the Stone,
Shrouded in the sanctity of the Sisterhood,
Held safe from the Beast, and
Setting free those bound by Prophecy's
Past and impending doom.
Sacred Stone, released from the temple,
Sliabh na Cailli',
Portal to the Otherworlds.
Sisters of Chaos
Return to the belly of the Serpent

At the close of Nos Galon-Mai.
There, in the Circle of Fire
Lit by the Stone, bring together
Four Keys, marked by the Dragon
Angel of Chaos, mark and medallion
The Beast, banished only through
Sisterhood at Guardian's door
With the rite of the Fallen.
Open your arms, Mistress of Chaos
To usher in the havoc of the ages
Or close them and
Deny His thirst for eternity.

There are things we know. That I am the one called to find the Stone once hidden by the Sisters of Altus. By my ancestors. That freeing those bound by the prophecy means freeing myself as well as the keys—Sonia, Luisa, and, now, Helene. That it means freeing future generations of Sisters and liberating mankind from the dark chaos that would ensue should Samael arrive in our world.

And that Alice is working even now to prevent that liberation.

But it is the location of the Stone that Dimitri and I cannot seem to decipher, and I must have it to complete the Rite at Avebury. We have so far assumed that "shrouded in the sanctity of the Sisterhood" means it is hidden at a site deemed spiritually significant. It is possible we are wrong, but since the final page of the prophecy was buried in the cavern at

Chartres—one that also housed an underground temple revered by Sisters past—it seems the best of all assumptions.

The mantel clock chimes seven times, and I cross to the wardrobe, removing the scarlet gown from its depths as I continue thinking about the possible locations we have eliminated and the nine that are left. Pulling the gown over my head while I try not to disrupt my pinned hair, I chafe against the frustration that we cannot entirely discount even those sites we have crossed off the list. We have been looking for a place deemed important by our ancestors—one that can be linked to the history of our people or the prophecy. But we have only our research on which to base our conclusions. The smallest piece of forgotten history could change everything.

And there is something else that stands in the way of our deciphering the final page.

Return to the belly of the Serpent at the close of Nos Galon-Mai.

It is clear from Avebury's previous significance that the belly of the serpent is there, but we have been unable to find reference to the eve on which we are supposed to gather to close the gate to Samael. I had hoped to find it in one of Father's many reference books, but we have searched every book in the house and scoured the bookshops of London to no avail.

A knock at the door causes me to start.

"Yes?" I call out, looking for the shoes I had custom-made to be both comfortable and passably fashionable.

"Edmund is ready with the carriage," Aunt Virginia says through the door. "Do you need help dressing?"

"No. I'll be down in a minute."

I am relieved when she doesn't force the issue. Dropping onto the bed amid a rustle of silk, I spot my shoes peeking from under the mattress. I spend only a moment wishing for the comfort of bare feet before slipping into the little heels.

It could be worse. And there are some things even I cannot change.

2

I am in the carriage on the way to the Masquerade when I think I see her.

We are making our way through the streets of London, Sonia and Luisa sitting across from me as we clutch our masks. The lush fabric of our gowns fills the carriage, Sonia's deep blue rustling against Luisa's plum-colored silk. I look down at my own crimson skirt, feeling strangely unmoved by my decision to wear it. A year ago I would have chosen the emerald in an instant. I tell myself the scarlet gown was the only suitable choice for the mask I had commissioned before I began considering dresses, but I know it is only half true.

The red gown is more than a simple match for the mask. It is a mirror to my own feelings of power since Chartres. Since fighting off one of Samael's deadliest minions, one of his Guard.

I wonder how I can revel in that power even as I am uncertain it will be enough to face the future.

This is what I am thinking as I turn my gaze out the curtained window to the bustling streets. Darkness stalks the city, seeping from its corners toward the center of town. London's many citizens must sense its presence, for they seem to hurry ever faster as they make their way to their homes and places of work. It is as if they feel its breath on their neck. As if they feel it coming for them.

I am shaking this dark notion from my mind when I see a young woman standing under the gaslight near a busy corner. Her hair is arranged in a style that would be considered elaborate, even by Alice's standards, and her face is leaner than I remember my sister's. Still, I have not seen her in person for some time, and every morning I am faced with my own changing reflection.

I lean forward in my seat, uncertain if it is fear, anger, or love that gallops through my veins as I hope for a better view of the woman. I am half-ready to call her name when she turns slightly toward the carriage. She does not face me. Not entirely. But she turns enough so that I see her profile. Enough so that I am quite sure it is not Alice after all.

She turns to make her way down the street, disappearing into the smoke from the street lamps. I press myself back against the carriage seat, not knowing whether it is relief or disappointment that presses against my heart.

"Lia? Are you all right?" Luisa asks.

I steady my voice, aware that my pulse is racing. "Fine, thank you."

She nods, and I attempt a smile in the moment before closing my eyes, trying to calm my quickened breath.

It was only your imagination, I tell myself. *You have too long
been sought by Alice and the Souls. You see them on every corner,
every street.*

I wish suddenly that Dimitri was next to me, his muscular
thigh pressed against mine, his hand caressing my fingers
beneath the folds of my gown. Yet, even as I wish it, I force my
breathing to slow, my mind to clear. It is unwise to rely too
heavily on others.

Even Dimitri.

As Edmund pulls the carriage up to St. Johns, I cannot help
but marvel how normal everyone looks. Of course, the members of the Society *are* normal in many respects, but even still,
I have never seen so many of us in one place at one time. I
almost expect there to be a glow, a hum, something to mark
the sheer number of those with supernatural powers in
attendance.

But no. It looks like any gathering of London's wealthy and
overdressed.

"How on earth did Elspeth manage a church?" Sonia's voice
is very near my ear, and I realize that we have all leaned forward, craning our necks at the window in an effort to get a
better view of the men and women stepping from carriages and
making their way up the stone walkway.

"I have no idea how Elspeth manages half the things she

does!" Luisa laughs aloud, that dear, unselfconscious laugh that brings to mind the birth of our friendship more than a year ago.

"I must confess that I asked no questions about the Masquerade's venue, but now I find I'm quite curious," I say. "Surely the Queen would be displeased to find a gathering of such heathens at one of London's churches."

Sonia makes a "Psh!" sound before continuing. "Byron told me many concerts and balls are held at St. Johns."

Her words are delivered with such calm that it takes me a moment to register what she has said. It must take Luisa the same moment, for at once, we both turn to Sonia.

"Byron!"

She blushes, and I am surprised to find that after all that has happened, Sonia can still blush at the mention of a gentleman.

"I saw him at the Society after we returned from Altus." Her gaze cuts to Luisa. "He's the one who first told me about the Masquerade."

A burst of cold air assaults the interior of the carriage as Edmund, very dapper in formal attire, opens the door. "Ladies."

Shivering, Luisa pulls her wrap tight around her shoulders. "Let's go, shall we? It seems Dimitri isn't the only gentleman eagerly awaiting our arrival!"

It is easy to offer her a smile. No one but Luisa could be so gracious as to wish Sonia and me well when she has left her own beau in Altus.

The thought of the island is a warm breeze across my heart — a series of lightning-fast impressions. The smell of oranges,

waves crashing against the rocks below the Sanctuary, silk robes against naked skin.

I shake my head, willing myself toward the one person who brings me closest to all of it, though I am worlds away.

We don our masks in the carriage before stepping from its warmth and making our way to the cavernous hall. Slipping through the crowd packed at its periphery, I cannot help but feel I am in a strange kind of sideshow. The costumed faces of those around me seem suddenly garish, my own mask too snug against my face. The masks make conversation difficult, and I am relieved when a man, tall and thin as a rail, removes his disguise to reveal himself as Byron. He bows, taking Sonia's hand, and she smiles shyly as they move to the dance floor. A moment later Luisa departs with a fair-haired gentleman who cannot take his eyes off her. I watch my friends sparkle under the adoring gazes of the men twirling them across the floor and can hardly fathom that we are the same three girls who met in New York not so long ago.

I am considering the merit of making my way to the refreshments when I notice a man standing amid the crowd some distance away. I know it is Dimitri, though we agreed to keep our masks a secret from each other until tonight. It is his shoulders, I think, and the way he holds his body, as if ready to defend himself—and me—that make me certain it is him.

He turns, his eyes holding my gaze in the moment before he begins striding through the crowd with single-minded purpose.

His mask is exquisite, large and adorned with onyx stones set amid shimmering silver glitter and deep red feathers.

As if he knew I would choose the scarlet gown all along.

When he reaches me he takes my hand, but he does not bend to kiss it. Dimitri does not pretend to follow London's rules. His big hand enfolds my smaller one, and he pulls me close until I feel the hard plane of his body. He stares deeply into my eyes in the moment before he lowers his mouth to mine. His kiss is passionate and lingering, and without thinking, I bring my hand up to touch the dark hair curling at his neck. We part reluctantly, some of the people closest to us raising their eyebrows before turning back to their own business.

He leans toward my ear, his voice a secret meant just for me. "You look ravishing."

"Why, sir, how very forward of you!" Lifting my chin to look in his eyes, I bat my eyelashes, pretending to be coy. I give up, laughing, a moment later. "How could you be sure it was me?"

"I might ask you the same thing." He favors me with a grin. "Or am I to assume that you gawk at every gentleman in a feathered, bejeweled mask?"

"Never." My voice becomes serious. "I only have eyes for you."

Dimitri's eyes darken. I recognize the expression as desire from the many hours spent locked in each other's arms since our return from Altus.

"Come." He holds out a hand. "Let's dance. It won't be quite as it was on Altus, but if we close our eyes, we might pretend."

He pulls me through the crowd, carving a pathway with his

mere presence. As we near the dance floor, Sonia whirls past in Byron's arms. She looks happy, and in this moment I do not begrudge her the enjoyment.

"Good evening, Miss Milthorpe. I heard you might be in need of a particular kind of expertise." The voice, coming from just behind me, is not loud, but it gets my attention nonetheless.

Tugging on Dimitri's arm, I stop my forward progress through the crowd and turn to the man standing amid the revelers. He is aged, as evidenced by his white hair and the wrinkles that fold across his hands. His mask is black and green and surrounded by peacock feathers, but it is the midnight blue robe that gives him away, for he is fond of wearing it even at the more intimate gatherings of the Society.

"Arthur!" I smile as I recognize the elderly Druid. "However did you recognize me?"

"Ah, Miss. My senses are not what they once were, but I'm still a Druid, through and through. Even the extravagance of your costume could not hide your identity."

"You are wise, indeed!" I turn to Dimitri, trying to speak above the crowd without shouting. "I imagine you're acquainted with Mr. Frobisher, from the Society?"

Dimitri nods, holding out a hand. "We've met on several occasions. Arthur has been most welcoming since I've taken a room there."

Arthur shakes Dimitri's hand, admiration shining in his eyes. He speaks softly, leaning in to be heard. "It is always an honor to extend hospitality to the Brotherhood."

The introductions dispensed with, I remember Arthur's earlier words. "You mentioned expertise?"

He nods, pulling something from his pocket and holding it out toward me. "There is word underground that you are looking for information. This is an address for some acquaintances of mine. They might be able to assist you."

I reach out, feeling the smooth, crackly surface of folded parchment as it is placed in my palm.

"Arthur, who told you about our need for information?" Worry shades Dimitri's eyes. "Our inquiries are supposed to be kept in the strictest confidence."

Arthur nods, leaning in again as he clasps Dimitri's shoulder with a reassuring hand. "Not to worry, Brother. Word travels slow and careful in these circles." He straightens, gesturing to the parchment in my hands. "Call on them. They'll be expecting you."

Turning to go, he disappears into the crowd without another word. I would like to open the paper now, to see who might be the keeper of the answers we seek, but the name and address will be impossible to read while I am being jostled about at the Masquerade. Dimitri watches me as I fold the paper twice more before opening the drawstring bag that swings at my wrist. I set the paper amid the silk lining and tug the ribbons shut.

Its presence steals the lightheartedness I felt only moments ago. It is a reminder that there is still much to do. That no Masquerade, no ball, no dark-eyed man can render me free of the prophecy. That is something only I can do.

As if sensing my worry, Dimitri reaches for my hand once

again. "There will be time enough for that tomorrow." His eyes hold mine. "Come. Let's dance."

I let him lead me forward, to the center of the great room, where he does not hesitate before pulling me onto the dance floor. There is no room for worry as we spin among the brightly colored gowns, the feathers and jewels of the masks passing in a blur. Dimitri's strong hand is at my waist, and I give myself over to his lead, relieved to allow someone else to be in charge, if only for a dance.

The music builds to a crescendo and then turns into something else entirely. This time, I am the one tugging on Dimitri's hands, pulling him off the dance floor.

I speak close to his ear. "Let's get something to drink, shall we?"

He nods, grinning. "Have I made you thirsty, my Lady?"

I raise my eyebrows. "You might say that."

He throws his head back and laughs. I hear the echo of it even over the music and conversation in the hall.

We are making our way through the crowd toward the refreshments when a flash of cheekbone catches my eye. Angular and feminine, it rises to eyes so green I see them flash from across the room. I should not feel the jolt of recognition. Not from so far away. Not for someone whose face is almost entirely masked by swirling gold glitter and purple jewels.

And yet, I am almost certain, and I begin moving in her direction without so much as a word to Dimitri.

"Lia? Where are you—" I hear his voice calling out behind me, but my feet move of their own accord without care for

anything but the woman standing in an uncannily familiar manner just a few feet away.

I grab for her arm when I reach her, not even considering that I may be wrong.

She does not seem surprised. Indeed, she does not bother to look down at my hand, encircling her thin upper arm. No. She turns slowly toward me, as if my finding her is no surprise at all.

I know before she has fully turned. I see it in the proud line of her chin. The challenging flash of her eyes.

"Alice." I breathe her name. It is not a question. I have seen her in the Otherworlds, and in my own. I have seen her spirit presence during the months when her power grew strong enough to allow her passage from one world to the other. I slept beside her as a child and listened to her soft breath in the night. Even beneath the mask, I am certain it is Alice.

Her smile is slow and unsurprised. My sister has always enjoyed the subtle brand of power that comes from knowing things before others. And yet, there is something else there, too. Something guarded and indefinable.

"Good evening, Lia. Fancy meeting you here."

There is something in her eyes, something dark and secret, that frightens me more than the knowledge of her considerable power now residing in London.

I shake my head, still recovering from the shock of seeing my sister in person for the first time since leaving New York. "What are you doing here? I mean...I...Why have you come?"

There are other things I should say. Things I should shout and demand. But the Masquerade and my shock conspire to

keep me polite, even as a scream threatens to wrench its way free from my throat.

"I've come to do some shopping. To make preparations." She says it as if her purpose is obvious, and I cannot help but feel I have fallen into the Otherworlds, to a place that looks and sounds like my own world but is, in fact, a version twisted and wrong.

"Preparations? For what?" I feel like the village idiot. It is obvious Alice is toying with me, and yet I am helpless to walk away. She has me in her grip, as she always has.

Even here. Even now.

She smiles, and for a moment I almost think her sincere. "For my wedding, of course."

I swallow the foreboding that rises like a stone in my throat as she turns to the gentleman beside her. I have been so focused on her that I have not noticed her masked escort.

But I notice him now. I notice him and feel my insides hollow out in the blink of an eye.

He is already reaching up to remove his mask. It takes too long, his face and hair revealed inch by inch until I can no longer hope that I am wrong.

"Lia? Is it really you?" Shock is evident on his face, and his eyes search mine for answers I cannot give him.

"You remember James Douglas, don't you?" Alice takes his arm, possession clear in her grasp. "We're to be married in the spring."

And then the room tilts madly, the faces of the masked guests distorting into something strange and fearsome.

3

I am not the kind of young woman who swoons. I have traveled roads terrifying and dangerous. I have defended my life and the lives of those I love. I have sacrificed everything in the name of the prophecy and the fate of the world.

But this almost brings me to my knees.

I did not notice Dimitri's arrival, but he is there as my arm flings out of its own accord, searching blindly for something to grasp as I will myself to keep my bearings.

"Oh!" Alice says. "Is this your beau?"

I cannot look at James, but when I turn to Dimitri, confusion coloring his expression as he gazes from James to me and back again, I cannot look at him, either. I settle on Alice and fight the inappropriate urge to laugh aloud. The situation is dire, indeed, if I prefer to gaze at my sister over either man.

"This is Dimitri. Dimitri Markov." I swallow my shame and

continue. I owe Dimitri, and James, this much. "And yes, he is my beau."

Alice holds out her hand in Dimitri's direction. "It's a pleasure to meet you, Mr. Markov. I'm Alice Milthorpe, Lia's sister."

Dimitri is not surprised by the introduction, for who else would have a face exactly like mine? But he does not take her hand. Instead, he leans in so that the others standing nearby might not hear him speak.

"I cannot imagine what you're doing here, Miss Milthorpe, but I suggest you keep your distance from Lia." There is a hard edge to his voice.

"Now, listen here," James breaks in. "There's no reason to be impolite. I would like for us to get along—despite the strangeness of the situation—but I cannot stand by while you insult my fiancée." His voice is halting, confused. And then I realize why.

He doesn't know, I think. *Alice has not told him about us. About the prophecy. About the thing that stands between us.*

The knowledge that James is engaged to my sister is difficult enough to accept; that he is engaged to my sister with no understanding of the danger in which he has placed himself is unimaginable.

I turn to look at Alice, searching her face for the malice that must be there. She has seduced James, brought him to London, thrown their engagement in my face without warning. All of it, to spite me. There is no reason for her to promise herself to the man I loved, the man I once planned to marry, other than

to take something I once held dear. As if she has not taken enough from me already.

Yet, as she gazes up at James, I see none of it. There is only softness in her eyes.

But then I think of Henry. I think of his gentle smile and his little-boy smell and am reminded anew of what Alice is capable.

Pulling myself up straighter, I take Dimitri's arm. "I'd like to go now, please."

He nods, putting his hand over mine.

As we turn to go, James's voice sounds behind me. "Lia."

I look back to meet his eyes and see my own feelings of futility reflected in his gaze.

He sighs. "I'm glad you are well."

I can only nod. And then Dimitri is rushing me toward the front of the hall.

❧

"But what is she doing here?"

The carriage is dark on the way back to Milthorpe Manor, and Sonia's voice drifts from the shadows across from me. Dimitri offered to accompany us home, but it is difficult enough to address the questions of Sonia and Luisa. I am not sure I have the courage to face those in Dimitri's eyes. Not tonight.

I am grateful when Luisa breaks in before I have time to answer. "I'm sure Lia has no idea what Alice is doing here. How can anyone know what Alice is thinking? Have we ever known?"

"I suppose not," Sonia says.

"There is a purpose to everything Alice does," I say. "I simply don't know what it is yet."

"I cannot believe—" Luisa starts but then stops abruptly.

I shake my head in the darkness, watching the smoky streets and the faceless figures that walk them. "Nor can I."

"I put nothing beyond Alice, but...marrying James?" Luisa says. "How *could* she? How could *he*?"

"I left." My voice is a murmur, and I wonder if I want Sonia and Luisa to hear me at all. If I want anyone to hear the truth about my abandonment of James. "I left without a word. I never even responded to his letters. He owes me nothing."

"Maybe not," Sonia says. "But of all the girls in New York, how could he marry Alice?"

I turn away from the window. There is only more darkness beyond its glass. "He doesn't know."

I feel Luisa's shock in the moment before she speaks. "How can you be certain?"

"I simply am. He has no idea of the thing that stands between Alice and me. No idea of the life he will lead with Alice if she has her way."

Sonia leans forward in a rustle of silk until her face is illuminated by the weak light of the street lamps. "Then you must tell him, Lia. You must tell him, to save him."

Despair rises in me like a flood. "What if he won't believe me?"

Sonia reaches out and grasps my hand. "You must make him believe you. You must."

I look down at our intertwined hands, pale against the blue

of Sonia's gown and the red of mine. Resting my head against the seat, I close my eyes. I close them and see Alice, standing like a queen in emerald silk, a perfect foil to the scarlet gown draped across my own shoulders and hips.

Of course, I think. *Of course.*

In the deep green gown, with James on her arm, Alice is the Lia that might have been. I see the two of us standing side by side at the Masquerade, and in my mind's eye it is difficult to tell which girl is my sister and which is me.

Standing outside the door in my nightgown and robe, the cold of the floor seeping through my slippers, I am startled to hear voices coming from within the room.

I waited patiently for the house to quiet before making my way to Aunt Virginia's room, but it seems I have not waited long enough. Still, going back to my chamber is not an option. I need my aunt's counsel. More than that, I need her understanding, for only Aunt Virginia can truly understand my horror at standing next to Alice as she explained her engagement to James.

Raising my hand to the door, I knock as quietly as possible. The hum of voices ceases, and a moment later Aunt Virginia opens the door, a look of surprise on her face.

"Lia! I thought you'd gone to bed!" Her hair, unbound, tumbles nearly to her waist. She looks quite young, and I flash on the painting of my mother over the fireplace at Birchwood Manor. "Come in, dear."

She steps back, holding the door as I enter her chamber,

scanning for the owner of the other voice. When I find it, I am more than surprised. I am not sure who I expect, but it is not Edmund, sitting comfortably by the fire in a tall-backed chair covered in thick burgundy velvet.

"Edmund! What are you doing here?"

Aunt Virginia laughs softly. "Edmund was simply telling me about Alice's appearance at the Masquerade. I'm glad you're here. Doubtless you will be able to tell me more."

She casts a glance at Edmund, and I have the distinct impression that this is not the first time they have conversed in Aunt Virginia's chamber in the dark of night.

Moving farther into the room, we sit on the small sofa in front of the fire. We do not speak right away, as we each ponder our own thoughts. It is Aunt Virginia who breaks the silence, her voice full of tenderness beside me.

"I'm sorry, Lia. I know how much James meant to you."

"*Means* to me," I say, gazing into the fire. "Just because I was forced to set him free — because I have since found Dimitri — doesn't mean I no longer care what happens to James."

"Of course." She reaches over to take my hand. "Had you no idea about his relationship with Alice? Didn't he mention it in any of his letters?"

I shake my head. "We stopped corresponding some time ago, even before I left for Altus."

"I simply don't understand how he could become engaged to Alice. The last time we saw her before coming to London, she was well beyond the point at which I could reach her."

"James Douglas is a good man. A smart man," Edmund says.

"But he *is* a man. Alice looks like you, Lia. And James was very lonely when you left." There is no accusation in his eyes. He is simply stating the facts.

"Edmund tells me you don't believe James knows about the prophecy," Aunt Virginia says. "What makes you think he doesn't?"

I look into the fire, remembering James. His gentle smile as he touched his lips to mine. His eagerness to protect me from harm. His simple *goodness*.

Turning back to Aunt Virginia, I am more certain than ever. "James would not be party to such a thing. Not to Alice's place in it."

Aunt Virginia nods. "If that is true, can you not simply tell him? Tell him everything, and beg him to get as far away from Alice as possible, for his own good?"

I worry my lower lip between my teeth, trying to imagine telling James about the prophecy.

"You think he won't believe you," Edmund says.

I meet his eyes. "Do you?"

He speaks slowly, considering his words. "You didn't trust him once before, and it does not seem that you've made peace with it. Perhaps it's time to try something else."

I look down at my hands, at the hated mark on one wrist, the medallion around the other. "Perhaps."

We sit in silence for another moment before Aunt Virginia speaks again. "And what do we do about Alice? Do you think she's come because we're close to having all four keys?"

"Even if she knew, it would seem too small a thing to bring

her all the way to London. Having *almost* all of the keys is hardly enough to worry Alice. We could spend years looking for the last one, to say nothing of the Stone."

"And the Rite," Aunt Virginia says, referring to the ritualistic ceremony required to bring about the end of the prophecy at Avebury — a ceremony of which no one seems to have heard. "Although I'm having tea with Elspeth at the Society tomorrow to go over some of the old books on Spellcasting there. Perhaps I will find mention of it in one of them."

"I hope so." I stand to leave, suddenly exhausted and overwhelmed at the thought of the tasks still ahead. "Arthur Frobisher gave me an address for someone who might have knowledge of the Stone's location. Dimitri and I are going to see what we can find, though I do wish Arthur had given me a name in addition to the address. I'd rather like to know whom I'm meeting."

"Well, if you don't, you'll be meeting them with me by your side," Edmund says. "I can't have you traipsing about meeting strangers without protection, especially now."

I do not remind him that I fought the Guard at Chartres. Instead, I simply smile my thanks, bidding them good night and making my way toward the door.

"Lia?" Aunt Virginia's voice stops me before I step into the hallway.

"Yes?"

"What *will* you do about Alice? She is undoubtedly waiting for you to make a move."

I contemplate my options before speaking.

"Let me give it further thought," I finally say, my voice hardening. "I'll not allow Alice to push me toward a decision I'm not ready to make."

Aunt Virginia nods. "Perhaps we will both make progress tomorrow."

"Perhaps." I leave the room, closing the door behind me without voicing the thought that springs to mind. *We must. We must make progress now. Whatever it takes.*

4

I am preparing to close the door the next morning, the cold London air stealing my breath, when I hear Luisa's voice behind me. "Where are you off to so early?"

She is standing on the bottom step of the great staircase, her midnight blue gown making her full lips seem even redder than usual. I try to ignore the almost-hidden note of accusation in her voice.

"I have an errand I must run with Dimitri." I smile at her, already feeling guilty. "It's just a quick outing. I'll be back in time for tea with you and Sonia, and we can talk all about Helene's arrival tomorrow."

"And would your errand have to do with the prophecy?"

Her resentment is suddenly obvious, and my own temper flares.

"What does it matter, Luisa? If it pertains to you and Sonia,

I'll fill you in later." I know how much this hurts her, how much it would hurt me, even as I say it.

A bitter sound escapes her throat. It is nothing like her usual carefree laughter. "What does it *matter*? I cannot believe you would say such a thing, Lia. It *matters* because once, we shared all things related to the prophecy. Once, you recognized its burden on all of us and sought to ease our fear as you sought to ease your own."

Her words find their way through the armor around my heart. I know they are true, however much I might wish to deny them.

"Lia? Is something wrong?" Dimitri's voice calls out from near the carriage. I turn to him, grateful for the few extra seconds in which to find an answer to Luisa's accusation.

I hold up a hand, telling him to wait.

Turning back to Luisa, I say the only thing I can. "I'm sorry. I'm trying to forgive Sonia so that we might all be friends as we once were. It is..." I look down at my boots while I try to find the words. "It is not as easy as it sounds."

She steps off the staircase and makes her way to me. I expect her to be kind. To offer an embrace of friendship and patience, as she always has.

But Luisa's patience is at an end. "I am *not* Sonia. I did not betray you. I don't need to seek your forgiveness." Her voice is as icy as the wind blowing into Milthorpe Manor from the streets of London. "But if you are not careful, you will find it necessary to seek mine."

She turns and makes her way down the hall, leaving me in

the chill morning air. Her words drop like a stone on my heart, and shame heats my cheeks despite the cold.

Straightening my spine, I close the door and make my way down the path to the carriage.

She does not understand, I think. *I keep things from her for her own protection. For her own peace of mind.*

But even as I think the words, I know they are a lie.

Dimitri and I sit side by side in silence as Edmund guides the carriage through the city. It is some time before Dimitri speaks.

"I've been aware of your previous relationship with James Douglas for some time, from the weeks when I was watching you in New York on behalf of the Grigori."

I nod, gazing out the window. "I know."

"You needn't feel ashamed or embarrassed," he says.

I turn to look at him, indignant that he would think me either. "I'm not. And it is insulting that you would think such a thing. Should I be ashamed for loving someone before you? Embarrassed that I'm not a delicate English flower with no knowledge of men?" My words bite through the shadows of the carriage.

He does not seem surprised at my outburst, and it almost makes me angry that he knows me so well. "Of course not. I've never expected you to be a...what did you call it?" A smirk begins to lift the corners of his mouth. "A 'delicate English flower with no knowledge of men.'"

Something about the way he says it causes me to fight the

urge to laugh. But it is no use. He sees the smile sneak its way onto my lips despite my effort to repress it. Soon my shoulders are shaking with the strain of stifling my laughter.

"I must admit," he says, his own laughter escaping heartily, "that I've never thought of you in quite those terms!"

Now we are both laughing hysterically, and I reach over to swat his arm. "Why, thank you! You likely..." I am laughing so hard I can hardly get the words out. "You likely say that to all the girls!"

This brings about a fresh howl of laughter, and I clutch my stomach until our merriment dies down a few moments later.

"Lia." Dimitri moves closer, his breath still coming fast on the heels of our laughter. He reaches for my hand. "I only wanted to say that I'm sorry for last night. For the way things have happened between your sister and James. It must be very difficult for you. And I never want anything to be difficult for you."

I meet his gaze. "Thank you. But it... Well, it was a long time ago that I thought my future was with James."

He brings my hand to his lips, opening my fingers and kissing my palm. The sensation sends a lick of fire from my stomach all the way up my spine. "Yes, but old feelings are not so easy to extinguish, I imagine. It would be impossible to put aside my feelings for you. Ever. I wouldn't blame you if some of yours for him remained, even after so long a time and all that's happened."

I hear the hesitance, carefully disguised as understanding, in his voice. Pulling my hand from his, I take his face in my palms

and look into his eyes. "It's true that I once loved James. But that love was based on a part of me that no longer exists. Even if I end the prophecy, I'm not the same person. I can never go back to the Lia I once was. Too much has changed. And this Lia, the one who walked Altus's rolling hills and kissed you in its groves and lay with you beneath its flowering trees... Well, this Lia would not be happy with James."

I am surprised to feel the truth of it. Surprised that I mean it with such certainty, despite my lingering affection for James.

The relief in Dimitri's eyes is obvious, and I lean forward, touching my lips to his. Our kiss, meant to be a gentle reminder of my loyalty and affection, quickly turns passionate. The rocking of the carriage and the shadows within it only serve to transport me further from reality, to a place where nothing exists except Dimitri's mouth on mine, his body pressing against me until I am almost lying down in the back of the carriage.

I do not know how much time passes before we feel the carriage slowing, but its changing pace brings us both back to reality. We pull apart, hurriedly straightening clothing and hair just in time for Edmund to bring the carriage to a complete stop.

Leaning toward me, Dimitri gives me one last kiss just before Edmund opens the door. As I step from the carriage, I make small talk in an attempt to ignore the feeling that he knows exactly what has transpired during our ride.

"Where are we, Edmund?"

He looks disapprovingly at the dirty street and rough men

hanging about the walk. "Nowhere good. But this one," he tips his head at a dingy stone building, "is the address on the paper given to you by Mr. Frobisher."

Peering up at it, I would swear it is leaning just the slightest bit to the right. Even still, after everything I have experienced, it will take quite a bit more to strike fear in my heart than an old building and questionable company.

"All right, then. I suppose that is where we must go."

I take Dimitri's arm as we follow Edmund across the dirty ground and up the crumbling stairs toward a wooden door painted a surprisingly crisp shade of red. It has nary a mark or scuff and stands in stark contrast to the neglected neighborhood around it.

Edmund looks none too pleased, despite the jaunty door. "Mr. Frobisher should not have sent a respectable young woman to this part of town without so much as a name," he mutters, lifting a hand to rap on the door with his knuckles.

His knock is met with silence, and he is lifting his hand once more when we hear the sound of footsteps making their way toward the front of the house. I cast a nervous glance at Dimitri as the steps become louder. All at once the door is pulled open to reveal an elegant woman, as smartly dressed as if she were on her way to tea. She surveys us with a patient smile and not a single word.

It takes me only a moment to place her. When I do, I meet her smile with one of my own. "Madame Berrier? Is it really you?"

5

Her smile widens. "But of course. Were you expecting someone else?"

Madame Berrier steps back to allow us entry, her twinkling eyes speaking of a secret kind of mischief. "Come. The gentlemen on the street will do you no harm, but it would still be wise to keep our own counsel, would it not?"

"Yes. Yes, of course." I am still disoriented by the fact that Madame Berrier has made her way from New York to London and is standing before me at this very moment.

We follow her into the town house and she closes and locks the door behind us. Edmund, looking entirely unfazed, says nothing, and I wonder if he remembers Madame Berrier from our first meeting, when she revealed my identity as Angel of the Gate.

Turning back to us, Madame Berrier nods appreciatively at Dimitri. "And who might *this* be? Hmmm?"

"Oh! I'm sorry. Madame Berrier, this is Dimitri Markov. Dimitri, Madame Berrier. She was of great help to me in figuring out my place in the prophecy." I turn back to Madame Berrier. "And Dimitri has been of great help to me since."

She smiles slyly. "I'm quite sure he has, dear."

My face heats at the innuendo, but I do not have time to come up with a witty retort before Madame Berrier turns, making her way down the central hall toward the back of the house.

"Come along. I expect the tea will be ready by now." Her voice, accented with the mysterious mixture of French and something else I am still unable to name, grows steadily fainter as she moves away from us.

Edmund, Dimitri, and I walk quickly to catch up, and I hope for Madame Berrier's sake that the rest of the house is better appointed than the hallway. It is dismal, lined with peeling wallpaper and lit only by the frail light leaking in from the adjoining rooms.

But I needn't have worried. Madame Berrier turns to enter a parlor on the right, and I suddenly feel as if I have landed in a strange fairy tale. The room is lit with several beaded lamps and the glow of a fire flickering in the firebox. The furnishings are well worn, but it is apparent that in this room, at least, Madame Berrier has made herself quite comfortable.

"Goodness, the tea smells delicious!" She makes her way to a small table set with cups and saucers in front of the sofa. "You are a dear for preparing it."

The comment catches me off guard, and from the confusion on Edmund and Dimitri's faces, it is obvious that I'm not alone.

We glance at one another as Madame Berrier settles herself on the sofa. She prepares to pour tea from the pot sitting on a silver tray as if there is nothing at all strange about her thanking someone who isn't there.

But as I peer more closely at the shadows lurking around the edges of the room, I realize that we are not, in fact, its only occupants. In the corner, near a bookcase with shelves sagging from the weight of many books and indiscernible objects of all shapes and sizes, is a slightly stoop-shouldered silhouette. Edmund and Dimitri follow my eyes to the figure, both of them tensing when they realize someone else is in the parlor.

Madame Berrier turns her head in the direction of the figure. "Put your musty books away and join us, will you? I'm quite certain it is you Miss Milthorpe has come to see, although I am, of course, delighted by her company."

The figure nods, turning. "Aye. My apologies for being coarse."

I did not think it possible for Edmund and Dimitri to become more tense, but as the figure makes its way out of the shadows, I can almost feel their defenses rise around me. I have to bite my tongue to keep from reminding them that I protected myself at Chartres and am not in need of rescue every time a stranger enters the room.

It is obvious the figure is a man, and he shuffles somewhat slowly forward, becoming visible all at once as he steps into the light of a lamp atop one of the many small tables.

"There you are, then! It has been some time and many miles since I've seen you!"

I blink for a moment, rooted to the floor as I try to take in yet another surprise.

"Mr. Wigan?" My voice rises shrilly, and I think I must sound a fool, for, of course, it is Mr. Wigan.

His laughter is welcome music in the silence of the room. "It is me, indeed! Come across the sea with my dear Sylvia, I have!"

He continues to the sofa, settling himself comfortably next to Madame Berrier as she hands him a cup of steaming tea.

Dimitri and Edmund stand stiffly and politely by, but shock has stolen my manners. I move toward Mr. Wigan and Madame Berrier, dropping without pretense into a chair across from the sofa.

"I am afraid we've caught her off guard, darling." There is humor in Madame Berrier's voice. "And here I thought we were being indiscreet while in New York."

"Indiscreet?" I repeat. *Darling?*

She takes a sip of her tea before answering and becomes distracted by something in its brew. "Alistair, dear, what is it I taste today?"

A smile breaks out across his broad face. "'It's almonds, my love. And a wee bit of chocolate."

Madame Berrier nods approvingly. "Most delicious." She meets my eyes and continues. "I've never liked tea. But Alistair is simply magnificent at brewing it. We have been . . . *together* for some time now. It was one of the many reasons I was shunned by the people in that narrow-minded little town in New York. And one of the many reasons I was in need of a change."

She looks up at Edmund and Dimitri in surprise, as if she

has half-forgotten they are there. "Do sit down. I should think it obvious that we do not stand on ceremony."

They sit on command, and I turn to Dimitri, gesturing to the little man sipping tea contentedly across the table. "This is Mr. Wigan. From New York. He helped us figure out that Luisa and Sonia were two of the keys." I look at Mr. Wigan. "And this is Dimitri Markov, Mr. Wigan. He is a...friend."

Madame Berrier gazes at Mr. Wigan mischievously. "I daresay they are 'friends' much as we are, darling!"

My cheeks flush hot with embarrassment and I avoid Edmund's eyes, though surely he understands the nature of my relationship with Dimitri better than anyone after traveling all the way to Altus in our company.

"I *am* happy to see you both," I say, seeking to change the subject. "But I don't understand why Arthur sent us here."

Madame Berrier places a cup of tea in front of me, handing some to Dimitri and Edmund as well. I remain silent as she busies herself passing them cream and sugar, having no doubt that she will continue when she is ready.

But it is Mr. Wigan who speaks first. "I wouldn't like to sound excitable, but I might be just the person to help you. That is, I do lay claim to knowledge not held by every man."

Hearing the indignation in his voice, I realize that I have wounded his pride. I set my tea down and smile. "Why, of course you do, Mr. Wigan. In fact, had I known you were in London, you would have been the very first person I would have called upon for answers."

He hangs his head modestly. "Not that I know everything,

mind. But this particular question, well, you might say it falls into my area of expertise."

"It certainly does," I say. "How much *has* Arthur told you, then? And how did he come upon you?"

"He found me through an old associate." Mr. Wigan bites into a cookie, turning to Madame Berrier. "These are quite good, my luscious. Quite good."

Edmund shifts uncomfortably next to me.

"Mr. Wigan?" I ask.

He looks up, his eyes far away. "Yes?"

"Arthur? And how much he told you about our quest?"

"Oh, yes. Yes! Most certainly!" He polishes off the cookie in one bite, chewing and swallowing before continuing. "I didn't speak with Mr. Frobisher. Not directly. He made inquiries, you see, discreetly to hear it told, about the matter at hand. But no one was able to help him. Each person passed the question on to someone else until it finally made its way to me. When I heard the nature of the information being sought, I knew right away that you must be behind the matter, what with all that business in New York."

Madame Berrier leans toward him. "What you mean to say, my dear man, is that *we* knew right away."

Mr. Wigan nods vigorously. "Quite right, my ravishing rosebud. Quite right."

"So, can you give us the information we need?" Dimitri's voice surprises me. I almost forgot he was in the room, so focused was I on the exchange between Mr. Wigan and Madame Berrier.

Mr. Wigan shakes his head. "Oh, no. I'm afraid not."

"I don't understand." I try to recall the conversation in which Arthur said he had found someone who might have the answer to my question. "I'm quite sure Arthur said you could help us."

Madame Berrier nods. "But of course we can."

"Then I don't . . . I don't understand." I feel helplessly lost, as if I have landed in a strange country in which everyone speaks a foreign tongue and looks at me as if I should know perfectly well what they are saying.

Mr. Wigan leans forward. His tone is conspiratorial, as if he's afraid someone will overhear. "I didn't say I couldn't help you. Only that I don't have the answer myself."

Madame Berrier rises, smoothing the skirts of her gown. "Seeking answers elsewhere has served us quite well in the past, has it not?"

I look up at her, wondering what she means to do. "I suppose so."

"Come, then. I presume you have use of a carriage?"

6

The house is imposing and at least as large as Birchwood Manor.

"What a lovely home," Madame Berrier exclaims, gazing up at the stone facade covered in deep green ivy.

We have traveled beyond the city, according to the instructions given to Edmund by Mr. Wigan, who has remained secretive about our journey. Dimitri's growing frustration with Mr. Wigan's refusal to name the person with whom we'll be meeting is evident, and he starts for the stone steps leading to the door without comment.

"Well, then," Mr. Wigan says. "It seems your young man is an anxious one."

I look up at him as I follow Dimitri. "We are all anxious, Mr. Wigan. There is much at stake, and much that has already been sacrificed."

His nod is slow. "Aye. I was sorry to hear of your brother. I don't like to contemplate the loss of one so young."

I feel Edmund stiffen beside me at the mention of Henry.

I nod at Mr. Wigan. "Thank you. It was very difficult."

Even now the words come with effort.

Madame Berrier touches my arm as we climb the steps after Dimitri. "Your brother is not gone, my dear. He is simply transformed and waiting for you in a better place."

I nod again, forcing away the grief that is already permeating my soul at the mention of Henry. He is in a better place. A place that will become better still when he crosses into the final world with my parents. It is not his fate I fear, nor my own death. Nothing as simple as that.

No.

My greatest fear is that I will be caught by the Souls on the Plane. That I will be imprisoned in their icy Void, never to see my brother again. That I will be *denied* death, forced instead to watch the skies of the Otherworlds for eternity, trapped in a hell of the Souls' making.

But of course I say none of this. What would be the point?

Instead, I smile into Madame Berrier's eyes. "Thank you."

It is all there is to say in the face of her sympathy.

We reach the top of the steps and Dimitri turns to Mr. Wigan. "I'd like to knock, but since I have no idea whom we have come to call upon, I think it best that you do the honors."

The sarcasm in his voice seems evident only to me.

Mr. Wigan steps forward. "Right you are, my boy. Right you are."

Mr. Wigan lifts his hand to the carved door, taking the enormous brass knocker in one hand and bringing it down on the plate until we hear the clatter echo through the halls of the house on the other side of the door.

Standing in the silence left by the absent knocking, we glance around, taking in the sleeping gardens and leafless trees. I imagine it must be beautiful in summer, but now it is empty, and slightly frightening.

The door creaks the smallest bit as the wood shifts and I realize that someone is on the other side. I think myself alone in the realization until Mr. Wigan speaks, rather loudly, to the wooden door.

"Victor? It's Alistair. Alistair Wigan. I've traveled across the sea to your doorstep, my old friend. Open the door, now."

I wonder at the coaxing tone in his voice, for he sounds as if he is speaking to a stubborn child. But it does no good, in any case. The door remains firmly closed.

"It's me, Victor, and a couple," he looks around at our group, "a few people who would like to make your acquaintance for a matter of great importance."

The wooden door creaks yet again but still does not open. Edmund and Dimitri glance at each other, some silent communication passing between them.

Mr. Wigan sighs, turning to me. "He has a bit of a worry, you see. He doesn't like to go outside, or even to open the door." He leans in close to my ear. "He's afraid."

"I am not afraid!" I jump a little as the voice startles me from the other side of the door. "I simply was not expecting you."

Madame Berrier presses her lips together before looking at Mr. Wigan. "Alistair, my darling, perhaps I should try. A woman's touch might do wonders."

Mr. Wigan seems to be considering the idea when the voice probes from the other side of the door.

"A woman? Do you mean to say there is a woman with you, Alistair? A proper lady?" The voice is incredulous, as if Mr. Wigan has announced that he has brought a rare beast to call.

Mr. Wigan leans toward the door. "Better," he says. "There are two of them."

"Now see here," Edmund begins. "It isn't proper to use the ladies as a—"

But he does not have time to finish, for the door swings open and, all at once, we are staring into the blinking eyes of a small, rather delicate man.

"You might have said you had women in your company. I would not have been so rude."

"It would have been a right bit easier to mention if you'd only opened the door," Mr. Wigan grumbles.

The man named Victor ignores him, bowing his head slightly toward Madame Berrier, and then to me. "My apologies, dear ladies. Please, join me for tea. If Alistair has brought you to my door, it can only be that the matter at hand is urgent indeed."

"You must forgive me. Most of the servants have gone, but I do manage a simple tea quite well."

I watch as Victor pours tea. He is slight and fair-haired, with an unusually soft manner. He hands each of us a delicate porcelain teacup, and we gaze around the richly appointed library as he passes tea to the men.

He gestures to the tray. "Please, do take some refreshment. I remember the journey from London as long, tiring, and, if I am to be honest, rather boring!"

I find myself laughing at his candor. It is a relief, and I realize I do not remember the last time I laughed in the company of anyone but Dimitri. Reaching toward the tray, I take a delicate biscuit.

"Thank you for the tea." I smile at him, thinking it has been a very long time since I have liked someone so immediately.

He waves my thanks away. "It is my pleasure, young lady. And the least I can do after my atrocious behavior at the door. I do apologize."

I swallow the bite of cookie I am chewing. "Don't you care for company?"

Victor sighs, his smile full of sorrow. "On the contrary; I like it very much."

"Then why didn't you open the door?" Dimitri's voice is surprisingly gentle.

"Well, it is rather complicated. You see, I have trouble with . . . I cannot . . ." He takes a deep breath, starting again. "It's difficult—"

"It seems you're afraid." Edmund's declaration is simple and holds no malice.

Victor nods. "It seems I am."

49

"Afraid of what, if you don't mind my asking?" I don't wish to be intrusive, but I've never met someone who was afraid to leave his home.

He shrugs. "Illness, criminals, carriage accidents, skittish horses. Everything, I suppose."

"But how do you obtain the things you require?" Madame Berrier asks, gazing around the lavish room.

He turns his palms to the sky, as if everything he needs will fall into them from the library ceiling. "The servants see that I have food and firewood. My tailor comes to the house to fit my clothing. I have everything I need, I suppose." But his is not the voice of one who has everything he needs.

Madame Berrier sets her teacup back on the saucer. "Except for company," she says kindly.

His smile is grateful. "Except for company."

Madame Berrier takes Mr. Wigan's hand in hers. "Then we shall endeavor to visit quite often — if you don't think you will mind the intrusion, of course."

Victor nods, genuine pleasure in his eyes. "I won't mind it a bit." He leans forward toward her. "Although I do hope you'll be patient if it takes me a few extra moments to open the door."

She laughs, her head tipped back, and I see the young woman she must have been. Certainly she was beautiful and wild. I think we would have gotten along famously, even then.

"Of course," she says.

"Now." Victor sets his own teacup on the saucer. "You have brought me great enjoyment with your visit and have been

kind enough to overlook my peculiarity. What can *I* do for *you?*"

"The young ones are trying to solve a riddle, you see," Mr. Wigan begins. "It's of some importance, and while I have no small knowledge of these things myself, I cannot find mention of it in any of my books."

"What is it, exactly? A map? A date? An obscure relic? I have plenty of time." He laughs, sweeping one arm to encompass the seemingly endless bookshelves lining every wall. "And I spend it here, reading book after book. I am well-read on many subjects, but most notably on alternative history."

Edmund's voice echoes through the room. "'Alternative history'?"

Dimitri turns to him. "I believe Victor refers to more controversial explanations for historical events, religious happenings. . . . Things of that nature."

Victor nods. "Precisely."

"Then you just might be the person to help us." I look around our small group, wondering that fate would bring such an odd assortment of people together in such an unimaginable circumstance. "We're trying to find the meaning of two phrases: *Nos Galon-Mai and Sliabh na Cailli*." I shake my head. "I don't even know if I have the pronunciation right. I've only ever seen them written, you see. But I do think they may be locations."

Victor nods with authority. "*Nos Galon-Mai* is the old word for Beltane, of that much I'm certain."

I meet Dimitri's eyes with a smile. To close the Gate, we must convene at Avebury on the eve of May first with Alice,

the keys, and the Stone. It makes perfect sense given that the keys were all born at midnight on Samhain, a holiday whose meaning stands in opposition to that of Beltane.

The prophecy began with Samhain. It will end with Beltane.

That we should so quickly find one of the answers to the prophecy makes my spirit soar with hope, but any expectation of a quick answer to our remaining question is dashed a moment later when Victor continues.

"The other word—Sliabh na Cailli', was it? That one doesn't ring a bell." Victor rolls it across his tongue, as if speaking it slowly will help him find its meaning. "You say you've seen it written?"

I nod.

"Could you write it for me?" he asks.

"Yes, of course. Do you have a pen and parchment?"

Victor rises. "Come."

I stand to join him and cannot help but be irritated when both Edmund and Dimitri stand as well.

A wry smile touches Victor's lips. "My, my! Aren't you important, then! Do they ever leave you alone?"

I roll my eyes. "On occasion."

Victor takes my hand, leading me around the tea table. "Gentlemen," he says to Dimitri and Edmund, "I assure you that I needn't take Miss Milthorpe to the ends of the earth for a simple writing implement. I have one in the desk near the window, though you're welcome to join us if you like."

They both glance at the writing desk, not ten feet away. I hope they feel at least as ridiculous as I. They settle back into their seats and I follow Victor to the desk. Once there, he pulls

the string on a lamp and a pool of softly colored light spills from its stained-glass shade. When he opens the shallow drawer at the front of the desk I catch a glimpse of the perfectly ordered interior, holding identical pens in a neat row, several inkwells, and a stack of parchment. Removing one of each, he sets the parchment on the desk and hands me a pen.

"Try to get the spelling just right. Sometimes I remember things the way I first saw them, and if they're off by a letter or two," he shrugs. "I simply don't make the connection."

I nod. I will never forget a single word of the prophecy. It is a part of me now.

Victor removes the lid from the ink pot and sets it upon the writing desk. Dipping the nib into the deep blue ink, I bend over the desk and write the words found on the final page of the Book of Chaos. The words that disguise the hiding place of the Stone. *Sliabh na Cailli'*.

Straightening, I hand Victor the pen. "There you are."

He reaches past me, lifting the parchment from the desk and leaning over to hold it nearer the light. His lips move as he mouths the strange words.

"Was there anything else? Anything surrounding the words that might help me identify them?" he asks.

I chew my lip, remembering. "It said, 'released from the temple, Sliabh na Cailli', portal to the Otherworlds.'"

I speak only those words necessary to discover the answer we seek. It is a habit to protect the prophecy from the eyes and ears of others. And to protect others from the workings of the prophecy.

Victor's brow furrows, his lips still moving in silent prayer to the words we do not understand. All at once he sets the parchment back on the desk and moves to one of the bookshelves that reach all the way to the ceiling stretching far above our heads. Seeing the sense of purpose on his face, I feel hope bloom inside me and follow him without being asked.

He reaches a wooden ladder and slides it to an adjoining shelf. Looking up to follow its progress, I see that it is attached to a track that runs the circumference of the room, giving the ladder access to each and every shelf. I have seen such contraptions before, of course, but never in a private library. I cannot help but be impressed.

"Do you know what it means?" Dimitri's voice sounds from across the room, but I am not surprised when Victor doesn't answer. I recognize his single-minded concentration.

He suddenly stops the ladder and begins to climb. I wonder if his many fears will prevent him from reaching the tome he seeks, but none of his anxiety is evident as he rises swiftly up the ladder's rungs.

Near the top he finally stops climbing and reaches toward the shelf closest to the ladder, his fingers caressing the spines of each book in turn. Finally, his fingers cease their dance, settling on one book that, from my vantage point, looks like all the others. But he seems to recognize it, and he holds it close to his chest with one hand as he descends the ladder. When at last he steps to the floor, the air seems to escape his lungs all at once.

"Well!" He stands a little straighter. "Let's take a look. If I remember correctly, the answer will be here."

7

But it is not. We wait while Victor pages through the book, first quickly and then more patiently as he seems to scour each word, and still he is unable to find the mention for which he is looking. After a few more tries with different books, a clock chimes in a distant area of the house and we grudgingly decide to head back to London, no closer to an answer than we were this morning.

Consternation creases Victor's face as we say our goodbyes. It's apparent that he is unused to failure in matters of research, and he promises to continue investigating and to send word immediately if he happens upon the phrase.

We are silent on the ride back to London, the sun hanging low in the sky behind the clouds that lie over the countryside. Even Mr. Wigan lacks his usual enthusiasm, and I am relieved when we leave him with Madame Berrier at the dingy brownstone in front of which Dimitri and I arrived only a few hours ago.

"I'm sorry, Lia," Dimitri says as the carriage jostles through the streets of town toward Milthorpe Manor. "I know how much you had hoped that Arthur's contact would hold the answer, likely even more so once you discovered it was Mr. Wigan and Madame Berrier."

I sigh. "It will be all right." My words do not sound as convincing as I had hoped, and I look into Dimitri's eyes. "It *will* be all right, won't it?"

I detest myself for voicing aloud my fear that it will *not* be all right. That we will never find the answers we seek. That the Souls and Alice will rule the world in darkness after all.

"Lia." Dimitri takes my hand. His eyes hold the answer, but he says it anyway. "You have Lady Abigail's adder stone. It will protect you from harm while we search, and search we will, until we find every answer to the prophecy. You have my word."

I manage a reassuring smile, feeling the falseness of it. I do not tell him that the adder stone grows cooler with each passing day. I do not tell him that Sonia, Luisa, and I may not be able to maintain our alliance long enough to fight the prophecy together, to say nothing of Helene, arriving tomorrow and throwing yet more uncertainty into our mix.

And I do not share my biggest fear of all: that as each day passes, my own resolve grows weaker. That I become more an enemy to myself than Alice could ever be.

With Dimitri back in his quarters at the Society for the night, I spend the ride home worrying over Luisa and Sonia's reaction to the hour of my return. Darkness has claimed what little remained of the daylight. My promise to be home in time for tea, to spend our last afternoon together before Helene arrives in the morning, was an empty one.

But I needn't have worried. Luisa and Sonia have retired to their quarters, leaving the house silent save for the ticking of the grandfather clock in the entry and the faint sound of servants' footsteps in the kitchen.

The absence of my friends is a recrimination, and I settle on the sofa near the fire. I am not ready to face my chambers and sleep. There is no peace in slumber. Instead, I turn my thoughts to the endless requirements of the prophecy, paging through them in my mind—the last key, the location of the Stone, the invocation of the Rite necessary to end the prophecy should I discover the answers to everything else. The questions drift on the breeze of my subconscious. It is not unpleasant, and I let my thoughts take me where they will, knowing that sometimes the answers come when you least expect them.

A soft knock from the entry shakes me from my reverie and I rise from the sofa, gazing into the hallway and wondering if I imagined the sound. No one else seems to have heard it. I am a breath away from making my way back into the parlor when I hear it again. This time I'm certain it is knocking.

And it is coming from the front door.

As I look left and right down the hallway, it quickly becomes apparent that no one else has heard the knock. The servants can still be heard moving about the house, but none of them seems to be heading for the door. As I make my way down the hall, I find I am glad. I somehow know this visitor is meant for me.

My reflection is distorted in the door's large bronze handle. I do not allow myself to hesitate before opening it. When I do, I am somehow not surprised to find my sister on the doorstep.

I hardly notice the rush of cold air that invades the house in the moment before Alice speaks.

"Good evening, Lia. I . . ." Alice hesitates. "I apologize for the late hour. I hoped you would be awake so that we might speak alone."

I search her eyes and do not find hostility in their depth. Besides, I am far more vulnerable on the Plane, even in sleep, than I am standing in the entry with a host of servants — and Edmund — in the house behind me.

Stepping back, I open the door wider. "Come in."

She steps into the house carefully, looking up at the ceiling as I close the door.

"I don't really remember this house," she murmurs. "I believe we were here with Mother and Father when we were young, but it's completely unfamiliar to me."

I nod, slowly. "It was that way for me when I first arrived as well. It was too long ago, I suppose."

She removes her gloves. "Yes, I suppose it was."

"Where are you staying while in London?" I regret the question as soon as I ask it. It is one more commonly asked between acquaintances during a formal social call.

She does not seem to mind. "We've taken rooms at the Savoy. I knew I would not be welcome here, of course."

We stand without moving, surveying each other until I begin to feel ridiculous. There is a world between us, but Alice is still my sister.

"Let's go to the parlor." I turn to make my way down the hall without waiting to see if she will follow, but I feel her eyes on my back and know that she does.

Once we are in the fire-warmed room, I settle myself on a chair, leaving Alice to the sofa I occupied only minutes before. She surveys the room, and I wonder if she is comparing it to the parlor at Birchwood.

"What are you doing, Alice?" My words surprise me with their softness. They hold only a question, without the accusations I feel lurking in the corners of my heart. "Why have you come?"

She takes a deep breath, looking at her hands before answering. "You're my sister, Lia. My twin. I've often wished that I could share these past weeks with you."

The reference to her engagement brings forward the anger lying in wait within me. "I wouldn't expect my participation in the premarital festivities, if I were you. Especially since you're engaged to my former beau." My voice is hard, and I suppose I should not be surprised that it is bitter.

"You're angry," she says.

A brittle laugh escapes my throat. "Did you think I would throw a party in celebration? Wish you well?"

She looks up, meeting my eyes. "I suppose I hoped you would find it in your heart to be happy for me, Lia, whatever else lies between us."

Her words cause me to jump to my feet, and I stalk to the mantel, trying to calm the sudden shaking of my hands.

"Happy? You thought I would be happy for you?" I cannot find words for the incredulity that floods my mind.

"I suppose." Her voice is harder than it was only moments ago. "You left him, Lia. *You left him.* What did you expect? That he would wait with bated breath for your return?"

I turn on her, the heat of my fury hotter than the flames in the firebox at my back. "You left me no one to return *to*, Alice. Nothing to stay *for*."

Her eyes flash as she rises. "Don't be simple, Lia. I'm not alone in my culpability. We both made choices. You could have asked Henry for the list and given it to me, to protect him. You could have aided the Souls, as is your duty as Gate. You made choices, too." Her voice grows colder. "And you are no innocent."

I cross the carpet in three angry strides, stopping directly in front of her. I am quivering with rage. "How dare you. *How dare you speak of Henry.* You have no right, Alice. You have no right to ever speak of him again."

She begins pulling on her gloves, her breath coming so fast that I see the rise and fall of her bosom. "I see this was pointless. I simply hoped that we could set the prophecy aside in

matters more personal. That you could find it in your heart to give me your blessing."

"My *blessing*? You want my blessing?" My laughter is colored with hysteria. "Oh, Alice, I assure you that you will not require my blessing for anything at all."

She tips her head. "Why is that, Lia?"

All at once, the hysteria passes. My voice grows calm as I look into her eyes. "Because there will not be a wedding. Not with James."

She smiles. "That's where you're wrong, Lia. There *will* be a wedding. One in which I will become the wife of James Douglas."

"Really?" I ask. "And are you certain he will make you his wife when he learns of your place in the prophecy?"

Her body becomes very still. "How do you know he isn't already aware of it?"

I smile at her. "Because, Alice, James Douglas is a good man. A man who would never marry someone with a heart as black as yours — if only he knew how black that heart is."

She flinches, the color draining from her cheeks, in the moment before she composes herself for my benefit. "He won't believe you."

"Are you certain? Truly certain? Are you certain that James would not look into my eyes and see the truth?"

Her throat ripples as she swallows hard against my threat. "James loves me. It's true that for many months I saw your shadow in his eyes, but all of that is forgotten." She lifts her chin defiantly. "Even if you tell him, even if he believes you,

James will stand by my side as he would once have stood by yours. If only you'd had the courage to tell him."

Her words are a dagger to my heart. She's right. I have my own part in all that has happened, not the least of which is James being used as a pawn in the prophecy. Had I trusted him, had I told him everything, he likely *would* have stood by my side and would not now, at this very moment, be my sister's betrothed.

But then I would not have Dimitri. And that, too, is unimaginable.

"I suppose we'll see, Alice."

She smooths her skirts. "I suppose we will."

She starts for the entry and I follow her out of the room and down the hall. Placing one hand on the doorknob, she turns to me.

"It was never easy, you know."

"What wasn't?" I ask, even though I don't care. Not really. I simply want her gone.

I think I catch a flash of pain in the moment before the veil of hostility again descends over her face. "Seeing the adoration in everyone's eyes when they spoke of you. Knowing that Father, James, even our own mother, preferred you to me. Is it so difficult to believe that perhaps James has made peace with your abandonment? That he may well and truly love me? That maybe, just this once, you are not adored above all others?"

I shake my head. "I don't know what you're talking about, Alice. I've been in your shadow since the moment of our birth. James's love for me was one of the few things that was mine

alone." I hear the dismay in my voice. Alice has always been the chosen one.

Beautiful. Vibrant. Alive.

Her smile is without the conciliatory warmth from the parlor. "You are so very stubborn, Lia. And so unwilling to see things as they really are where it doesn't suit you. I cannot imagine why I always hope things will be different. They never are."

"No. And they never will be, Alice. Not where the prophecy and my place in it are concerned. Not where the fate of those I love is concerned."

I fear the smile that touches her lips. It is the one I remember from our many meetings on the Plane, the one that speaks of Alice's allegiance to the Souls, even at the peril of mankind. "It surprises me that you can still be so self-righteous, Lia. That you still don't see the truth."

I cross my arms in front of my chest. "What truth is that, Alice?"

She tips her head, as if it is very obvious. "That you're not so different from me after all. That you become more like me every day."

She pulls the door open, slipping through it and closing it behind her.

I stand there for some time, staring at the door, thinking of my sister and James and the prophecy. Of how tangled our web has become.

When I finally turn to make my way up the stairs, I try to focus on James and what I will say to him. I try to focus on his

fate, and the importance of saving him from Alice. But all I hear are Alice's last words. They echo through my mind until I'm not sure if they are hers or my own.

I do not sleep well. My dreams are full of dark figures and of whispering that seems to come from inside my head.

Even as I drift through the landscape of half-sleep, I am aware of turning over the possible locations of the Stone in my mind. Victor is there, riding his ladder along its tracks from book to book while Dimitri stands below him, parchment in hand. In the moment before I wake, I feel the answer slip and slide through my fingers.

When I sit up in bed a minute later, I think I have it.

8

"Explain to me what we're doing again?"

Dimitri rubs a tired hand over his face, fighting a yawn as the carriage lurches through the countryside in the faintly blue light of early morning.

I lean toward him, grabbing his hand in excitement. "Don't you see? We've been looking at it all wrong." I chew my lip, considering my words. "That is, I *think* we've been looking at it all wrong. I suppose we cannot be certain until we speak to Victor."

Dimitri sighs. "Yes, you've mentioned that, but I'm unclear exactly *what* we've been looking at all wrong. You still haven't gotten to that part."

"We asked Victor and Mr. Wigan about the words from the prophecy's final page."

He nods. "Yes, because that is what we're trying to decipher.

But that still doesn't explain why we're on our way to Victor's at this ungodly hour."

I hold out my hand. "Did you bring the list?"

"Yes, of course. You asked me to, didn't you?" He reaches into his pocket and pulls out a folded piece of parchment, placing it in my hand.

Opening it, I read through the list of potential locations — the many we have crossed off and the nine remaining possibilities.

"On the final page, the location of the Stone seems to be written in another language." My voice is a murmur under the clatter of the carriage wheels over rocky ground, and I wonder how Edmund is able to keep us upright. "Searching for it based on that reference alone, a reference we don't even understand, is rather like looking for a needle in a haystack."

"That is rather obvious, love, and the reason we haven't yet uncovered the location of the Stone." Dimitri is trying to keep the impatience from his voice, but I hear it nonetheless.

"Yes, but that is why we've been looking at it all wrong." I pull my eyes from the parchment, meeting Dimitri's gaze. "We haven't been using what we have already."

"And what's that?"

I wave the parchment at him. "This. There are only nine locations left."

His brow furrows. "Yes."

"If we give the list of nine locations to Victor, perhaps he can research only those nine, looking for a reference to Sliabh na Cailli'." I pause, suddenly feeling that my idea is not as profound

as it seemed in the quiet of my chamber two hours ago. "It's no guarantee, I suppose, but it's better than starting from nothing, isn't it?"

Dimitri is quiet in the moment before he leans over to kiss me on the lips. "It's far more than we had before. And so simple it's brilliant."

I try to absorb his enthusiasm, attempting to recapture the hope I felt upon waking with the idea to bring the list to Victor. But all at once, I'm not so sure. It seems a tenuous thread on which to hang our hope for answers, and with all the questions that remain, there is one thing of which I am certain: Beltane is only two months away.

And we are running out of time.

"Ugh! There are too many! We'll never get through them all!"

I lean back in the upholstered wing chair, knowing it's unladylike but not caring.

After some coaxing, Victor finally answered the door—a full twenty minutes after we began knocking. He listened to our explanation over a tray of tea and toast and began pulling books from the shelves of the library almost as soon as we showed him the list.

"Psh!" Victor says in response to my frustration. "You may speak for yourself, young lady. Now that I have a direction in which to work, I will not cease looking for your answer until I've researched each and every location on that list."

I scan the room, settling on the enormous pile of books stacked on the reading table in front of us. "But we'll be here all day!" The thought makes me sit up straighter. "Edmund? What time is it?"

His eyes find the clock on the mantel. "Nearly eleven. Why?"

Bolting out of the chair, I touch my hand to my forehead, realizing what I have done. "Helene. Helene is arriving this morning and is likely at Milthorpe Manor as we speak." I am already calculating the consequences to my relationship with Sonia and Luisa.

"Whoever this Helene is, she seems rather important," Victor says, standing. "Not to worry. I will continue searching, and I will send word the moment I find something."

I take in again the stack of books still waiting to be investigated. "Are you certain? It doesn't seem right to leave you alone with the task."

He laughs aloud, clapping his hands together. "My dear girl, I have little to occupy me in my hours alone. You do me a tremendous service, I assure you!"

I smile, leaning forward to kiss his dry cheek. "Oh, thank you, Victor! You're a dear!"

He flushes, and I wonder how long it has been since he has been touched by anyone. "Nonsense! It's my pleasure." He heads for the door of the library. "Come. I'll show you out."

We make our way down the hall amid hurried goodbyes, and a few moments later Dimitri and I are in the carriage, Edmund at the reins, on our way back to London.

"Do you think he'll find anything?" I ask Dimitri as Victor's house fades away behind us.

"I don't know. But it's more hope than we had yesterday."

The carriage ride goes much too fast. I prepare myself for meeting Helene and facing Sonia and Luisa by imagining the scene in my mind, but it does nothing for my nerves, which grow tighter and tighter the closer we get to home.

"Would you like me to come back to the house with you?" Dimitri asks, taking my hand as we enter London.

I resist the urge to say yes, for Sonia and Luisa will already be angry that I have not included them in my morning plans. Having Dimitri there would only be salt in their wounds.

"No, it will be better for me to greet Helene alone. I expect you'll meet her soon enough, in any case. She'll be living at Milthorpe Manor."

"How much did Philip tell her about the prophecy? About her place in it?" he asks.

Sighing, I turn to look out the window, feeling suddenly claustrophobic in the close quarters of the carriage.

"He told her the truth in as simple terms as possible," I say softly. "Whether or not she believes him, well . . . that is another matter entirely."

"She must believe him, at least in part. Why would she come to London otherwise?"

"Because she is haunted by dreams, as we all have been. She told Philip that she travels unwillingly in the dark of night. She feels the Souls at her back, though she has not been able to give them a name until now." I do not meet his gaze, though

I feel it even as I continue to look out the window, suddenly hesitant to allow him to see the fear in my eyes. "The prophecy has claimed her as it has claimed us all."

Dimitri's fingers touch my cheek, turning my face to his. When I look into his eyes, the love I see burning there is fierce. "It has not claimed you, Lia. And it *will not* claim you as long as I live."

He touches his lips to mine and I try to lose myself in his kiss. I try to let it drown out everything else. My worries and nightmares and darkest thoughts.

But it doesn't quite work. I have come too far to think it so simple. It is not within Dimitri's power to save me. My salvation will have to be my own doing, and I'll have to do it with the help of my sister.

The idea is inconceivable, and I push it aside, for if I think too long about the impossibility of bringing Alice to my cause, I will remember the futility of it all.

And if I remember the futility of it, I will have no choice but to wonder how long it will be before I find myself staring over the edge of a cliff. Just like my mother.

9

Stepping into the foyer at Milthorpe Manor, I hear the murmur
of voices in the parlor.

I hang my cape near the door, smoothing my skirt and
straightening the pins in my hair before making my way down
the hall. I am nervous, and I wish that I had allowed Dimitri to
accompany me home after all. Or at the very least, that Edmund
was beside me instead of outside, putting away the carriage.

The voices become clearer as I near the door of the parlor. I
recognize Sonia's soft cadence and Luisa's raucous, heartfelt laugh,
but underneath them is another I have never heard. Deeper and
richer than the voices of my friends, this voice speaks of a mystery
yet to be solved—of an unfamiliar life lived in a faraway land.

I take a moment, only a moment, to gather my wits before
stepping into the room. I don't know if it is meeting Helene for
the first time or the prospect of facing Sonia and Luisa's anger

that causes my heart to race, but standing in the doorway will not allow me to avoid either. Not for long.

Stepping into the room, I try to cross it with confidence, avoiding the eyes of Sonia and Luisa as I make my way to the unfamiliar girl sitting in the high-backed chair near the firebox.

"Good afternoon. I'm sorry for my late arrival. I had an errand this morning that took longer than expected." Her dark eyes survey me with veiled interest as I approach. Her hair, piled atop her head in a formal arrangement, is as black as the night sky above Altus. "You must be Helene Castilla." She blinks at my outstretched hand and I withdraw it, remembering that many young ladies find the shaking of hands overly masculine. "I'm Lia Milthorpe, and I'm so pleased to make your acquaintance. Did you have a pleasant journey?"

She nods slowly. "The journey was long, but not unpleasant. Mr. Randall saw to my comfort." Her English is accented with an exotic undertone. I think her very like Luisa in looks, though her manner holds none of Luisa's endearing approachability.

Turning to follow her gaze, I realize Philip is standing in the shadows.

"Philip!" I make my way to him, leaning in to kiss him on the cheek. "I didn't see you there! How was your journey?"

He smiles, the wrinkles around his eyes deeper than when I last saw him. The prophecy has taken its toll on us all.

"The crossing was difficult. We were cursed with rough seas the entire way, though Miss Castilla was quite stoic about the whole thing." He flashes her a smile, and I wonder if it is my imagination that her eyes soften as she returns it.

"But why are you standing?" I ask him. "You must be exhausted. Come and sit. Have you eaten?"

Philip shakes his head. "It is a pleasure to stand. I've been sedentary far too long on the ship." He casts his eyes to Sonia and Luisa. "We were offered refreshment, but alas, we are too tired even to eat. I imagine Miss Castilla would like to see her room. We were simply awaiting your return."

There is no recrimination in his voice, yet I feel a flush of shame for being so careless with the time at Victor's. "Of course." I turn to Luisa and Sonia. "Have Helene's bags been taken to her chamber, then?"

Luisa nods, her mouth tight. "The staff has settled her into the yellow room upstairs."

Her obvious anger sparks an irrational response of my own, for even as I acknowledge the unfairness of excluding Sonia and Luisa from the morning's journey to Victor's, I am loath to seek their forgiveness.

I force a smile, attempting to let go of my ill feelings. "Would you and Sonia mind seeing Helene to her room while I walk Philip out?"

She nods, standing, and I turn to Helene, holding out a hand and hoping, this time, that she will accept the gesture of friendship. "I *am* glad you've come. Please make yourself at home, and don't hesitate to ask the staff, or one of us, if you should require anything at all. Perhaps after a rest you will join us for dinner and we can become better acquainted."

She rises, her smile so small it is nearly invisible. "Thank you."

It is all she says before following Luisa and Sonia out of the

room, leaving me alone with Philip. A sigh escapes my lips as they disappear into the hall.

Philip makes his way toward me. "Is everything all right? You look tired."

I turn away from his probing eyes and move toward the fire-box. "Everything is as well as can be expected, I suppose. I think we simply grow weary of the prophecy and its demands."

"After all that has happened, you are certainly entitled to be weary. Is there anything more I can do to help?" he asks.

I turn to meet his eyes, feeling a rueful smile touch my lips. "I would say 'Find the last key,' but I know you are working to do just that."

He nods slowly, his brows knit forward. "I've gotten word from a small village of another young woman with the mark. I have some things to attend to here in London but should be able to investigate the claim in a few days' time."

I study his face. "Is it my imagination that you don't sound optimistic?"

"It isn't so much a lack of optimism as it is lack of information. I've already been told, you see, that the girl no longer resides in the town. Apparently her mother died giving birth to her, and her father took her away some years later."

I shake my head. "I don't understand. Why would you go if she isn't there?"

There is resignation in the shrug of his shoulders. "She's the only clue we have at the moment. I'm hoping someone will be able to tell me where she has gone. It is unlikely that it's her,

given our luck in the past, but it seems only prudent to follow every lead to its end."

I study my hands, the mark of the serpent revealed in a sliver from beneath the sleeve of my gown. Philip's words are no revelation. It is only practical to assume that our leads are reaching an end in the search for the keys. There are only so many girls who would be reported as having such a strange mark. Even still, the energy leaves my body in a rush, seeming to seep into the carpet at my feet until I am left with an all-consuming exhaustion.

"Yes," I say quietly. "We must be diligent in investigating every clue, however far-fetched. Take the time you need to recover from your journey with Helene. You've worked hard on our behalf, and you look quite tired yourself."

He smiles, heading for the parlor door. "No more than you, my dear. No more than you."

I link my arm in his. "Come, I'll show you out so you can go home to a proper rest."

We make our way to the front hall, where Philip plucks his coat off the rack near the door.

"Thank you for escorting Helene to London, Philip. Really. I cannot imagine what I'd do without you." I hope he sees the affection in my eyes.

Returning my smile, he places a hand on the doorknob. "Your father was a good friend. The prophecy, and your deliverance from it, has become my life's work. I only pray that I'm up to the task."

I move to speak, to assure him that if anyone can find the final key, it is him. But he is gone before I can say another word.

I intend to retire to my chamber to rest before dinner, but I find myself at a standstill a few feet past Sonia's room. I know that Sonia is on the other side, likely resting or running a brush through her hair or reading one of the books from Milthorpe Manor's library. The closed door fills me with sadness, for once I would have rushed in to share the events of the day.

No. Once, Sonia would have accompanied me anywhere and everywhere. There would be no need to fill her in, for she was my companion and friend in all things. The loss of it is suddenly unimaginable, and I make my way back to her door, knocking softly before I have a chance to change my mind.

She opens it a moment later, the curiosity on her face turning to surprise in the second it takes her to register my presence. "Lia! What are you...? Come in!"

Her obvious shock at seeing me in the doorway to her chamber fills me with guilt. I cannot remember the last time I sought her company.

I step into the room and Sonia closes the door behind me. "Come and sit. Sarah has just stoked the fire."

Making my way to her bed, I ignore the sitting area near the firebox. It is the only place I have sat on the rare occasions I have found myself in Sonia's chamber since her return from Altus. But this time, I lean against the plush mattress, studying the carpet under my feet as I remember when we sat comfortably on each other's beds, confiding and laughing and contem-

plating the future. In this moment, I want only for things to be as they were.

Sonia sits carefully next to me, as if afraid that I will change my mind and leave at any moment. "Is everything all right?"

I take a deep breath, looking up to meet her eyes. "I suppose things have not been right for a while now."

She nods. "Yes, but we are working to make them right again."

"I simply wanted to say that…Well, that I'm sorry." It is more difficult than I expect to say the words.

She takes my hand. "I know."

Her voice is not unkind, but her lack of denial causes a burst of indignation to rush through my veins. I attempt to quell the bitterness. It is a living thing that threatens to eat me alive.

I smile, though it feels like a mask over my face. "I'm trying, as you are trying, to make things as they were."

Her returning smile is sad. "Yes, but there is a difference."

"What is it?"

She turns her palms upward in a gesture of surrender. "You seek answers to the prophecy and work to forgive me, while I simply anticipate my fate." She shrugs. "You control everything. It is all I can do to wait. "

I want to refute her words, to deny their truth. But Sonia is right. I have held close all the power since leaving Altus. And as I nod, rising to leave her chamber, I cannot help but wonder if I hold that power because I fear betrayal — or because I have come to enjoy the feel of it in my hand.

Dinner is at first an awkward affair. Aunt Virginia attempts to make conversation by sharing Elspeth's gossip from the night of the Masquerade, but the underlying tension is felt by all.

I feel strangely paralyzed. My worry over the location of the Stone, the words exchanged with Sonia, and my impending conversation with James all conspire to make me silent, my words unable to compete with the thoughts in my head.

Finally I gather my wits, trying to remember how a proper hostess behaves.

"Is your chamber comfortable?" I ask Helene as I lift a glass of wine to my lips.

Setting her fork down, she nods. "Yes, thank you."

"And were you able to rest from your journey?"

"Yes."

Her face is closed, and I wonder if she is making things difficult on purpose or if she is simply unable to sustain a conversation.

"It must be painful, leaving your home behind." Sonia's words are soft. They bring to mind the memory of the girl she was in New York.

"It is...necessary," she says. "But yes, it is not easy to leave all that is familiar."

I think I see the stoic facade crack, just a little.

"I know just how you feel," Sonia says. "I was sent away from my family to live with a stranger in New York. I was very young, but I still remember how disorienting it was to be in new sur-

roundings." She smiles at Helene. "I did become used to it, however, as I hope you will."

Helene sits up straighter, the wall dropping in front of her face once again. "I think you misunderstand. I don't wish to become used to London. I want to return to Spain as quickly as possible."

Luisa shakes her head, her eyes clouded with questions. "Then why have you come?"

Helene places her glass back on the table, her elegant throat rippling as she swallows the wine. "Because I want this madness to end. I'm weary of being hunted in my sleep, of thinking dark thoughts even in the brightest sunlight. It has only grown worse as I've gotten older. If coming to London and joining with you means that I may at last be free, then so be it."

Aunt Virginia's nod is full of understanding. I wonder if she is thinking of my mother and her failed struggle to fight the Souls. "And were you surprised when Philip found you?" she asks. "When he explained your place in the prophecy?"

Helene studies her plate, the food forgotten. When she speaks, I hear remembrance in her voice. "I have always been different. It was more than the mark. For as long as I can remember, I have heard the voices of those on the other side. They spoke to me even when I begged them to stop. And that was not all. Even as a child, I frequently had flying dreams. I knew it wasn't normal to bring things back from my slumber, but I often did. A stone, a feather, a blade of grass." She shrugs. "They found their way into my bed at night, and I knew my dreams were real."

I am lulled into a state of relaxation by the candles flickering at the table and the lilting accent of Helene's voice as she continues.

"But soon they became unpleasant. Soon I was chased through the landscape of those dreams, and I no longer brought back tokens of pleasure. Instead, it was bleeding feet or bruises suffered while trying to escape things dark and frightening." She pauses. "I didn't know how to tell anyone save my parents, and they already suspected something was wrong, based on the mark and all the other strange things that had happened since I was a child."

"Were they understanding of your abilities?" I hear the pain in Sonia's question as she recalls her own parents' unwillingness to accept her otherworldly gifts.

Helene nods. "As much as they could understand such a thing. But it isn't enough." She meets our eyes, one by one. "I'm nearly eighteen. And yet, I cannot allow myself to fall in love, to laugh in the companionship of other young women without watching my every word, for who would accept such a thing? And how could I begin to explain it?"

I think of James and understand.

"There are people here," Luisa says softly. "People in London, like us, with unusual abilities. It doesn't have to be so lonely."

Helene's voice is no longer distant. "It's kind of you to try and make me comfortable. To offer your friendship. But I don't want such a life. I don't want to be a curiosity. To reside on the fringes. I want only to bring this to an end so that I can return to Spain and live a life of normalcy."

I remember when my aspirations were so simple. Before Dimitri. Before the role as Lady of Altus was bequeathed to me by Aunt Abigail and the laws of the island.

Yet it doesn't matter whether our dreams are simple or elaborate. Whether we wish to live quietly as wives or visibly as rulers of many. In the end, we all want the same thing: to live. To live on our own terms, without the prophecy as a millstone around our necks.

10

I have dressed carefully, though it shames me to admit, even to myself.

Only Aunt Virginia and Edmund know what I mean to do. I cannot bear to tell Dimitri and see the worry carefully tucked away behind a mask of confidence.

"Would you like me to accompany you?" Edmund asks as I step from the carriage in front of the Savoy Hotel.

I shake my head. He wouldn't give me a choice were he referring to anyone else, but even Edmund knows I have nothing to fear from James.

I gaze up at the imposing facade of the hotel. "You can wait inside if you like."

I feel rather than see him shake his head. "I'll be here with the carriage when you're ready."

Pulling my eyes from the hotel, I turn to smile at him. "Thank you, Edmund. I won't be long."

The streets are bustling with morning traffic, carriages and horses jostling for space among the men and women who crowd the streets of London. But it is all at the periphery of my mind. My stomach seems to fold in on itself the closer I get to the entrance of the grand hotel. The closer I get to James.

I don't have the number of his room, and it would be unseemly to meet him there anyway, however well we were acquainted in the past. Instead, I make my way through the richly appointed lobby to the front desk, stopping before a portly, dapper gentleman who favors me with a smile.

"May I help you, Miss?"

I swallow my nerves. "Yes, I've come to call on James Douglas, please."

The man raises his eyebrows. "And who may I tell him is calling?"

"Amalia Milthorpe." It is strange to say my given name aloud. I have not been referred to as Amalia since I left New York and the Wycliffe School for Young Ladies.

He nods. "Very well."

I turn away to wait, surveying the lobby nervously for signs of Alice. She likely knows that I plan to speak with James, but it will be that much more difficult should she wish to insinuate herself in our conversation. Even still, I am not sure what feeds my nerves more, the prospect of seeing Alice or that of seeing James. How strange, I think, that they are both here in London.

That they are so near and staying together in this very hotel in preparation for their wedding.

"Lia?"

I start at the sound of the voice behind me. I prepare myself to see him with my sister, but when I turn, it is James alone.

I smile. "Good morning, James."

His face is different than I remember, and I realize with surprise that he has aged. It is not unpleasant, and an unbidden thrill runs through me at the knowledge that he is no longer a young man but a proper gentleman. His eyes, as blue as the sky under which we walked at Birchwood, ask every question I'm afraid to answer.

"I'm happy you've come." He says the words, but he does not smile.

I nod, gazing around at the busy lobby. "Could we . . . ? Would you mind going for a stroll? It will be difficult to have a proper conversation here."

He does not hesitate. One moment we are standing in the lobby of the Savoy and the next he is placing my hand on his arm and making for the door. And then we are outside on the streets of London, as alone as we have been in the year since I left New York.

We don't speak as we make our way through the busy streets. The muscles of his arm are tight under my hand, and he leads with confidence, as if he knows exactly where he is taking me. I don't feel the cold in the air, though I can see the breath leave my body in a cloud of vapor.

Some time later we come to a park, hidden behind the branches of many trees and bushes. The sounds of the city fade as we pass through an iron fence into the sprawling refuge, and I feel some of the nervousness leave my body. I miss the peacefulness of Altus, of Birchwood Manor, though much of the time I am too busy, too worried, to notice the tension that creeps into my shoulders when I am in London for too long without respite.

We make our way down a cobbled pathway, secluded from the rest of the park by far-reaching trees on either side. The sounds of the city dim to a hush. Without the crowds of people, the rattle of carriages, and the clatter of horses clopping through the streets, I am even more aware of James's presence. I swallow hard against the memories that come flooding back with the feel of his body so near to mine.

"You didn't write." His voice breaks the silence so suddenly that it takes me a moment to realize that he is, in fact, speaking to me.

"No." It is not enough, but there is nothing more I can say.

We continue walking, rounding a bend in the pathway until I see a stretch of water up ahead.

"Didn't you... Didn't you love me?" he finally asks.

I stop, pulling his arm until he stops, too. Until I can look into his eyes. "That was not it, James. I promise you."

He shrugs. "Then what? How could you leave me with so little word? Why didn't you write when all the while you've been perfectly well and living in London?"

It's not that way, I think. *You're making it sound all wrong.*

And yet, with the limited information he has, that is exactly how it must seem.

I cannot look too long into his eyes, and so I pull his arm until we are walking once again. "I've been far from 'perfectly fine,' James, though I realize how it must seem to you."

We have reached the edge of a small pond that reflects the gray sky and laps rebelliously against the shore. It is colder by the water, but I note the chill with detachment even as my body begins to shiver.

James turns to look at me, removing his overcoat and draping it around my shoulders, underneath my cloak. "I shouldn't have brought you here," he says. "It's far too cold."

The familiarity of his touch makes it seem as if no time has passed at all. As if we are standing, at this very moment, on the banks of the river behind Birchwood Manor, listening to Henry laughing with Edmund in the background.

"I'm fine. Thank you for the coat." I turn to the iron bench standing guard at the edge of the pond. "Shall we sit?"

His thigh brushes mine as he lowers himself to the bench. I wonder if I should pull away, if I should distance myself from him out of regard for my relationship with Dimitri and James's engagement to Alice. Yet, I find I cannot. I enjoy the solid feel of him next to me. Allowing myself so small a comfort can do no harm.

Taking a deep breath, I begin as I must—at the beginning. "Do you remember the book? The one you found in Father's library after his death?"

His brow furrows in concentration. "I found many books in your father's library while cataloguing them after his death, Lia."

It has not occurred to me that James might not remember. For him, the Book of Chaos was simply one of many interesting finds, even as it changed my life — and his — completely.

"The one you found right after the funeral. The Book of Chaos? It was written in Latin?" I hope to jar his memory. It will be difficult enough for James to believe in the prophecy with the book as his guide. Without it, I imagine it will be next to impossible.

He nods slowly. "I think I remember. It was only one page?"

I breathe a sigh of relief. "That's right. You translated it for me, remember?"

"Vaguely," he says. "But, Lia, what does this have to do with —"

I raise a hand to stop him. "This is so difficult to explain, James. Could you just listen? Listen, and try to open your mind?"

He nods.

"The story in the book? The one about the sisters and the seven plagues?" I continue without waiting for an answer, struggling to find words that will not be too fantastical to believe. "It's not just a story, as we first thought. It's...It's more of a legend. Except that it's real."

He studies me, his face blank. "Go on."

I speak a little faster. "Thousands of years ago there was a legion of angels sent to watch over mankind, but they...they fell in love with mortal women and were banished from heaven." I cannot read the expression on his face, and I continue before I lose my nerve. "Ever since, the descendants of

those women, all twin sisters, have been part of a prophecy. A prophecy that claims them, one the Guardian, one the Gate, just as it said in the book."

"One the Guardian, one the Gate." His voice is a murmur, and I wonder if he really remembers the words in the Book of Chaos or if he is just repeating mine.

"Yes. My mother and Aunt Virginia are descendants of those women, James, as are Alice and I. My mother was designated as Gate, marked to usher Satan's followers, the Lost Souls, to our world, where they wait for his return. As Guardian, it was Aunt Virginia's task to keep my mother in check. To ensure she didn't allow passage of the Souls, or at least to minimize the number that gained entrance through her. But Virginia couldn't stop my mother from fulfilling her role.

"It wasn't what Mother wanted, but she couldn't fight it, James. It ate away at her until she believed she had no choice except to sacrifice her life. But that just meant the prophecy passed to Alice and me."

"What has this to do with your leaving, Lia?" His voice is gentle but tinged with something I already fear is skepticism.

"Alice is the Guardian, James, and I am the Gate." I say it quickly. "Except I'm not just any Gate. I'm the Angel of the Gate, the one Gate with the power to allow passage to Samael himself. I'm...I'm trying to fight it. To find a way to bring it all to an end, but Alice rejects her role as Guardian and instead covets mine.

"She has worked in concert with the Souls since she was a child, and even now works to bring about the end of the world

as we know it." I take his hand. "You cannot marry her, James. You cannot. You will be by her side when the world falls, and though you will be safe because of your allegiance to her, everyone you love, everything you value, will turn to dust."

I hold his gaze, staring deep into his eyes. I want him to believe that I speak the truth. I want him to feel it. To see it in my eyes.

He returns my stare for a moment before standing and walking to the edge of the water. The silence stretches between us, long and fragile. I dare not speak.

"You needn't have done this." His voice, cast out over the water, is so quiet I have to lean forward to make out the words.

"What?" I ask. "I needn't have done what?"

"Concocted this...this...story." He turns to look at me, and I want to weep at the anguish in his face. "I still love you, Lia. I've always loved you. Will always love you." He crosses the space between us, dropping before me and taking my hands. "Are you saying that you still love me as well? Is that what this is about?"

I study his face, his eyes, looking for something I might have missed. Some shred of belief in the prophecy. In me. But there is only the adoration, the love that would once have been enough.

"You don't believe me."

He blinks in confusion. "Lia, it doesn't matter, don't you see? You don't need this story. I have only ever wanted you."

I cast about for something—anything—that will make him see. Make him believe.

"I know it's difficult to believe." I reach down, rolling my sleeve as I speak, looking into his eyes with every ounce of truth inside me. I thrust my hand toward him. "But look at this, James. I bear the mark of the prophecy. Have you ever seen it on my hand before now?"

He glances reluctantly at the mark on my wrist, as if he does not want to lay eyes on anything that will give credence to my story. His gaze remains there for only a second before returning to mine.

"I've never noticed it before, Lia. But it doesn't matter. It doesn't change anything."

I let my hand fall into my lap and turn away from the fever in his eyes. It is not the fever of love but of denial.

"This is why I didn't tell you." My voice is heavy with bitterness. "I knew then you wouldn't believe me. I've carried the guilt of leaving you all these months, when I was right all along."

He shakes his head, looking wounded as he scrambles for words. "I will believe you, Lia. If that is what it takes to get you back, to prove my love, I'll believe anything."

My throat hurts as I swallow the knowledge that Alice was right. James will not believe me. Despite his words, there is not a shred of doubt in his face. Not a glimmer of possibility. Only a desperate willingness to tell me what I want to hear.

"It's not that simple, James. Not anymore."

He shakes his head. "I don't understand."

I pull my hands from his, pushing past him to stand by the water as a strange sensation builds inside me. It is nothing I

expect. Not sadness for all we have lost or fear for James's safety.

It is anger at the regret that has consumed me since leaving New York. Since leaving James. Anger at the hours spent agonizing over my inability to tell him the truth all those months ago.

I turn, removing his coat from my shoulders as I walk back to where he stands. "I'm sorry, James. This was a mistake." I hold the coat out to him, my voice catching in my throat. "It was wonderful to see you again. I wish you well."

Turning away, I hurry up the path, his voice following me every step of the way.

"Lia! Lia?"

I try to ignore it, to hurry ahead without looking back. But he catches up to me in no time at all, stopping me with a hand on my arm.

"I don't understand. I love you. That was once all that mattered. If my believing you means the difference between our being together or not, I'll believe."

His face is earnest, and I wonder that he can look so sincere while proposing that we base our renewed relationship on a falsehood. I think of Dimitri, of his utter willingness to accept all the darkest and most dangerous parts of me.

"It would be a lie," I say.

His jaw tightens as he looks away, considering. A moment later he turns back to meet my gaze. "I don't care."

His words free me, and all at once it is not so difficult to let go.

"But that's just the thing, James." I touch my hand to his cold cheek. "I do."

I turn to leave. And this time, he does not give chase.

The letter is waiting when I arrive back at Milthorpe Manor. Seeing the sender's name, I tear open the envelope with eager hands, not even bothering to remove my cape. My heart beats wildly as I read the words written on thick parchment, and seconds later I am back out the door and calling to Edmund.

I stare out the window as we make our way through the streets of London, daring to hope that we are finally moving toward the prophecy's end. When the Society's building finally comes into view, I step from the carriage before Edmund has time to come around and open the door.

"I'll be back in just a moment!" I call out as I hurry up the steps to ring the bell.

The butler smiles when he sees me standing on the door-step. "Good morning, Miss. He's in the library."

"Thank you." I return his smile, edging past him as I have more times than I care to remember.

But this time is different. This time I come bearing answers.

Dimitri looks up as I enter the library. "Lia! What is it? Is something wrong?"

I am not surprised to find him at the reading table near the window, books spread out in every direction. I cross the room until I am standing right above him.

"No. Nothing is wrong." I wave the parchment. "In fact, I'd say that, finally, something is right."

He plucks the paper from my hand, his eyes scanning the words until he looks up to meet my gaze. "But this means..."

I nod, smiling. "That we're going to Ireland?"

He meets my grin with one of his own. And suddenly, nothing is impossible.

11

Because I haven't told anyone about my planned attire, I am prepared for their reaction. Even so, my cheeks become hot as I make my way down the steps toward the waiting horses.

Aunt Virginia watches with open shock as I approach, recovering only after I come to a stop before her. "You are wearing breeches?"

She does not mention the man's hat under which my hair is hidden or the fact that I have done all I can to disguise the fact that I am a woman at all. Apparently, these infractions pale in comparison to the shock of my breeches.

I look down at them and smile before raising my eyes to hers. "It must seem strange to see me dressed in such a way. But I've been wearing them riding for ages, and it is difficult to move quickly with a skirt about my legs." I do not tell her that I *must* move quickly. That the adder stone grows cooler by the day and that all our lives depend on my ability to find the Stone and close the Gate as soon as possible. She knows it all too well.

She hesitates before nodding slowly. "The fate of the world is entrusted to you, dear niece." She leans forward, wrapping me in an embrace. "I think you're capable of choosing your own attire in any situation, and most certainly in this one."

Taking a deep breath, I allow myself to sink into her embrace for just a moment. In the absence of my mother, Aunt Virginia has offered me endless wisdom and support. I will miss her presence now more than ever, but someone must stay and look after the other girls while Dimitri and I make our way to the ancient stone caverns at Loughcrew, Ireland. That Victor found an ancient mention of Loughcrew in connection with an unusual turn of phrase may be only coincidence, but in the absence of other possibilities, we would be foolish to ignore it.

I pull away, looking into Aunt Virginia's eyes. "I'll be back soon." I lower my voice, casting a glance at Sonia, Luisa, and Helene, who wait near the horses. "Please look after everyone, and be watchful of anything untoward."

She nods, and I know we are both thinking of Sonia's betrayal. I lean in to kiss her cheek before making my way toward the others.

Sonia and Luisa huddle near each other, with Helene just a few inches away. I cannot help but approach them with hesitation as I recall my conversation with Luisa the day I sought Madame Berrier and Alistair Wigan. The resentment still lingers in her eyes, and for one fleeting moment, I question my decision to leave the keys in London.

But it does not last long. Riding with a group would be too cumbersome. Time is a luxury we do not have, and it would be foolish to allow Helene access to the possible location of the Stone when we have only just become acquainted. It was difficult enough to discover the connection between the ancient cairns at Loughcrew and the prophecy. I'm not about to put that knowledge at risk.

And then there is the other thing. The thought I push away, forbidding it to take root in the fertile soil of my lingering distrust.

As much as I think it wise to withhold important information from Helene until we come to know her better, neither do I want to divulge anything crucial to Luisa or Sonia. Even as I acknowledge that it may be wrong, I know without a doubt that I cannot afford to take the chance.

I come to a stop before them, looking down at my riding boots. Laced at the ends of my trouser-clad legs, they do not seem like they belong to me.

When I finally look up, I take the coward's way out and first address Helene. "I'm sorry we've not had time to become better acquainted, but you're in good hands here. I hope you'll make yourself comfortable. If all goes well, we will be much closer to bringing this all to an end when I return."

She nods, her face impassive, as it always seems to be. "I trust you're doing what you must. Don't concern yourself with me."

I smile at her before turning to Luisa. "I'm ... I'm sorry to be traveling without you. I will miss your company. Will you be all right while I'm gone?"

Her mouth, once set in a hard line, softens. She looks away before turning her gaze back to mine. "Everything is well in hand here, Lia. Do what you must."

The defeat in her voice wounds me like nothing else. Luisa has always been an endless source of optimism and humor. It seems the prophecy has taken even that. Either that or it is my doing alone.

I nod, forcing myself to swallow around the tightening in my throat. We stand awkwardly before each other, and I reach out to take her hand, squeezing it before I turn to Sonia.

I don't know how long we stand in silence before Sonia finally speaks. When she does, I am startled by the anger in her voice.

"Do what needs to be done, Lia. Do it, and end this thing." She turns, stalking away from me with her arms folded across her body against the cold.

I stand, stunned into immobility, until Dimitri reaches me. He takes my hand and leads me to the horses. "She is hurt and angry, Lia. It will pass when this is all said and done."

His words do not make a dent in my sadness, but I follow him nonetheless.

Edmund hands me Sargent's reins, and I reach up to stroke the horse's nose.

"I still don't like the idea of the two of you traveling alone," Edmund says.

I smile. "As much as I would welcome your presence, you're needed here more. It cannot fall to Aunt Virginia alone to care for the other girls and get them to and fro. And with Alice so close..."

He gestures to the satchel draped over my shoulder. "You have your bow and dagger?"

I nod, and he turns to Dimitri. "You'll look out for her."

Dimitri's face is somber as he clasps a hand to Edmund's shoulder. "With my life, Edmund, as always."

Edmund looks at the ground, his shoulders rising in a sigh of defeat. "All right, then. You'd best be going."

Dimitri climbs into his horse's saddle as I lift the satchel over my head so its strap crosses my body. Giving Sargent's nose one last stroke, I move to his side and place one foot in the stirrup, swinging my leg up and over in one easy motion.

Dimitri turns his horse, his eyes meeting mine. "Ready?"

I nod, and we spur the horses to action. I do not look back as we make our way down the street. I am too busy trying to ignore Dimitri's question, simple though it was, and my own lingering concern that I am not ready at all.

For the journey to Ireland, or anything that is to come.

☙

My spirits lighten as we make our way through town. Exhilaration courses through my veins where before there was only worry over the journey ahead. It takes me a moment to place the feeling, and when I do, I cannot help but smile.

Freedom, I think. *I feel free.*

Released from the constraints of my skirts and petticoats, I feel closer to free than I have since leaving Altus. The breeches are not as welcome as the robes of the island, but they are a close second. Summer is two months off, and though there is

still a noticeable bite in the air, it is invigorating rather than unpleasant. It will almost certainly be colder once we reach the woods, but even this knowledge cannot dampen my mood as Dimitri and I make our way through the city—first by way of the busier thoroughfares and then by increasingly small, less populated ones.

It was far easier to prepare for the journey to Ireland than the one to Altus. Dimitri and I discussed our plans at length with Edmund, arranging for supplies and maps in just a few short days. We packed light, carrying everything we need on the flanks of our two horses.

I pass the morning in a pleasant state of absentminded thought. Dimitri and I make comment of the people on the roads, the carriages and horses, the buildings. The sun is high overhead when I realize the city is well behind us. Roads that were once dusty and crowded have turned to winding lanes through outlying villages, and the air that was ponderous with smoke and scent has become clear and sweet.

"Are you hungry?" Dimitri says from my left.

I didn't notice my hunger before the words were spoken, but now my stomach tightens. I nod.

He tips his head at the road in front of us. "There's a farm up ahead. Let's stop and see if we can purchase something to eat."

I do not have to ask why we shouldn't use the supplies in our packs. The journey to the Loughcrew cairns will take us nearly two weeks, and there will undoubtedly come a time when food and places to purchase it will be scarce. It is only wise to save what we carry as long as possible.

We walk the horses to the thatched-roof farmhouse, where Dimitri secures bread and cheese from a pretty young wife in exchange for a few pence. She directs us to the barn behind the house, urging us to make use of the buckets of water, and we wash our faces and hands before leading the horses to drink. They slurp noisily as Dimitri walks the length of the barn, looking for a place to sit and take our lunch.

"Here." He waves me to the back of the barn. "There's an empty stall with some hay. It will make a fair enough seat, I think."

I smile, both amused and heartened that even here, Dimitri looks after my comfort.

The stall is dim and touched with shadows, and I sit on the floor, opting to lean back against the bales of hay rather than use them as a seat. After hours in the saddle, it feels good to slump against the straw, scratchy as it is. I don't even feel self-conscious about my bad manners around Dimitri.

He sighs, stretching out on his side and supporting himself on one elbow. "This is heaven. I could stay here for days with no one but you and the horses for company."

I take a bite of the cheese, marveling at the clean, sharp tang of it in my mouth. "Me and the horses, is it? I suppose you wouldn't be happy with just me, then?"

He throws a piece of bread into the air and catches it in his mouth before turning back to me. "You're wonderful enough, of course, but sometimes...Well, there's just nothing like a good horse to keep a man company."

"Oh, really?" A smile tugs at the corners of my lips. I toss a

small piece of bread at him. "I'll keep that in mind tonight when we make camp. Perhaps Blackjack can keep you company in the tents."

He plucks the bread from the hay near his thigh and tosses it into his mouth. "Perhaps. And I'm happy to give you my blanket if you think you'll be cold all alone."

I laugh aloud. "I'll take it under advisement."

His eyes sparkle with mischief for a moment before turning serious. "You've no idea how much I love to hear you laugh."

Swallowing the bread in my mouth, I look into his eyes. The sun breaks through the roof in places, setting alight shimmering motes of dust as they dance through the air between us.

"I shall endeavor to laugh more, then, if it pleases you."

He crooks a finger in my direction. "Come."

I remain in my spot, still teasing. "Why, sir, I'm otherwise engaged with my bread and cheese."

He doesn't answer, but the desire in his eyes speaks the only words I need, and I scoot down next to him a moment later.

"Lia...Lia..." He traces his fingertip across my brow.

He does not move, but his gaze draws me toward him until it is I who lean forward, touching my lips to his. I let my mouth linger softly for a moment, the breath moving between us in a whisper.

A groan escapes from his lips, and I lean forward, kissing him with all the pent-up urgency of the past days and weeks. Days and weeks in which we have been ensconced inside parlors and libraries and eyed by the staff at the Society and Milthorpe Manor.

He presses me back into the hay. I can hardly breathe as his hands linger just above my body, not quite touching me but close enough that I would swear I can feel his fingers on my skin.

Reaching up with my arms, I wrap them around his neck, pulling him to me until his body is stretched long and tight against mine.

"Did you arrange this, Dimitri Markov? So that we could finally be well and truly alone?" My voice is a murmur in his ear, and I feel the goose bumps rise at the back of his neck.

He kisses his way down to the place where my bare skin disappears beneath the cotton of my shirt. "I would do that and more," he says, "to have you to myself for a moment."

His lips work their way back up my neck until I think I will perish with pleasure. I know we should leave, but I push aside thoughts of anything but this moment. This moment when there is nothing else in the world. No prophecy. No Stone. No Souls.

Just us. Dimitri and I alone in a world of our own making.

I give myself over to it, ignoring the voice inside me that whispers: *Hold this moment. Your time with him is not long.*

12

"What causes you to think with such concentration?" I jump at the sound of Dimitri's voice beside me. He speaks softly, but his words echo in the dark night around us.

I look up, placing a hand to my chest so that I can feel my runaway heartbeat beneath my fingers. "However do you *do* that?"

"What?" He sits down next to me on the fallen log near the fire.

"That," I say. "Sneak up on me so quietly."

He shrugs. "I didn't mean to startle you. And *you* are changing the subject."

I laugh softly, my voice an intruder in the deep night. "I'm not changing the subject. I was only thinking about the cairns and wondering if the Stone will really be there."

He sighs. "Yes, well, I suppose we won't know for sure until we arrive and have a look around, but Victor's discovery is the closest we've come to a connection between any of the sites on our list and the prophecy."

"Loughcrew." I murmur the word, sending it out into the darkness like a prayer. "Portal to the Otherworlds."

"Yes." Dimitri's voice is soft. I hear the hope in it.

Victor's skilled research, together with the list of nine possible locations, revealed what weeks of disorganized, hopeful digging on the part of Dimitri and I had not: Loughcrew was once referred to as "the Portal to the Otherworlds." We cannot be certain it points to our Otherworlds rather than an abstract, mythical idea, but it cannot be ignored.

Even still, I hesitate to voice my fear aloud. It seems that speaking the words will only give them more credence. I quickly discount the notion. The possibilities are all before us, whether or not we name them.

"What if it's not the right place?" I ask.

He doesn't say anything right away, and I know he is contemplating an answer that will maintain some semblance of hope.

In the end, he chooses honesty. "I don't know. I suppose we'll have to find the answer if, and when, that comes to pass. But one thing is certain."

I turn to look at him. "What is that?"

"Every step we have taken has had a purpose. Even those that seemed only obstacles at the time led us to something else." He turns away, speaking to the fire. "Regardless of whether

we find the Stone at Loughcrew, it is one more step in our journey to end the prophecy. And with every step we take, we are that much closer to the end."

The camp is quiet as I settle into the blankets. Dimitri's shadow, distorted by the tent and the firelight beyond, is a comfort, though I would prefer his presence beside me. We argued the point for some time — Dimitri insisting on keeping watch while I disputed his ability to make the journey without at least some rest — until we agreed on a solution for the dilemma: Dimitri will stay awake, guarding the camp until first light, after which he will sleep for a short while before we break camp. It means a later start each morning, but even Dimitri must rest eventually, and convincing him to sleep beside me has been futile.

My body is already stiff from being atop Sargent, and I know it will be days before I am once again accustomed to the rigors of riding for long stretches. It has been many weeks since our trip to Altus, and though I have ridden alone at Whitney Grove, it has only been to the targets to work with my bow.

Reaching for the adder stone around my neck, I test it for warmth. Attempting to gauge the stone's remaining strength has become a cruel pastime. I do it even as it becomes increasingly difficult to tell whether the adder stone is, in fact, cooler than it was yesterday, or the day before. Certainly, it is much cooler than it was when I awoke on Altus to feel it burning feverishly at my chest, but the change from day to day is nearly impossible to discern. Yet it does not stop me from trying, as if receiving confirmation of its waning power will somehow prepare me for the time when it will be gone for good.

Letting go of the stone around my neck, I slip the fingers of my right hand around the medallion on my left. The adder stone is a reminder that I am a Sister. That the light of the Sisters on Altus and the many who have come before them courses through my veins.

But I cannot ignore the medallion, for it is a part of me, too. It whispers to the pieces of myself I keep hidden, locked away for fear that if anyone were to see them as they really are—to see me as I really am—the fate of the world would never again be trusted in my hands.

I am conscious that I am dreaming even as I sleep. I stand in a circle, the warmth of others' hands in each of my own. The figures on either side of me are robed, their hoods pulled forward to hide all but the shadowy planes of their faces.

Strange words rise from my throat. Both fear and exhilaration race through my body, and my own robe billows about my legs as a hot wind blows from the center of the circle. I am forced to stop my chant as something tugs at the core of my body, wrenching itself free as if it has been long hidden, long quiet, long sleeping. Crying out, I drop the hands of those next to me even as someone calls to me from very far away.

"Don't break the circle."

But I do. Overcome with my own fear and pain, I break the

circle. I stumble into the center of it and see the hands join behind me, merging the figures together as one.

As if I were never there at all.

The tugging continues until I feel as if I will be pulled in two—as if I am being pulled apart from the inside out. I fall to the ground, and the black sky, shimmering with ageless stars, unfolds above in the moment before something clamps my wrist. Turning to my side, I lift my hand to see the mark.

The serpent.

It writhes and twists, searing deeper into my skin until I feel as if it melts away the flesh at my wrist completely.

I cry out for it to stop, but it doesn't. It burns and burns and burns.

"Lia! Wake up, Lia."

I open my eyes to the voice and find Dimitri looming above me in the tent.

"You were crying out in your sleep." He smooths the hair back from my brow.

The fingers of my right hand hold my left wrist in a viselike grip, and I lift it to my eyes, trying to make out the mark in the little illumination the moon provides inside the tent. It is no deeper. No darker. I imagine I feel the residual burning from my dream but do not trust myself enough to give the idea merit.

Taking a deep breath, I try to calm my racing heart before answering Dimitri. "I'm...I'm sorry."

"You're sorry?" He scowls. "Lia, you don't need to apologize. Ever."

I have a flash of the circle in my dream, the robed figures, my own voice speaking unfamiliar words. "I had a nightmare."

His face softens, and he lowers himself to the ground, stretching his body out beside mine and taking me into his arms until my head is pressed to his chest.

"Tell me," he says. "Tell me your nightmares."

The silence between us is a weight on my heart, and I am reminded of another instance, another time when I was urged to speak of my fears. Of the things growing wild and dark in the fortress of my consciousness. Alice is right; we have both made decisions that have informed the places in which we find ourselves now. James once gave me the opportunity — more than once, in fact — to tell him what was happening to me.

But I didn't trust him. I didn't trust his love.

Dimitri, his voice a murmur in my ear, speaks to my hesitation. "I love you, Lia. We don't speak of it often, but know it now. Know it, and tell me your fears so that I can rid you of them."

I take a deep breath, inhaling the scent of him. It is the scent of Altus. Of the most beautiful of all the Otherworlds. Of my past and future. It gives me the strength to look into his eyes and tell him.

I tell him of my nightmares. Of their increasing frequency. Of my inability to forgive Sonia — to find one shred of love for her in the aftermath of her betrayal. Of the decreasing heat and strength of Aunt Abigail's adder stone. I tell him of Alice's

visit to Milthorpe Manor. Of her assertion that we are not so different.

And then I speak of my biggest fear of all: the belief that Alice is right and it is only a matter of time before the prophecy turns me against all that I hold dear.

13

"Did you sleep well?"

Dimitri's voice is clouded with tiredness as he kisses the top of my head.

"As well as possible," I tell him, burrowing farther under the blankets and enjoying the moment of quiet before we will have to pack up camp and spend the day riding yet again.

He says nothing but pulls me closer to him in understanding.

I am still surprised by Dimitri's reaction to my confession. I'm not sure what I expected. That he would despise me? That he would not look upon me with the same admiration?

I don't know. But in the four days that have passed since the night I told him everything, I have searched his face for signs of suspicion or repulsion. Yet even in the moments when his thoughts have been elsewhere, I have found nothing but devotion in his eyes.

I feel both liberation and sadness when I realize that it would not have been the same with James. Finally, there is no room for regret. James would not have believed me then as he does not believe me now.

All there is to do now is to save him.

And to save him—and the world as I know it—I must stop Alice and the Souls.

Dimitri and I do not speak as we pack the camp and eat a quick breakfast before resuming our travel. Our meals on this journey are considerably simpler than they were on the way to Altus. With only the two of us to consider and the need to pack light, we subsist largely on cheese, bread, apples brought from London, and the occasional small animal one of us is able to hunt with my bow.

Five days into the journey, we are more than halfway to the water that will take us to Ireland. The landscape changes by the day as we move away from Southern England. Rolling hills and farmland have given way to scrubby, barren moors. They are an apt reflection of my increasingly dark mood, and I find myself staring at the bleak landscape and thinking of my sister. It is true that our relationship has always been woven with complex thread—laced with love, fear, awe, and, yes, even hatred. But as I think of Alice now, I am filled with an unsettling anxiety. It is too vague to place, but it grows by the hour. By the time we make camp and finish dinner, I am certain something is wrong.

I should not be concerned for Alice's welfare, but it seems everything that happens to Alice somehow happens to me as well. We are as intertwined as ever, whether I wish it or not.

Our fates have lasting implications for the prophecy and all who are held hostage by it. The worry nags at me as I prepare for bed and kiss Dimitri good night. I fall quickly into sleep, and am unsurprised when my spirit being rises into the night sky of the Plane.

I can hardly remember a time when traveling was unfamiliar, yet I feel a thread of foreboding as I realize that I am being summoned by my sister. The wiser part of me realizes that I should deny the call and make my way back to my slumbering body with haste. But even as I think it, I know I will not. My earlier unease will not allow me to hide from a potential explanation, and I fly above the ground, the dark fields passing below me in a blur as I make my way back through the landscape of the Midlands and into Southern England.

I see London long before I reach it. Smoke, visible even against the night sky, hovers like a great monster over the city. Yet, locating Alice is instinctual. Even now, my soul gravitates to hers until I find myself approaching the hotel where I met James two weeks ago. The facade of the building is imposing in the night sky, but I float through it without effort, touching my feet with relief to the thickly carpeted floor. I feel Alice's presence like a tug of absent memory and drift through the doorway to the grand bedchamber beyond.

A fire blazes in the firebox, casting a flickering orange light over the room. I cannot feel the heat of the flames in my spirit body, but I sense their energy and know the room must be warm. Scanning the shadows, it takes me a moment to place my sister, but I finally spot her slight figure in the shadows cast

by the canopy of a thickly blanketed bed. Even from my vantage point near the door, I see her shoulders shaking, her body wracked with sobs.

The sight alarms me, for I cannot think of a time when I have seen Alice cry. Not when our mother died after flinging herself from the cliff over the lake at Birchwood. Not when Father's body was found, his face frozen in a silent scream. Not when we laid Henry's small, broken body to rest in the cold ground surrounding Birchwood Manor.

I am drawn to her — this shattered Alice, this more human version of my sister — even as I am shocked to discover myself in the physical world. It is possible, of course, to cross the veil between the worlds so that one might be seen when traveling. Alice has proven it can be done, even in violation of the Grigori and their ageless rules. I could do it, too, if I wished it. I have become powerful enough.

But it is a burden I do not want. Had she lived, my mother would have had to answer to the Grigori's council for her use of forbidden magic. Alice, tutored by the Souls in the use of their dark powers, has only added to the cloud of suspicion surrounding our family name. Should I survive to take my place as Lady of Altus, it will be difficult enough to earn the trust of the Sisters. It would be foolish to violate the laws of the Grigori now. And while I admit to being curious, I do not wish to force a confrontation with Alice. There is nothing to be gained. I want only to discover the cause for my disquiet and am grateful that I was summoned here through no intention of my own.

I approach her carefully, stopping a couple of feet from the bed. She is curled up on her side, her face hidden by one arm thrown over her head. The position brings with it a flash of memory, and I see Alice at six years old, after our mother's funeral, lying on the bed, her arm draped across her face in exactly this manner, but without the tears.

Bending down, I peer more closely at her, tuning my ears as I catch the hint of words hidden in her sobs. At first I think I am imagining it, but a moment later I hear them again and have to restrain myself from shouting for her to repeat them.

Her hair, shimmering chestnut in the light of the fire, has fallen over her face. My hand lifts without thought, the urge to push it back from her brow nearly overpowering me.

And then, all at once, her words become clearer and I understand what she is saying.

"He doesn't love me. Will never love me."

I stop my outstretched hand a few inches from her face as she goes on, her body wracked with fresh sobs at the sound of her own words.

"I will never be...enough." Her voice is broken. Despair leaks from every word. "It will always be you."

I am surprised to feel the sting of tears at my eyes. I blink them away, feeling disloyal to Henry. If I must take responsibility for my part in where we now find ourselves, so must Alice.

Her crying slows in the moment before she moves her arm, giving me a clear glimpse of her face, moist with tears. She seems to gaze directly at me, though there is not enough light

to reflect the green of her eyes. They are black as ebony in the dim glow of the fire.

I peer closely at her, watching her lips move with whispered words. I lean in a little closer, trying to make them out. When I do, when I hear them at last, I pull back with a start.

"It is all your doing. He will never love another, least of all me."

I swallow my fear, for even now, as she lies before me seemingly broken, I fear her. I tell myself that she cannot see me, but then she speaks again, her eyes meeting mine. I feel suddenly trapped in a very strange and dangerous dream.

"I see you." Her voice is a twisted singsong breaking the near silence, and I am reminded of the little girl who first gave me the medallion. "I know you rejoice in my suffering, Lia, but remember this: If James will not be mine, then I truly have nothing left to lose."

14

The waterfront is not as I imagined it, but I am too tired to care. Nine days on horseback coupled with eight cold, dream-riddled nights have left me on the verge of exhaustion. By the time we pass the horses off to the men hired ahead of the journey, I am anxious for a change of scenery and eager to board the boat that will take us to Ireland. I kiss Sargent's nose, patting his smooth flank one last time, and take Dimitri's hand.

"We're supposed to meet our guide near the wharf," he says, leading me around the rubbish, dead fish, and street urchins that populate the streets near the water.

The stench is overpowering, but I do my best to appear unfazed. Not everyone lives in the luxury of Milthorpe Manor. Still, the rough-looking men glance at me with something like hunger, and I cannot help but worry for our safety. I clutch the strap of my satchel more tightly, finding comfort in the proximity of my bow and dagger.

I look up at Dimitri as we walk. "But how will we know our guide?" I lower my voice. "How can we be certain he's not one of the Souls? It would be an easy matter to hide behind the guise of any of these men."

Dimitri's smile is sly. "Trust me."

I sigh as a small boy no older than six years of age approaches, his hand outstretched. "Anything to spare, Miss?"

His cheeks are sunken and his clothes hang about him in tatters, but his eyes are bright. Reaching into my pocket, I hand him a piece of dried meat left over from lunch. I expect his hand to be grimy, but it is smooth and dry.

"Thanks be to you, Miss!"

I watch him scamper away, thinking of Henry. For all his privilege in many things, fate dealt him a blow in making him my brother. I am not surprised to feel my heart grow heavy. Henry's death is a loss that never dims.

"You miss him." Dimitri's voice pulls my thoughts from Henry.

I meet his eyes. "How did you know?"

He squeezes my hand, his voice low. "I simply do."

I look away from the tenderness in his eyes and take the opportunity to scan the pier upon which we now stand. It is old and worn, the wood faded and splintered from many a storm. We walk its length, heading toward the place where it drops off into the water.

"Are you certain we will——"

He sighs. "We'll recognize our guide, Lia. I promise."

I stifle my annoyance, though I am not sure if it's aimed at his interruption or the fact that he has anticipated my question.

We stop at a slip near the end of the pier and I lean out over the water. A small sailboat is tied on, its owner bent over the bow, deep in concentration. He rises when he hears us behind him, and suddenly I understand.

"Gareth!" A smile breaks across my face. It feels foreign and unfamiliar, for there has not been much cause to smile during the long journey from London to the waterfront. "What are you doing here?"

His hair glints gold even in so gray a light, and he is as tan now as he was on our journey to Chartres. I wonder again how he can be so brown while the sun struggles to break through the clouds that seem to make their home over England.

His own smile outshines mine by a mile. "Brother Markov sent word that a trusted guide was needed to escort an important Sister across the water. No Sister is as important as you, my Lady, and no Brother more trusted than I." I laugh aloud as he punctuates his statement with a wink.

Dimitri crosses his arms over his chest. "Ahem."

Gareth holds out a hand. "Present company exempt, of course."

Dimitri's face remains serious, and I wonder if the spark of rivalry from our trip to Chartres has been ignited once again. But a second later, he is grinning and reaching out to clasp Gareth's hand.

"It's good to see you, Brother. Thank you for coming."

"I wouldn't miss it." Clapping his hands together, Gareth stabilizes the boat by holding on to the pier. "Now climb in. It's a long trip across the water. Let us make use of the daylight."

I stare at his outstretched hand without moving. With only the sailboat rigging and a few planks for sitting, the boat is not large, and the water beneath it is murky and dark. Water always gives me pause, but this is too close to the memory of our boat ride to Altus. It is impossible to think of it without remembering the kelpie's trick on that journey and my own dark descent beneath the water after I reached out to touch its glimmering skin.

Gareth's eyes soften. "Come now, my Lady. You are far too brave to bow to the intimidation of the Souls and their monsters. Besides," he says, "the Lady of Altus must always walk through her fear."

I take his hand and step gingerly into the boat. "I have not yet accepted the appointment," I grumble.

"Yes, yes," says Gareth, leading me to a seat inside the boat. "I believe you've mentioned that."

Dimitri drops in behind us, and within moments Gareth has freed us from the pier. We drift away, Gareth and Dimitri busying themselves with the sails, and I wonder if there is anything Dimitri can't do.

I watch the water while remaining as far as possible from the side of the boat. I think of the crystal sea, smooth as a looking glass, that cradles Altus. This is a different ocean entirely. I cannot see beyond the flotsam-covered surface, and stray pieces

of rubbish bump up against the sides of the boat as the water moves beneath us. I am not eager to know what lies below.

It is well past midday when we clear the port. Dimitri and Gareth finally sit, and we enjoy a leisurely lunch as they compare notes on word from Altus. Gareth has heard that Ursula is campaigning for support in the hope that I will fail. As a distant relative, she would be next in line should I be unable to assume the role vacated by Aunt Abigail upon her death. It is no secret that Ursula wishes to claim the seat of authority that is rightfully mine, nor that she wishes to see her young daughter, Astrid, succeed her.

I worry my lower lip between my teeth, taking in the news from the island I have come to love. It causes me great disquiet to think of Ursula grappling for position even as I risk my life and the lives of others to bring an end to the prophecy that binds us all.

But it is just the thing, just the reminder, I need.

I cannot afford to give in to my fear—of Samael's monsters, of the Souls, or of my own dark nature. There is too much at stake, and though I may question fate's decision to give the responsibility to me, it is mine.

One way or another, I will accept it.

❦

I pass the rest of the day observing Dimitri and Gareth work the sails, listening with interest as they explain how the various contraptions work. I think I might like to try sailing on my own one day, and I imagine sailing with Dimitri on the crystal waters off Altus.

By the time we finish our meager dinner, the boat's course is set and we are carried along on a steady wind. It is colder still on the water, and I lean back against Dimitri for warmth, watching the sky darken a little at a time. The novelty of the boat has worn off, and I begin longing for the luxuries of home.

I crane my neck to look at Dimitri. "Do you know what sounds lovely?"

"Hmmm?" His voice is lazy.

"Guinea hen. A giant roast guinea hen with crispy skin and meat so moist it falls off the bone."

I feel the laughter in his chest and twist to look at him. "What's so funny? Aren't you hungry for something other than dried meat and bread?"

"Yes, yes, I am." His voice is still warm with humor. "I've simply never heard you pontificate about food."

I slap his arm playfully. "I'm hungry!"

"She has a point," Gareth says from the other side of the boat. "I'd like some of the apple pudding from Altus, straight from the oven and hot enough to burn my mouth."

I look up at Dimitri. "What about you? What would you like?"

His voice grows serious. "I don't need anything else. I have everything I want right here."

I look up at him with a smile. Something quiet but profound moves between us in the moment before he opens his mouth to speak again. "Although a roast guinea hen and hot apple pudding would be welcome."

It is my turn to laugh, and I lean back again, reveling in the feel of his strong body against mine. As we sail toward Ireland beneath the deepening sky, I am not conscious of being tired. I am simply content, and in the moment before the darkness of sleep claims me, I do not have time to wonder at the oddity of finding peace in the middle of the Atlantic with nothing but two able men—one already a friend and the other something far more.

❧

I expect to be handed off to another guide upon arrival in Ireland and am happy to learn that Gareth will be our escort all the way to the cairns at Loughcrew. He maneuvers the boat expertly into a small slip at the dock and we make our way to the teeming waterfront, where Sargent, Blackjack, and a horse I recognize as Gareth's are handed off to us by a ginger-haired young gentleman. His mouth lifts in a shy, respectful smile when he meets my eyes, and I wonder if he, too, is a Brother of Altus. I do not bother asking how the horses made the crossing. I have become used to the many mysteries of the Sisterhood and the Grigori and am satisfied to leave them as such for now.

After mounting our horses we pass through the crowded waterfront and continue into Dublin proper. Then the city is behind us, and the endless Irish countryside is a lush green carpet in every direction.

Dimitri and Gareth determine that it is safest to avoid the main roads, and we spend the day crossing verdant meadows

and rolling hills. Although cold, it is a pleasant day's ride, the wild, open beauty of the landscape illuminating some of the darkness lurking in the corners of my heart.

I turn to Gareth. "How long will it take us to reach the cairns?"

"A day or so, provided we don't meet with any trouble."

I nod, disappointment dampening my serenity.

"Do you think you'll decide soon?" Gareth asks a moment later. "About the position as Lady of Altus?"

I look over at him, stepping carefully around the details of the prophecy that he does not know. "It seems foolhardy to think of it when there is still so much unfinished."

I feel the weight of Dimitri's silence and avoid his eyes. We are both aware that my decision involves more than simply my place on the Isle. I have not yet formally accepted Dimitri's offer to be together should I survive the prophecy. At first it was because of James and my uncertainty about my feelings for him. Now it is uncertainty over my own future, and a superstitious fear of taking too much for granted.

Gareth's brow furrows. "The workings of the Sisterhood and the Grigori remain something of a mystery, even to me. Although I'm often entrusted with critical tasks, no one is told everything. Yet..."

He hesitates, and I prompt him. "Yet?"

"It seems once this business is concluded, you will have to make a decision rather quickly, does it not?"

I nod slowly. "I suppose so."

"Well, then—with all due respect, of course—should you

not make your decision in advance so that you might accept or refuse the role when the time comes?"

I try to smile. "You are most wise, Gareth. I'll give it further thought."

And all that day, I do. Gone is my earlier sense of peace, for Gareth is right: It is foolish to hide from the truth. I have done that too often in the past—hidden from the realities about Alice, Sonia, my very own family. It has done me nothing but harm, and it doesn't take long to come to at least one conclusion.

When all is said and done, there are only two possible outcomes: end the prophecy and make a decision that will change the course of my life forever—or die trying.

15

I feel our approach to the cairns before I see them. It is a pull originating from the center of my body, one that draws me forward so powerfully that I'm quite certain I could find my way even without Gareth. I am surer than ever that the Stone is there, for why else would I have such a powerful reaction to a place I've never been? I try to find comfort in the belief as we come upon a pathway spilling out of a small forest.

"This will be the road leading to the house. I don't know about you, but I cannot wait for the comfort of a proper bed," Gareth says, leading us into the sparsely wooded forest.

I try to smile through my weariness. "I'm most hoping for a bath."

"I will take both of those together with a good meal," Dimitri adds.

The pathway is too narrow for us to stay abreast of one

another, so we ride single file as we make our way through the trees. For a while, I lose all sense of time and place. I am almost startled when we finally emerge into a clearing, the house visible in the center, its gray stone nearly blending into the steely winter sky beyond. I cannot help but smile at the tendrils of smoke that rise from the chimney.

Looking over at Gareth and Dimitri, I grin. "Warmth!"

They return my smile, and we walk the horses over to the fence at the front of the house.

"We'll tie them here for the time being," Gareth says. "Let's go meet our hosts."

Dismounting, I secure Sargent to the fence post, taking a moment to nuzzle his neck. "Thank you," I whisper, patting his flank before joining the men at the walkway leading to the house.

"What is the caretaker's name?" I whisper to Dimitri as we stand on the stoop, waiting for a reply to our knock.

"Fergus. Fergus O'Leary."

I nod, repeating the name under my breath as a sudden knot of nervousness ties itself around my stomach. I have become accustomed to keeping my own counsel. To Milthorpe Manor in London, to Dimitri, and to those with whom I've become familiar. It will be strange to stay in someone else's home while searching for the Stone.

Gareth is raising his hand to knock again when the door is opened. I am expecting to see an older man and have to blink a few times at the sight of the girl standing in the doorway before us. Then I remember. Dimitri said the caretaker has a daughter.

"Good afternoon." She nods her head, a soft Irish lilt touching her words. "You must be Mr. Markov and company."

Dimitri nods, meeting my eyes in a silent reminder to use only my first name. All of the accommodations were arranged by Dimitri, and we have agreed that it is best to keep secret as much as possible about the purpose of our journey—and my identity.

"These are my associates, Lia and Gareth." Dimitri nods at each of us. "Gareth will only be staying the night."

I look at him with a start. I should not be surprised, for Gareth has not been told the purpose of our stay at Loughcrew. As before, when we made our way to the missing page, Gareth can be allowed only a glimpse into the prophecy's workings. It is the way Aunt Abigail wished it, and so it will remain.

"Please, come inside." The girl steps back, allowing us passage into the house before closing the door behind her. "I'm Brigid O'Leary. My father is waiting in the parlor."

She turns and we follow as she makes her way down the hall. Candles flicker along the walls, casting their light on Brigid's hair. At first, I thought it blond like Sonia's, but now I see that it is threaded with burnished copper.

The hallway is narrow and dim. I cannot keep from peeking into the rooms as we pass. The furnishings are not nearly as grand as those at Milthorpe Manor, but I note their well-worn comfort and decide I like the house already.

"Here we are." Brigid leads us through a doorway on the right and we emerge into a small room. A gray-haired gentleman sits at a reading table, a large book spread before him as he bends his head to a piece of parchment, his right hand moving across it with a pen. "Excuse me, Father. Our guests have arrived."

He looks up, his eyes clouded. I recognize the expression. It is the look my father used to get when he was deeply immersed in research in the library. The look of one returning, reluctantly, from another world.

"What do you say there, Daughter?" He peers at us in confusion, and I wonder if Brigid has somehow forgotten to tell him of our impending arrival.

Her voice is gentle. "Our guests, Father. They've arrived. Remember, Mr. Markov sent word that he would require rooms during his study of the cairns?"

Dimitri and I have concocted a story that we are scholars preparing an important report on the historical significance of the cairns. It will allow us to move about freely, asking questions that might lead us to the location of the Stone without arousing too much suspicion.

"Mr. Markov?" He looks at us questioningly for a moment more before understanding lights his eyes. "Ah, yes! Mr. Markov. We've been expecting you." Standing and moving toward us, he says it as if he was not, just moments ago, staring at us without recognition.

He walks straight to Dimitri, arm outstretched, and shakes his hand carefully before turning to Gareth and doing the same. But when his eyes settle on me, I think I see a wall drop. I cannot help but think there is suspicion in his gaze. "Look here, Brigid. 'Tis a lass! It seems Mr. Markov's friend will be good company for you."

Two fiery spots of red appear on Brigid's creamy cheeks, and she ducks her head. "Shush, Father! I'm sure Mr. Markov and his associates have important work to attend to and will have little time for leisure."

Dimitri nods. "We are on a bit of a deadline. We need to complete our research and be on our way as quickly as possible. But," he winks at Brigid, "I'm certain there will be ample time for friendly conversation."

She nods without enthusiasm.

Mr. O'Leary clasps his hands behind his back. "There now, you see? It will be nice for you to have the company of a young woman, Brigid."

But even as he speaks, it does not seem that he thinks it will be nice, and I feel suddenly as if I have fallen down the rabbit hole and landed in another world altogether. It may be sheer exhaustion, but there seems to be hidden meaning behind every word the O'Learys speak, every glance they cast at each other when they think we're not paying attention. I scold myself inwardly for being overtired and melodramatic, but I am relieved nonetheless when Mr. O'Leary claps his hands together and speaks.

"Well, now. Let me see to your horses while Brigid shows you to your rooms. You do have horses, don't you?"

Gareth nods. "The horses are out front, tied to the fence. I'll come along and help you get them settled."

"Tsk, no. Clean up and rest from your journey. 'Tis well in hand."

He turns to go, but Dimitri's voice stops him in his tracks.

"Mr. O'Leary?"

"Yes?"

"I understand you have five rooms for rent?" Dimitri reaches into his pocket.

Mr. O'Leary nods. "Yes, but there are only three of you, are there not? Until tomorrow, when this one leaves?" He gestures at Gareth. "Though we can certainly prepare additional rooms if you've a need."

Dimitri stretches his hand toward the older gentleman. "I haven't a need for more rooms, Mr. O'Leary, but my work is very important and must be done in silence. I would like us to remain the only guests for our duration here. I will, of course, pay for the empty rooms."

Mr. O'Leary hesitates, looking at Dimitri's hand with something like distaste, though surely he must not get many visitors to the cairns in the months of early spring. I wonder if we have offended him, but a moment later he takes the money from Dimitri's hand. He says nothing further before turning to go.

Dimitri's eyes meet mine in the faint light of the room, and I know we are thinking the same thing: No one is above the suspicion of working for the Souls. Not even Mr. O'Leary and his daughter.

"Is there anything else I can get you?" Brigid has filled a large copper tub in the center of my chamber. Steam rises and curls above it, disappearing like ether into the softly lit room.

"No, thank you. The bath is lovely."

Brigid nods. "We serve dinner at six, if it's all right with you."

I notice that her sleeves, far too long, are damp at the cuffs from running my bath. I feel a pang of guilt for my earlier criticism, however warranted, of the O'Learys.

I smile. "It's perfectly fine. Thank you for everything."

We stand in a silence made awkward by the length of time it stretches between us, and I cannot help but feel as if she has something else she wishes to say. I wait, and a moment later she says it.

"You've come from London, then?"

"That's right." I purposefully avoid elaborating. Vagueness is a friend to those with something to hide.

She casts her eyes downward, chewing her bottom lip as she contemplates her next words. "And will you be here long?"

It is only idle curiosity, I tell myself. *She is alone in the middle of nowhere with no one but her aging father for company.*

Even still, I harden my voice, hoping to deter further questions. "As long as is necessary to complete our work."

She nods once more before turning to leave. "Enjoy your bath."

I stand, unmoving, trying to stem the tide of suspicion that has risen in the wake of our arrival at Loughcrew. Something plucks at my subconscious until I'm certain an important clue is hidden there.

I realize what it is sometime later as I tip my head back against the copper tub, the bathwater cooling against my skin.

Dimitri and I are not from London. Not really. In fact,

neither of us has been in London long enough to develop a Londoner's accent. I still speak enough like an American that I routinely garner strange looks from those who come from the city. Gareth, for his part, is a drifter, traveling widely on behalf of the Brothers and Sisters of Altus. He has even less accent than I. We are all in rough dress, having purposefully avoided anything fine to prevent drawing attention to ourselves.

And if all of that is the case... if all of that is the case and Dimitri was careful not to let slip our origins, there is no reason for Brigid to assume that we have come from London. Which means she has either taken a wildly accurate guess, or she knows more about us than she should.

16

Dinner is an awkward affair. Whether due to shared suspicion or unfamiliarity with our hosts, we eat mostly in silence, with only the occasional attempt at friendly conversation by Gareth. Brigid has changed into another too-large gown, and her sleeves come perilously close to dragging in the various dishes and sauces on the table before us. I feel a moment's sadness for her solitude and obvious lack of feminine guidance.

Despite the strangeness of the company, we eat enthusiastically. Brigid, with the help of an old woman from a town some distance away, has cooked us a wonderful meal. It is simple in preparation but extravagant in quantity, and I eat heartily in portions that would give any proper young woman pause. We are sipping ale after dessert when Mr. O'Leary finally mentions our purpose for coming to the cairns.

"I expect you'll need a guide, then." I am almost certain I catch a hint of hopefulness in his voice.

I have not found an opportunity to fill Dimitri in on my conversation with Brigid, and I speak before he has a chance to answer. "Actually, we prefer to work alone, though we do appreciate the offer."

Dimitri casts a glance my way, and I try to send him a look that says, *I'll explain everything later.*

Mr. O'Leary's nod is slow. "I expect you'll have a map of the site."

"We do, as a matter of fact," says Dimitri. "But I'm sure we will have need of your expertise as we get further into our research."

Brigid speaks from her father's right. "Father knows much about the cairns. If there is anything specific you seek, he'll be able to help you find it."

Mr. O'Leary's laugh is a cold wind in the candlelit dining room. "Daughter, you have forgotten; Mr. Markov and his party seek only historical knowledge of the cairns. And that is easy enough for any man learned in the ways of research." The sarcasm in his voice is obvious, and he turns to look at Dimitri. "Isn't that right, Mr. Markov?"

Dimitri holds his eyes. "That's right."

There is a moment of silence in which the two men stare each other down. I almost wonder if they will come to blows, so intense is the hostility between them, but a minute later Mr. O'Leary pushes his chair back from the table.

"It has been a long and tiring day, for you more than any.

Please make yourselves comfortable. Brigid serves the morning meal at seven."

He disappears into the hall and Brigid rises with an awkward smile. "My father is unused to company. We rarely have guests, and it's easy to forget how to behave among others. Please forgive him."

Dimitri sits back in his chair, at ease now that Mr. O'Leary has gone. "Think nothing of it."

Brigid nods. "Is there anything else I can see to before retiring for the evening?"

"I can speak only for myself," Gareth says, "but I have everything I need in the mattress that awaits me upstairs."

"We're fine, thank you." I try to smile at her. To force down my unease with the reminder that we are all tired and skittish.

"Very well."

We say our good nights but remain around the table in silence until she has been gone more than a minute.

Gareth leans forward in his seat, his voice a loud whisper. "What was *that* all about?"

Dimitri shakes his head. "Not here." He rises, gesturing at us to follow. "We'll have to speak in one of our chambers, and we'll have to do it quietly."

We follow him up the stairs, past the rooms assigned to him and Gareth upon our arrival. He stops at the door to my chamber, pushing it open. He lifts his eyebrows in silent question and I nod, giving him permission to enter my room though he is asking only for Gareth's sake. Dimitri is welcome in my room, and he knows it.

Once we are all inside, Dimitri closes the door and we move farther into the room. A fire has been lit in the firebox, and we cross to the small sofa and set of chairs that sit before it. Gareth sits in one of the high-backed chairs, covered in threadbare tapestry, while I curl up at the end of the sofa. Dimitri drops to the carpet before the fire, stretching his long limbs with a sigh and leaning back on his forearms.

"Now," he says softly. "What do you suspect?"

I take a deep breath. "I'm not sure. It's just that Brigid asked if we came from London. But not in the way one asks when one needs to hear the answer."

"I must be confused about the nature of an inquiry, then." Gareth's voice is tinged with humor. "Isn't that the only way one asks a question?"

I level my gaze at him, trying to keep the exasperation from my voice. "No. Sometimes one asks a question to confirm something one already knows."

"So you think Brigid already knew we came from London?" Dimitri asks from the floor.

"It certainly seemed that way." I look from one to the other of them. "Are you sure that neither of you let slip our origins?"

"Positive," Dimitri says without hesitation. "I've taken great care to protect our identities, our backgrounds, anything and everything beyond the story we concocted. After what happened on the way to Chartres, I take no chances with your safety, Lia." His voice is full of something deep and rich, and I feel my cheeks flush with heat.

"Gareth?"

He shrugs. "I don't know enough about your reason for being here to give anything away, and I've not had the time or inclination to babble on about London. You and Dimitri are both well-spoken, and many scholars probably do come from London to study the cairns. Isn't it possible that she simply guessed?"

"Perhaps." I gaze into the fire as if it holds the answer to all our questions. "It is possible, I suppose. I . . ." I look up, meeting Gareth's eyes. "I simply feel that they know more than they're letting on."

"I agree with Lia." Dimitri speaks softly into the room. "It may well be nothing, but we cannot afford to take chances. We'll have to keep a close eye on them while we're here, and guard carefully any discovery."

"Would you like me to stay?" Gareth asks. "I can at least keep watch and see to your safety."

Dimitri meets my eyes, leaving the question to me. He knows well my desire to see to things the way Aunt Abigail would have seen to them, at least until such a time as I know enough to do them differently.

Yet, I am tempted. Since Sonia's betrayal, the people whom I trust have dwindled to an alarmingly small number.

But Aunt Abigail did not wish Gareth to be told. When she assigned him as one of our guides to Chartres, she entrusted him with only a small piece of the journey, just as she did with the other guides. It is impossible to believe that I, with my small experience and knowledge, would know better than she.

I smile at Gareth, reaching out for his hand. He looks at my outstretched arm in surprise, looking to Dimitri as if for

permission. When Dimitri gives him a small nod, Gareth takes my hand in his.

"Dear Gareth, if there were anyone with whom I could share my secrets, it would be you. It's for your safety and my own that I must decline. But I heartily wish it were not so."

He nods. "I'm always at your service, my Lady." Squeezing my hand, he grins before I can reply. "And you needn't bother to remind me that you have not yet accepted the appointment. The people of Altus, *your* people, need you. No true Lady can turn away from the call of her people, and there is no truer Lady than you."

I swallow against the emotion that fills my throat, but Gareth stands, saving me the embarrassment of trying to speak around it. "I'll leave you to rest. Good night."

"Good night, Brother." There is both respect and affection in Dimitri's voice as Gareth makes his way from the room.

Dimitri and I sit in the silence left by Gareth's departure, the crackling and shifting of the logs in the firebox the only sounds in the room. When I look over, Dimitri is watching me, his eyes dark and inscrutable. Leaning back on his arms, his white shirt stretches taut across his chest, the undone tie at the collar revealing a smooth stretch of skin. If I were to undo the remaining laces, I could push the shirt from his shoulders and kiss his chest, his stomach.

"Why do you look at me so?" I am caught in the tide of his eyes, unable to deny the desire in my voice.

The passion in his gaze is a reflection of my own. "Can I not look at you for the simple pleasure of doing so, my Lady?"

I look away. "Don't call me that, Dimitri. Not here. Not now. I don't wish to be Lady of Altus. Not yet."

He pats the carpet next to him. "Come." His voice is thick with longing.

I go to him, crossing the few feet that lie between us and dropping next to him on the floor.

"Closer." He speaks the word so softly I almost cannot hear him.

Moving toward him, I stop when my face is a few inches from his.

"Closer still," he says.

I smile and move closer until our lips are but an inch apart. "Here?"

His own smile is sly and dark. "That will do." He reaches for me, lifting my face just a little to meet his. "Even when the time comes for you to reign, you will never simply be Lady of Altus. Not to me."

He lowers his mouth to mine, his lips soft in the moment before they slide to the sensitive skin of my neck. My head tilts back and I fight to keep a moan from escaping my mouth.

"What, then?" I whisper. "What will I be?"

He speaks against my skin. "That is a simple question. You will be my love. My heart." His lips continue their journey, making their way to the soft spot at the center of my collarbone. "However strong you must be when you face the world, with me you may lay yourself bare and come to no harm."

My body is afire, lit from within by the spark of his mouth and the soft words spoken in a whisper. Sliding down so that I am lying half on top of him and half on the carpet, I push him back against the floor. My hair is a dark curtain around us, the firelight only barely visible through the shimmering strands.

"I think I would like to lay myself bare before you, Dimitri Markov." This time it is my mouth on his, and I linger there, feeling his lips move against mine.

When I pull away, he touches a finger to my kiss-swollen mouth. "I can wait, Lia. I'll never stop waiting."

17

I sleep poorly, haunted by strangely contrasting dreams. One moment I am back within the fire-lit circle, the mark on my wrist burning and burning. The next I am in Dimitri's arms, my skin bare and warm against his. By the time I emerge from my room the next morning, I am grateful for the lack of a looking glass in my guest chamber. I am certain I would not like the reflection gazing back at me.

I hear the murmur of voices below and follow them down the simple staircase to the main hall, reassured by the weight of Mother's dagger in the drawstring bag swinging from my wrist. Paranoia may have led me to bring it, but I would rather have it and not need it than the other way around.

Making my way toward the back of the house and the parlor I remember from our arrival, I am surprised to see only Dimitri, his head bent to a book. The chair in which he sits is dwarfed by his sturdy frame, and I feel a flash of desire as I remember being locked in his strong arms only hours ago.

"Good morning," I say softly in an effort not to startle him.

He looks up, his eyes alert. "Good morning, my love. Did you sleep well?"

The endearment is new, and a rush of pleasure courses through my body as, all at once, I realize that I *am* his love. And he is mine.

I cross the room toward him, stepping into his arms as he stands. "No. Sleep is not my friend these days, I'm afraid."

He tips my chin up, studying my face as carefully as if it were the book he was reading. "Ah, yes," he says, nodding. "I should have looked before I asked. It's plain to see that you have not had a restful night."

I give him a gentle shove. "Why, thank you! Am I supposed to be flattered by such an observation?"

He kisses the tip of my nose. "It isn't meant as an insult. You're lovely to me at any time of the day or night, in any condition. I worry about you, that's all. You're looking gaunt and tired, and we still have much work ahead."

I smile, touched by his concern. "It's nothing some fresh air and a good meal won't cure." I step away, looking toward the hall. "Where is everyone?"

"Mr. O'Leary and his daughter are seeing to household matters." Dimitri hesitates, rubbing the stubble at his chin. "I'm afraid Gareth has gone."

"Gone?" I shake my head. "Whatever do you mean?"

He leans toward the tea table, picking up a folded piece of

parchment. "He doesn't like goodbyes, he said. He departed early this morning, and he left this for you."

He hands me the parchment and I turn to the fire, unfolding the thick paper and adjusting my eyes to the slanting script.

My Dear Lady,

I am sorry to leave without saying goodbye, but I've never liked them, least of all now. I wish you could entrust me with your task, for it is obvious that it weighs heavily on your heart. Please know that if, at any time in the future, you need assistance or simply a trusted friend, I am at your service and pledge my devotion.

Regardless of the path you choose, you will always be the rightful Lady of Altus to me.

Your faithful servant,
Gareth

I fold the parchment slowly, feeling the loss of Gareth as an unpleasant surprise though I knew he was leaving today. So many of the losses I have suffered have been sudden, forced upon me with no time to say the many things I wished to say.

I suppose I wanted, just this once, to say goodbye.

"I'm sure he meant only to spare you both sadness." Dimitri's

voice comes from behind me. "It's clear you've come to mean a great deal to him."

"And he to me." I speak the words softly into the fire, taking a deep breath before turning to face Dimitri. "Shall we take breakfast in the dining room and begin our day, then? I'm sure we have much to do."

"Breakfast is certainly in order." He smiles, reaching for my hand. "But not in the dining room. Come. I have a surprise."

The fields lay magnificently before us as we gallop across the countryside, the hills rolling this way and that in every direction. The sky is unusually blue, and as I look up, marveling at its clarity, I feel the world tilt until I think I will drown in the sea of it.

The cairns watch us from a distance, the strange hills and rocky outcroppings dotting the lush plain. We drive the horses toward them, and with every step I feel the same strange familiarity I felt at Chartres. By the time we stop at the base of the largest cavern, my nerves are humming with awareness. I feel myself bonded to this stark landscape and its underground caves, but it fills my heart with a melancholy I cannot explain.

Dismounting from Sargent, I scan the outcropping and surrounding fields before turning to Dimitri with a smile. "While this is a lovely surprise, I hardly think you can take credit for the cairns. They have, after all, been here for centuries."

He pulls a bundle from his saddlebag and makes his way to

a spot in the sun, very near the sloping, grassy wall of the hill that houses one of the caverns.

"You've grown comical, Lia." He nods his approval. "I quite like it. But the cairns are not your surprise, silly girl."

I hold out an arm in a sweeping motion to take in the landscape around us. "Well, this *will* be difficult to top, but I'm certainly willing to give you the benefit of the doubt."

He shakes out a bundle of cloth and I see that it is a woolen blanket, crisscrossed with beige and green plaid. "Now I'm afraid to tell you what it is because you're right — it will pale in comparison to so lovely a morning in so lovely a place."

I make my way to him, rising on tiptoe to place a kiss on his lips. "Nonsense. You've brought me all this way. And without breakfast! I demand my surprise."

He sighs in mock weariness. "Very well, then. I'll do my best to meet your expectations."

Reaching into a sheepskin bag, he begins removing parcels wrapped in cloth. A moment later I join him on the blanket as he unwraps boiled eggs, fresh bread, cheese, apples, and a small earthen pot of honey.

He surveys the arrangement of food, moving the pot of honey a little to the left and the eggs a bit to the right before speaking. "Now, let us eat."

I drop next to him on the blanket, taking his face in my hands. I touch my lips to his before speaking. "It's marvelous, Dimitri. Really." I look into his eyes. "Thank you."

He returns my gaze before rising to a sitting position and

reaching for the bread. "I wasn't eager to repeat last night's dinner debacle—especially on our first morning at the cairns."

I sigh, taking a piece of the bread he hands me and reaching for the honey pot. "A very wise decision indeed." Drizzling honey over the bread, I replace the lid on the pot and take a bite. It is unlike any bread I have tasted, dry and crumbly and full of butter. "So. Where shall we start?"

"I think we should spend the day getting the lay of the land. It's difficult to get a sense of the place with only the map on parchment."

I nod, reaching for the cheese. "Yes, and it would help if we could discover the significance of any one of the caverns. If the Stone is here, it would likely be hidden someplace important, would it not? As with the final page at Chartres?"

"That would be my guess, though I haven't found anything specific in the little research I was able to do before we left. I even asked Victor, but he sent word that this site, like many in England and Ireland, has been left to deteriorate for some time." He takes a bite of one of the apples. "It seems no one in recent history has made meaningful study of it."

I sigh, attempting to stifle the frustration that is already rising within me. It is far too soon for that. "Well, then, if there is no easy answer, I suppose we should begin."

Dimitri nods, jumping to his feet. "Quite right."

We wrap our rubbish and place it back inside Dimitri's saddlebag before mounting the horses. The site is large, and it takes us the morning and some of the afternoon to cover it. We do not enter any of the cairns. Not yet. This is simply a day to

get our bearings, and we spend it riding the fields. We stop from time to time, and I recite for Dimitri the basic physical structure of the hills and caverns so that he can make note of it for later. We cannot be sure their outward appearance is important, but anything that might set one cavern apart from another might be helpful.

By the time we head back to the house, the light has grown blue-gray with the setting sun. Although we have not made any discoveries this day, we have taken the first, important step to locating the Stone.

And it is here somewhere. I can feel it.

18

That night we are prodded with questions throughout another dinner with Mr. O'Leary and Brigid. I finger the hilt of my dagger through the fabric of my bag as they repeatedly ask about the cairns. This, despite Dimitri's early assertion that we did nothing but scout atop horseback. It is only after dessert that Mr. O'Leary seems to accept the explanation of our day, and I cannot tell if I see relief or disappointment in his eyes.

I am anxious to leave the table and am relieved when enough time has passed that Dimitri and I can bid the O'Learys good night without seeming rude. We ascend the stairs together, stopping in the doorway to my chamber for a hurried but passionate good-night kiss before Dimitri heads to his room down the hall.

It is a relief to pull off my breeches and shirt. They are more comfortable than gowns and petticoats, but it is still heavenly to feel the slide of my nightdress over my bare skin.

Slipping into bed, I pull the wool blankets all the way to my chin, grateful for the fire in the firebox. I wonder if it is Brigid's doing, for I have seen no household help other than the woman who comes to cook supper. I do not bother to check the adder stone. I have given up the habit of testing its heat these past days. It has become too difficult to deny its waning strength. Instead, I allow myself a moment of denial and slip into the abyss of sleep.

I am certain that I am inside one of the caverns at Loughcrew, though there is nothing to mark it as one of the cairns. I know it in the inexplicable way one knows things in dreams.

At first I am alone, making my way through the cool, damp interior with only the light of a torch to guide me. I am looking for something—or someone—I cannot name. It is but a shadow of thought, and I continue forward, my eyes searching the rocky walls and floors as I make my way deeper and deeper into the belly of the cave.

I hear the whispering first. Not the strange murmuring I used to hear before waking when Alice was casting spells in the Dark Room, but the simple whisper of conversation. It grows louder with each step I take, and as I round a corner of the cavern, I see them.

The girls walk side by side, holding hands. They are nearly

identical, even from behind. One of them is at once familiar to me.

I see in a flash the little girl in New York, handing me the medallion for the very first time.

I see her on the path just outside Birchwood, handing it to me yet again, soaking wet, only moments after I threw it into the river.

Finally, I see her in a dream, her angelic face morphing into Alice's just before I left for Altus.

I have come to view the child as my dream Alice, despite the golden hair that stands in contrast to my sister's real chestnut waves.

The girl on the right is exactly the same size, but her hair falls in auburn curls. She turns to look at me, her eyes meeting mine. Even by the faint light of the torch I can see that they are as green as my own. Aside from her brown hair, she is physically identical to the little girl who has played such an important part in my darkest moments with the prophecy. Yet this girl's face is somehow softer and more innocent.

"Will you come with us? Please?" Her voice trembles, fear evident on her small, delicately featured face.

I nod, though my own heart beats faster. I know that the other girl is the child from my nightmares, and I do not relish the thought of following her farther into the cave.

A second later she turns, her smile full of secrets. "Yes, come with us, Lia. I'll show you both." Her voice has the uncanny lilt that I remember—a child's voice, almost falsely naive.

I do not have time to ask to what she is referring, for she turns away once again, pulling the other girl by the hand. I follow them, feeling the air grow damper still as a metallic scent drifts on a humid breeze from up ahead.

"We're almost there." The child Alice speaks without stopping or turning around.

The other girl, pulled hurriedly along, cranes her neck to look at me. The terror in her eyes causes my heart to drop like a stone. She stumbles, turning forward to right herself. She takes a few more steps before stopping suddenly, and I understand when I hear the faint sound of water up ahead. It is a combination of drips, all falling in quick succession against the stone of the cavern.

Little-girl Alice does not stop walking. She only pulls harder on the other girl's hand. "Come, now, don't be afraid. It's only water."

I don't want to follow them. Twice I have nearly met my death at the hands of water. Only my sister frightens me more.

Even still, I keep walking, watching as the terrified girl is pulled farther and farther into the cavern. Her fear will not allow me to leave, even in my dream.

The cave suddenly goes very dark. I no longer see the girls, for my torch illuminates only a couple of feet in front of me. Everything beyond that is blackness, until we round another corner and the space suddenly opens up before us.

The room feels deceptively large due to the ceilings that rise far beyond our field of vision. But it is not large. In fact, it is

rather small, lit with an eerie red glow that illuminates a pool of water only steps away from us. Drops fall from some unseen place above our heads, bouncing around the cave walls on their way into the basin of water. They have a long way to go, for the water's surface does not lie at the ledge where we stand. No. The ledge drops off into a yawning stretch of stone that only meets the water, black as pitch, far below.

I don't even have to think about stepping away from it. My body shakes with fear, and I have to force myself to keep hold of the torch. All I really want to do is clutch the cave walls and feel my way out of the dream as quickly as possible.

But I am riveted. I cannot leave because something is about to happen.

And I am here to watch. It is the only thing one can do in such a dream.

"Come closer, Lia," my dream Alice says. "I want you to see."

I would like to refuse her, but the other girl's eyes are pleading, as if my proximity can somehow save her when I already know it cannot. Will not.

Still, I have to try, and I inch forward to offer the terrified girl a hand. To pull her away from the watery abyss that stretches below her.

Except I do not get the chance. I am only inches from her, my arm outstretched toward her small, quaking frame, when Alice lets go of her hand. For a moment I rejoice, thinking she is being offered freedom.

Then my dream Alice steps toward her, reaching out with

both hands. The push is so gentle, so graceful, that it takes me a moment to realize the brown-haired girl has gone over the side of the cliff.

I lurch forward, my own fear forgotten. She is still falling when I reach the edge. There is no scream, no sound at all as she falls. Only the slight flailing of her limbs and the eerie calm of her face. But not her face alone — her face turning into mine as she falls.

❦

Mr. O'Leary gives us a new map after pronouncing Dimitri's hopelessly out of date. It seems Mr. O'Leary's duties as caretaker include updating the map with each new discovery and passing it along to those who come to study the site. He has done so over a period of years as explorers and scholars have made their way to the cairns, and while he does not seem happy to aid us, he clearly feels obligated to provide us with the most current version. We are hesitant to accept his assistance, but it seems only wise to use all the tools at our disposal.

Having debated the matter for some time, we begin with one of the largest cairns. I believe the Stone might be hidden in a less grand location in order to ward off discovery by a casual explorer, but Dimitri is of the mind that it will be in one of the most significant spots at Loughcrew, and that likely means one of the bigger caves. I finally give myself over to his theory. We will have to search them all, in any case, until we either find the Stone or eliminate the cairns as its potential hiding place.

We approach on horseback the first large cairn, sitting a bit to the left of the first grouping. It is still unnerving to see the grass-covered mounds rise above the landscape in odd formation across the sweeping hills. It seems impossible that such a place could hide an elaborate, labyrinthine cave, but as Dimitri and I anchor the horses and step into the cool interior, we find that it does.

The fact that we don't know, exactly, what it is we seek both hampers and speeds our progress, for while we begin slowly, looking every which way for anything out of the ordinary, our pace quickens as we wind our way farther into the first cave. There is simply too much to take in, and the longer we walk, stepping carefully around rocks that block the path and sometimes ducking because the ceiling is so low, the more things begin to look the same.

The rocky walls of the cave, sometimes augmented with large stones set in front of them, are covered with strange carvings. Spirals, holes dug out of the rock, zigzags—much of the interior is elaborately marked. I cannot help but wonder what it all means. At the same time, I pray the location of the Stone is not hidden in one of the illustrated riddles on the walls of the cave. I cannot even speak Latin well. We are truly doomed if I am expected to decipher these ancient carvings.

"The path ends here." Dimitri stops in front of me, and I almost run into him. "We should go back."

I sigh, whether with relief or discouragement, I cannot be certain. "All right."

"Don't give up yet, Lia. This is only the first one. There are still many more to explore."

"Exactly." I cannot keep the grumble from my voice as I make my way back through the cave, toward the entrance. "What if they all look exactly like this one? How will we ever make sense of it?"

"I don't know," he says, his voice echoing off the walls of the cairn. "But we'll figure something out."

His answer does nothing to soothe my worry, but I do not speak again until we are outside under the gray skies of spring once again. I survey the grounds in every direction, the smaller mounds to the right and left and the larger one in the distance.

"Which one is next?"

I can see Dimitri's mind working, as if more thought will actually increase our odds of finding the right cavern when it's becoming increasingly obvious the whole excursion may be a random exercise.

"Let's work our way toward the big one by moving to the smaller one there." He points to the right, and I follow his gaze.

I think I will see nothing but the verdant sameness that surrounds us in every direction, but as I scan the field, I see a flash of yellow near the smaller cave.

"Wait! Something's over there!" I point toward it.

Dimitri squints, following the direction of my finger. "I don't see anything."

I look closer, trying to find it again to show Dimitri. But it's gone.

"It's not there anymore. Perhaps I was only imagining it."

He shakes his head. "I'm sure that's not true. You're quite practical. If you say you saw something, you must have seen it. Let's head over and take a look, shall we?"

It takes us only a moment to reach the next cairn. We could have left the horses at the last one and walked, but the strange landscape leaves me feeling deeply unsettled. And though there is no one but us as far as the eye can see, my habits remain. I am forever preparing for my escape and planning for my defense.

It is almost impossible to properly explore the smaller cairn. The ceilings are low, the passageway inside nearly nonexistent. We make an attempt to inch our way in while also trying not to disturb anything, but it is not long before we give up entirely, opting to regroup over lunch.

"Now what?" I try to keep the despair from my voice.

We are sitting on the grass outside the smaller cairn. I try to work up the enthusiasm to enjoy the food Brigid packed for us, but my frustration over our lack of progress does nothing for my appetite.

Dimitri sighs. "Let's call it an early day and head back to the house. As much as I hate to admit it, we're ill prepared. I don't exactly trust Mr. O'Leary, but we may have to avail ourselves of his offer to be our guide."

The thought of spending the day with Mr. O'Leary among the darkness of the caves sends a shiver up my spine, but Dimitri may be right.

"Well, I suppose it wouldn't hurt to allow him to accompany us in the beginning. Maybe we can learn something from him and then continue our exploration alone."

Dimitri nods. "It's the wisest of all our options, I think. Besides," he stretches and yawns, "I could do with a rest before supper. I don't sleep well in this place."

I turn sharply to look at him, for in all the situations Dimitri and I have found ourselves together, I cannot recall him sleeping poorly.

"Why not?"

"I feel . . . disturbed. I don't know if it's because we're near the Stone, because this place may have ancient ties to our people, or because of the strangeness of Mr. O'Leary and his daughter, but I find myself unable to rest comfortably."

I nod. "I feel the very same way."

He reaches over to take my hand. "Still having bad dreams?"

"A bit." It's more than a bit, of course, but I do not want to alarm Dimitri, nor give him further cause to lose sleep.

He lifts my hand to his mouth, placing a gentle kiss on my knuckles. "You can always come to me if you're afraid."

His tenderness makes me smile. "Thank you. It is manageable for now."

He stands, pulling me to my feet. "Come. We'll speak to Mr. O'Leary about accompanying us tomorrow."

We make our way back to the house under an increasingly familiar gray sky, and all the while I ask myself which is worse, not finding the Stone at all, or risking our lives by trusting someone like Mr. O'Leary?

19

"That is a lovely bracelet," Brigid says as I reach for my wine-glass. "Simple, but striking."

My eyes drop to the medallion, and I pull my arm a little farther into my sleeve. I have been careful thus far to keep it and the mark on my other wrist hidden.

"Thank you." I try to make my tone dismissive, bored. "It is simply a ribbon, actually."

"A ribbon?" She reaches for the potatoes, and I wonder if it is my imagination that her tone is forced. "What an interesting accessory."

"Yes, well, I've never been fond of jewelry." I take a bite from the dish in front of me, some kind of cabbage fried with meat, and attempt to change the subject. "Mmm! This is quite good!"

Brigid's gaze grows hard. "Thank you. It's an Irish dish. I'm glad you enjoy it."

"And how did your day at the cairns go?" Mr. O'Leary asks. His boredom sounds overdone. As if he's trying too hard.

"Actually," Dimitri says, taking a sip of his wine, "we were wondering if you wouldn't mind accompanying us tomorrow. It seems you were right; Loughcrew is a large site. We could use some help to get our bearings. It would just be for the day, if you're willing. We can manage on our own thereafter."

Mr. O'Leary looks into Dimitri's eyes. "Didn't find what you were looking for, then?"

Dimitri eyes flare with suspicion. "We aren't looking for anything specific, but we'd like an overview of the site to put in our report, and it's difficult to determine what is important and what's not when everything looks so much the same. I imagine a man with your knowledge of the cairns would easily be able to make that determination."

It is a blatant attempt at flattery on Dimitri's part. I am half-surprised when Mr. O'Leary nods, though it is entirely possible he simply wants to keep an eye on our activities.

"It would be my pleasure to show you around the cairns tomorrow," he says. "'Tis a large site and best explored with a full day. We'll leave at sunrise."

❦

The sky, soft orange and palest pink, hangs above us as we ride across the fields. Mr. O'Leary is riding an old gray gelding and leading the way, and though I wish Dimitri and I had the expertise to explore the cairns alone, we are already better prepared than we were yesterday. Mr. O'Leary packed three torches, an elaborate lunch put together by Brigid, and a duplicate of the map he gave Dimitri that includes several circled locations. We will at least see well, eat well, and have some idea where we're going.

We begin at the same large cairn Dimitri and I started with yesterday. Dimitri protests, but Mr. O'Leary raises his hand in a gesture of silence.

"Did you enter the cavern through the front?" Still atop his horse, he guides us to the opposite side of the entrance.

"Well...yes." Dimitri's brow furrows in puzzlement. "How else would we enter?"

Mr. O'Leary stops his horse at the back of the mound, hopping to the ground. "That would be the most logical entrance, but there is another." He looks at us, still atop our mounts. "Are you coming?"

Dismounting, Dimitri and I anchor our horses next to Mr. O'Leary's. When we look up, he is halfway to the top of the grassy mound.

"Mr. O'Leary?" I shield my eyes from the brightening sun. "Whatever are you doing?"

He sighs, looking down at me with great weariness. "It would do us all good to save the questions. You asked me to be your guide, so please," he gestures to the hill as if extending a formal invitation to climb it, "follow me."

Dimitri steps onto the sloping dirt, rock, and grass first. Stabilizing himself, he extends a hand to me in an offer of assistance, but I am already nearly level with him. He smiles, and the admiration in his eyes brings me a rush of secret pleasure.

I manage to keep pace with both men as we continue up the mound. It is not steep, but the rocks, mud, and uneven growth of grass make the climb treacherous, and I step carefully along the way. Mr. O'Leary gets to the top first and stands still, gazing downward as if there is something fascinating at his feet. When Dimitri and I reach him, we understand why.

It takes me a moment to register the gaping hole in the mound. I am still staring downward when I speak. "What is it?"

"It's a large hole, of course." Mr. O'Leary sounds bored, as if it's quite common to be standing at the crest of an ancient cavern with a giant hole at the top.

"Of course it is." I try to keep the impatience from my voice. "But why is it here? Where did it come from?"

He shakes his head. "It's a shame, really. One of the gentlemen who first discovered the site took apart the top of this one. Was looking for a burial site, he said."

"Did he find it?" Dimitri asks.

Mr. O'Leary shakes his head. "He didn't. And the stones were never put back the way they were, either. If we drop into the cavern from here, you'll notice a piece of it that is invisible when you enter from the front."

I gaze back down into the cave. "But what of the site? Won't we compromise it by disturbing the displaced stones?"

"There is no one more careful than I when it comes to the cairns. We'll tread lightly, have a look, and exit without disturbing things. I'll hold the torches while you drop down, and will throw them to you once you reach the bottom."

It is a rocky drop to the bottom of the cavern, and I am not

at all confident in my ability to make the jump without injury. And then there is the matter of dropping into the cave without the torches, and with Mr. O'Leary looking on from above. My paranoia gets the better of me, my imagination twisting and turning until I become certain Mr. O'Leary plans to abandon us inside the cairn, perhaps even to push the displaced earth and rocks on top of us.

All these thoughts swirl through my head, but I already know I will not give voice to my fear.

"I'll go first." I do not look at Dimitri as I say it, and I am already lowering myself down the rocky ledge by the time he tries to stop me.

"What are you doing? At least let me go in ahead of you. I'll catch you as you drop."

"It's all right," I call up, my eyes still on the rocks as I make my way down. "I'm already halfway to the bottom."

"Be careful!" The worry in his voice is obvious, and I smile as I drop the last couple of feet to the cavern floor. I cannot help being pleased, and even more because I was afraid. My father's voice rings in my ear, as clear as if he were standing next to me: *One must never be a prisoner to fear, Lia. Remember that.*

Dimitri begins his descent and is beside me in moments, making the climb that felt perilous and slow as I made it seem simple in comparison. My nervousness over Mr. O'Leary's intentions lifts as he drops down the torches and it becomes clear that he intends to join us in the cairn. We wait as he makes the same climb. He is not much slower than Dimitri,

and I admire his speed and agility as he jumps to the floor like a man half his age.

"Let's go, then."

He hands us each a torch and we follow him deeper into the cave. Exploring with Mr. O'Leary stands in stark contrast to yesterday's aimless excursion. He holds the torch to the walls as we walk, illuminating the many carved pictures and symbols and providing us with various theories on their meanings. Along the way, we learn that some people believe the markings were meant to be a calendar of sorts, while others believe it has to do with the rising of the sun. No one is sure, really, and my soul goes silent and still as if out of respect for this sacred place.

It is interesting to listen to Mr. O'Leary's explanations as we make our way through the cave, but by the time we find the hole in the ceiling that marks the place of our arrival, we have found nothing to aid us in our quest. Of course, we would not like to find the Stone while in Mr. O'Leary's presence, but I am still disappointed that even this detailed journey through the past has led us to no new discoveries about the prophecy and the Stone.

The rest of the day is just as uneventful. While Mr. O'Leary takes us through another large cairn and three of the smaller ones, we discover no clues to the Stone's whereabouts. The spiral markings are everywhere, but there is nothing to indicate the presence of a sacred Stone.

We are silent as we make our way around the last small cairn of the day. I wonder what to do next, for we have already decided to head back to the house for the day, and I cannot

imagine how we might proceed tomorrow. Wandering from cave to cave will obviously do us no good.

Dimitri takes one last glance at the map before moving to put it inside his coat. All at once he stops, peering with concentration across the fields.

"What is that?"

I follow his gaze. The speck of yellow is the same as the one I saw yesterday, only this time I can see that it is a woman, her yellow cloak billowing in the breeze, near one of the larger cairns.

"By God," Mr. O'Leary mutters, stalking to his horse, "I've told her and told her to steer clear of the cairns."

"Whatever are you doing?" Rushing to Mr. O'Leary's side, I place a hand on his arm to stay the rifle he has removed from his saddlebag.

He furrows his brow as if he cannot understand why I would be concerned at the idea of him wielding a rifle in the direction of a woman. "It's crazy Maeve McLoughlin. She skulks about at all hours of the day and night even after I've told her this is private property."

"I cannot think of a need for the rifle." Dimitri levels his gaze at the older man. "Put it down now, will you?"

Mr. O'Leary scowls as he weighs the seriousness of Dimitri's tone.

Looking back in the direction of the figure, I am relieved to see that the woman named Maeve has disappeared. If nothing else, we have delayed Mr. O'Leary long enough to allow for her safety.

Following my gaze, he notes her absence and moves back to his horse, stuffing the rifle angrily back into his bag, grumbling all the while. "I wasn't going to shoot her. Just scare her off. It is my job, after all."

We mount our horses and head back to the house, thanking Mr. O'Leary for his guidance. As we lead the horses to the small barn at the back of the house, Dimitri asks a question not directed at me but at Mr. O'Leary.

"Is there a town nearby with a library?"

I look at him in surprise, wondering what he's thinking.

Mr. O'Leary leads his horse into one of the stalls without looking at Dimitri. "Oldcastle has a small collection of books, mostly local history and such. It isn't grand enough to be called a library, but I suppose it is the closest thing you might find within a day's ride." He turns to make his way out of the stall, surveying Dimitri with barely hidden curiosity. "But we have quite a collection of material on the cairns right here, if that's what you're looking for."

Dimitri leads Blackjack into the stall that has been his since we arrived at Loughcrew. "It's a more general query on local history. If you wouldn't mind directing us, perhaps Lia and I can make our way to Oldcastle tomorrow. Besides," he meets my eyes with a smile, "I imagine Lia might like to do some shopping."

I swallow my protest, knowing he is only trying to find a reasonable excuse for us to ride into town with a minimum of suspicion on the part of Mr. O'Leary. Even still, it raises my ire.

I force a smile. "Quite right. There are a few things I should like to acquire before we make the return journey."

Mr. O'Leary's nod is slow. "And when will that be? Your return, I mean?"

Dimitri takes my hand, squeezing it as if trying to impart a secret message. "Not long now, I would imagine."

20

"It's the map that has me wondering," Dimitri says as we make our way into Oldcastle the next day.

"Which one?"

I am practically dying of curiosity after spending another strange night with Brigid and Mr. O'Leary.

"Both of them." Dimitri guides Blackjack to the right, down a narrow road leading to a cluster of buildings in the distance. "In comparison to one another, to be more accurate."

I chew my lower lip, trying to decipher the meaning of his words. "Are they not the same?"

He nods his head. "They're nearly exactly the same, except for one small difference."

"And what is that?"

"The map we brought from London has one additional cairn. A big one not shown on the map Mr. O'Leary gave us."

In no hurry to arrive at Oldcastle, we are walking the horses into town. The soft clopping of their hooves on the hard-packed road would be soothing if not for the seed of unease taking root in my mind.

I turn to Dimitri. "Is it one we explored without Mr. O'Leary?"

Dimitri shakes his head. "I used his map the first day, assuming it would be more current since he claims to update it with each new discovery. I only checked them against each other after our first day out."

"But why didn't you say anything?" I cannot help but be annoyed that he kept the discovery from me.

"I thought it might be a simple error, but yesterday when we saw that woman near the cairn—"

"Maeve."

He nods. "Maeve. Well, she was at the cairn not shown on Mr. O'Leary's map. His reaction seemed unusually strong for such a simple infraction, don't you think?"

The picture becomes clearer, and I begin to hope we will get a break. "What does this have to do with Oldcastle's library?"

An older gentleman makes his way toward us on horseback, a young boy at his side. Dimitri nods his head to them in greeting, his eyes watchful as they pass. He waits until they are well behind us before continuing.

"Maybe nothing. But I hope the archives have some information about that cairn, the one not noted on Mr. O'Leary's map. I cannot help thinking he has something to hide, and I mean to find out what it is."

Although I have always thought of any repository of books as a library, even those within the walls of my own homes, it is difficult to think of Oldcastle's archives as such. In fact, we believe ourselves in the wrong building altogether after our inquiry is met with a blank gaze from the aging clerk. It is only after Dimitri says, "We'd like to see the records, please," that we are escorted to a room at the back of the building.

Along the way we pass several rough-looking men in the outer hall, one with a goat tied to a rope. They all appear to be waiting for something, though none of them follows us as we are escorted to the records. I duck my head as we pass, wondering if they see me as a woman with my hair tucked inside my hat, as I've grown accustomed to wearing it when I ride.

We are left without comment in a crowded room overrun with books and all manner of loose papers. None of it seems to have much order, but after careful inspection, we manage to make sense of three distinct categories—birth, death, and marriage certificates; legal proceedings; and land surveys.

We start with the land surveys, splitting them in half, with Dimitri working on one stack and I on the other. The records date back a hundred years or so, and we skim the pages for mentions of the Loughcrew land. The area outside Oldcastle is fairly undeveloped, and it is still early afternoon when we come to the end of both stacks.

"There's probably no point in looking at the marriage

certificates," Dimitri says, leaning back in his chair to stretch his body. "Let's jump straight to the legal disputes, shall we?"

The hours spent studying tiny, largely illegible handwriting have taken their toll, and I resist the urge to yawn. "But why would we find information about the mystery cairn in the legal disputes?"

He rights his chair with nary a sound against the wooden floor. "We may not, but perhaps there was a dispute over the land, or permission to study it, or something of that nature. It's one of our few remaining options. I think we should eliminate it as a possibility before we resort to a thorough search of Mr. O'Leary's study, don't you?"

I sigh. "I suppose. Here." I gesture to the stacks of paper at Dimitri's right. "Give me half."

I do not say what I am thinking: that a thorough search of Mr. O'Leary's library sounds increasingly promising. Regardless of my certainty that he and Brigid are hiding something, I would prefer to avoid a confrontation until we know more. If they are working on behalf of the Souls, as I am beginning to believe, I would rather find what we need and make our way back to London immediately.

Wading through the legal disputes is much more difficult than making sense of the land surveys. Where the surveys were often filled out by men of some education, the legal disputes are executed in cramped handwriting and riddled with misspellings so gross I sometimes cannot decipher the words at all. From what I gather, though, there are quite a lot of disagreements near Oldcastle having to do with stolen livestock, theft

in the small storefronts that line the streets of the town, drunken pub disputes, and unpaid debts.

But there is no mention of Loughcrew, and by the time Dimitri and I come to the end of our respective stacks, the older gentleman who first escorted us to the archives has twice attempted to close for the evening.

Disappointment is evident on Dimitri's face, and I try to sound cheerful as I stifle my own dismay. "Well, I still think it was worth the effort."

"I cannot say that I agree," he mutters, holding his arm out for me to grab. "But I *would* say I owe you a decent meal after forcing you to spend the afternoon in such boredom. We may as well see if there's an inn in which we can take dinner while we're here."

I know he is hiding his own ill feelings out of consideration for me, and I squeeze his arm as we step onto the street in front of the archive building.

"Let's see..." Dimitri surveys the street, trying to gauge the best possibility for a good meal as we start down the small road that fronts the shops and pubs of Oldcastle.

He is gazing to the right as I look to the left, attempting to do my part in the search for dinner, when I see a person disappear around a corner ahead. The figure would not command notice save for one thing: the yellow cape that flutters in the breeze, slipping around the corner in the wake of the person's disappearance. It stands out like a ray of sunshine amid the brown and gray clothing of the townspeople. Without thinking, I drop my arm from Dimitri's.

And then I run.

The ground is slippery underfoot, but I do not even try to temper my steps. The first tendrils of desperation have crept into my conscience. The prophecy does not allow us unlimited time. The adder stone is growing colder by the day, and my sister more powerful. If there is even a minute chance that Maeve McLoughlin holds the answers that we need, it is a chance worth taking.

"Wait! Stop! You, in the yellow cape!" I scream as I run, weaving through the crowd when possible and pushing when necessary.

It must not be uncommon to see one person chasing after another on the streets of Oldcastle, for no one pays me any attention save a laborer who yells, "You oughta have more manners!" as I shove past.

Trying to brace myself against a building as I swing around the corner, I hope and pray all the while that the woman named Maeve will still be in sight. I manage to keep my balance and am relieved to see her cape bobbing through the crowd ahead.

"Maeve McLoughlin!" I shout, pushing my voice as far into the crowd as it will carry. "Wait! I won't hurt you!"

She looks back at the sound of her name, and I catch a glimpse of a dirt-smudged face and frightened eyes. Snippets of conversation make their way to me as I run.

"*. . . crazy Maeve . . .*"

"*You know how she . . .*"

"*. . . those McLoughlins are!*"

And then there is Dimitri's voice behind me. "Lia! What are you doing?"

I run faster. Harder. I do not have time for the questions Dimitri will have if he catches me. They will have to wait until I catch Maeve McLoughlin.

The distance between us closes as she approaches the dusty intersection ahead, and I force my legs to move more quickly even as my lungs burn with the exertion of running so far, so fast. By the time she reaches the street, we are only feet apart, and I lunge, grabbing hold of the yellow cape just as she steps onto the road.

We both go down and the hat flies off my head, my hair tumbling about my shoulders in a thicket of curls as we hit the dirt. I pull the woman back a couple of feet just before a wagon clatters past, frighteningly near.

I turn her from her side to her back, my breath coming hard and fast as Dimitri comes up behind me.

"What in the Sisters' name are you do—" He stops short as he comes around to my side, catching sight of Maeve's arm in my hand as I try to keep her from fleeing yet again.

She doesn't speak. Not at first. She only looks into my eyes, her own bright with fear and a host of unspoken questions that I somehow know she has held close for many, many years.

"Please. Don't run." I make my voice as soft and kind as possible, despite the fact that I am still struggling for breath. "We won't hurt you. We only want to ask you some questions. Can I let go now? Will you speak with us?"

She stares deeply into my eyes for a long moment as the people on the street begin milling about once more, stepping over and around us as they continue about their business.

Finally, Maeve drops her eyes to my wrist and the small piece of the mark visible in the gap left by my shirtsleeve, now slightly askew. I mean to pull it down, to hide it from view. But when I meet her gaze, there is understanding in the moment before she nods her agreement, speaking the only words I need to hear.

"I will help you."

21

Making our way to a small pub on the outskirts of town, we order food for ourselves and Maeve, who looks as if she needs it. We sit in silence as she consumes with single-minded concentration two bowls of hot soup. It is only after a fresh pot of tea is brought around that she begins to speak.

"I'm not crazy." Her eyes are clear, and I cannot help but wonder if Mr. O'Leary misrepresented Maeve's intellect in order to throw us off her trail.

Dimitri does not immediately address her statement, inclining his head instead to the empty bowl before her. "Would you like another bowl of soup?"

Maeve looks down at the bowl as if considering the offer before shaking her head no. "'Tis pleasant to be full, though." Meeting his eyes, she nods. "Thank you."

Dimitri nods back, smiling. "You're welcome."

We sit in silence for a moment before I have the courage to ask the question, rude as it seems, at the forefront of my mind: "Why do they *say* you are crazy? If you're not, I mean."

I am relieved that she doesn't appear offended. "Because I walk about at all hours of the day and night. Because I love the cairns. And because..." She trails off, looking down at her dirty cloak and ripped breeches, not that different from mine, though a good bit more worn. "Well, because I don't dress like a proper lady, I suppose."

I smile, a thread of kinship moving between us. "I know just what you mean."

Her returning smile is not wholehearted, but I think I see a hint of camaraderie in her eyes.

"Why do you trespass about the cairns when Mr. O'Leary tells you to stay off the land?" I ask, gentling my voice before I continue lest she think my words are an accusation or a threat. "You might get hurt."

Her face puckers with distaste. "Psh! Old Fergus wouldn't see fit to shoot." Her brow furrows as she contemplates her own words. "At least, I hope not."

"Even still," Dimitri says. "What could be so important that you would risk it?"

She wraps a surprisingly small hand around the teacup in front of her. "Not important so much as special," she mutters.

"What is special?" I tread carefully, not wanting to scare her off by pushing too hard. "The cairns?"

She nods as if to herself. "The cairns, sure enough, but not simply them." Her words are softly spoken, with a strange

cadence that makes them seem repetitive even when they're not. I understand why ignorant townsfolk might label her mad, but I don't think it is an accurate assessment. "It's the one cairn. The one that's special."

Dimitri meets my eyes, and I know we are both thinking of the cairn missing from Mr. O'Leary's map.

I turn my gaze back to her. "And why is that, Maeve? Why is that one special?"

She fingers the bent spoon resting near her cup atop the table. It is difficult not to push. I sense that we are close to something, something that will bring everything to some kind of order, but I'm afraid if I become overeager we will lose the tenuous grasp we have on the possible answer.

Finally she speaks, though without taking her eyes off the spoon. "It isn't possible to speak of it. Not really."

"Why?" Dimitri's voice is probing but gentle. "Is it a secret?"

A short, wry laugh escapes from her mouth, and several people at nearby tables look over, their eyes hooded and suspicious. "A secret of some sort, that is true enough."

I take a deep breath. "Can you tell us the secret?"

The breath catches in my throat as she looks up, narrowing her gaze at me. There is too much understanding there. "Why don't you ask Fergus O'Leary?"

Dimitri doesn't take his eyes off her. "We're asking you."

Her eyes drift to my wrist before rising again to my face. "They've come here before, looking for it." Something darker than fear seeps into her expression. "Are you one of them?"

I don't know whom she means. Not exactly. I don't even

know if she is thinking clearly. But I know what I see. I know she fears whoever has come before us.

I shake my head. "No. I'm not one of them."

She sits back in her chair, surveying Dimitri and me before speaking. "We'll have to go tonight. I've been waiting, but it hasn't happened yet. 'Twill be any day now."

"It's freezing! Tell me again why we must wait through the night?"

Maeve's insistence that we wait inside the cairn until morning was initially intriguing, but hours spent huddled in the darkness at the back of the cave with only a small torch to keep us warm have dampened my enthusiasm.

"Because of the dawn. It isn't an exact thing. And if you miss it, you'll have to wait another year."

"And do you do this all year? Sit in the cairn waiting for the sun to rise?" The skepticism is obvious in Dimitri's question.

Maeve shakes her head. The black hair tangled about her shoulders gives some credence to the appearance, at least, that she is mad. "Only in March."

I raise my eyebrows. "Only in March? Why is that?"

She sighs, speaking as if to a small child. "Because that's when it happens. Godsake, you ask a lot of questions! If you simply wait, you'll see what I mean."

I'm able to maintain my silence for only a moment. "Forgive me, but—"

"Ack!" She throws her hands in the air. "What is it now?"

I straighten my back, trying to keep hold of my dignity even as I begin to feel foolish for my impatience. "I was just wondering how you could be sure this...event or...whatever it is will happen with this sunrise?"

She leans back against the cold stone of the cairn. "Nothing is ever certain, but I'm as sure as can be expected."

"Yes," Dimitri says, his own voice belying the hesitance even he feels to incite Maeve's ire. "But why? Why are you as sure as can be expected?"

Maeve's eyes remain closed as she speaks. "Because today is the twenty-second of March, and it didn't happen yesterday or the day before, so it has to happen today or tomorrow."

I draw absently with my finger in the dirt. "And it always happens on one of those days?"

It is increasingly difficult not to feel mad as we dance around the event of which Maeve is so certain but that seems more and more ludicrous the longer we sit, freezing, in the cairn.

"Well, not exactly. Two years ago it happened on the nineteenth day of the month, but that was unusual indeed. Now I come early, just in case."

"I see. And tell me again about the others. The ones who came before us." I have been afraid to ask, but it seems we have time to burn. We may as well pass it learning all we can.

Maeve lifts her head from the stone wall of the cairn. Her eyes, full of fire and mystery, find mine in the faint light offered by the torch. "I don't wish to speak of them."

I nod, sighing. "Fair enough, Maeve."

We fall into silence and I scoot closer to Dimitri, trying to absorb some of his body heat. After a while his breathing slows, and it is only moments later that sleep comes to claim me as well.

"Wake up! It's happening!"

I am awoken with a rude shaking and open my eyes to find Maeve's dirty face directly in front of mine. I don't have to ask to what she is referring. Even in the little half-sleep I was able to manage, my mind was alert, waiting for the event Maeve brought us here to witness.

Dimitri is on his feet in an instant, reaching a hand down to help me up from the floor.

"Where is it?" he asks Maeve, looking around as he pulls me to my feet.

"Right here. Right here!" She is unable to contain her excitement, and I look around the interior of the cave, wondering what I'm missing. "Come! This way."

She pulls me to the side, turning my body so that I am facing the rear of the cavern and the wall of stone that rises from its floor.

"Just wait." Her words come out in a breathless sigh, and I know that whatever she is waiting for will come.

It begins with the sun as Dimitri stands behind me, both of us to the side of the cramped path leading all the way through the cave to the place where we now stand. The cairn, before dark save for the minimal light offered by the torch, begins to brighten ever so slightly with the dawn.

The rising sun, lifting into the sky somewhere outside the

cairn, casts its rays straight through the cavern, a rectangle of golden light becoming visible in the back corner of the wall farthest from the entrance. It seems a small thing, but I cannot fathom how the light, sent from millions of miles away, can find its way through the twists and turns of the cavern in such a way as to light up the back wall of the cave.

And that's not all.

As we watch, the light moves from left to right, growing larger by the minute as it creeps toward the back of the cairn. When it reaches the center, the entire backstone seems alight with fire, the intricate carvings visible in all their sacred, mysterious glory. It is impossible to imagine how the people who created the cairns, thousands of years ago, managed to line everything up just so. The fact that it is designed to highlight the backstone only once a year is even more of a mystery, but a moment later, the words come to me as if on the mists of Altus: *the Spring Equinox.*

The cairn is designed so that the sun will light the backstone only during the Spring Equinox.

In this moment, I feel everything more acutely. Dimitri behind me, our bodies touching just enough for me to register the quickened pace of his breathing as he watches the sun make its journey across the writings on the cave wall. The cairn floor, cold and solid, centuries old, beneath my boots. The musty, metallic smell of the stone inside the cave, and the earth atop which it sits.

It takes a few minutes for the light to make its way from the center of the backstone to the right, growing smaller as it

continues its journey. We stand without moving or speaking, watching the light track across the stone until the cairn again grows dim, the rectangle of illumination becoming ever smaller until it is but a pinprick, as bright as a star, in the moment before it disappears entirely.

We do not move for some time. When I finally look up, twisting my head to look at Dimitri behind me, his eyes meet mine. In them is the bond of our shared history, the history of our people, and, yes, the future we both imagine together. His smile is a promise, and I am somehow certain that from this moment forward, we are bound through all space and time.

22

Gathering my wits, I turn to Maeve, still staring with rapt attention at the place where the last point of light disappeared. She must feel my gaze because she turns to look at me, her eyes clearer than I have seen them in the few hours since we met.

"Thank you." My words are a whisper. I want to tell her that I recognize the magic of the moment, even if it did not bring us the answers we sought.

Her face lights with a smile. "You shouldn't thank me yet. I still have to show you what you're looking for."

I think she will try to decipher the marking on the backstone, but instead she pulls me to the side of it and bends down to look at something very near the floor.

"It isn't the backstone itself, you see, though I wonder if maybe it says the same thing using symbols that are long gone."

She waves Dimitri forward, motioning for his torch, and he leans in, holding the flame very near the wall.

I don't see anything unusual. Only a small, flat ledge, indented in the middle, beneath a long stretch of rock reaching toward the ceiling of the cairn.

"Wait..." Dimitri reaches for the wall with his free hand, brushing away some of the dirt until it rises like dust motes in the light of the torch. When he speaks again, it is in a surprised murmur. "There *is* something here."

I look more closely, wondering if he is going round the bend, for I do not see any markings at all. But then Dimitri's hand moves ever so slightly, the light catching a divot in the wall, and I begin to see it.

Reaching forward with the hem of my shirt, I wipe the cairn wall more carefully near the place where I am just beginning to make out some kind of marking. It does not take long to see that Dimitri is right.

There is something there after all.

"Hold the torch." Dimitri hands it to me, and I point the flame in the direction of the wall as he leans forward.

He does not speak for a long moment, and I begin to wonder if perhaps we have gotten ahead of ourselves. If perhaps the markings have nothing to do with the Stone.

But when he turns to meet my eyes, I know they do.

"It's the prophecy. It's written here, *carved* here, in Latin."

"I told you." Maeve beams.

"Is that all?" I lean forward, wanting to see for myself despite

my unfortunate inability to speak Latin. "Does it say anything about the Stone? Is it hidden here?"

He traces with his fingers the letters carved into the wall. "Not exactly."

"Not exactly?" I don't bother trying to hide my impatience.

"It lists the prophecy, both the page you found in your father's library and the one we found at Chartres." He pauses, his voice growing grave with concentration. "And then it says, roughly, and in Latin, '*In the first light of Nos Galon-Mai free those bound by the Fallen with the power of this Stone and the words of their Rite.*'"

I shake my head. "Wait a minute . . . 'the words of their Rite'? Do you mean to say that it refers to the Rite of the Fallen? Does it state what the Rite is?"

His brow furrows as he leans still closer to the wall. "It's . . . it's possible. It says something about . . . let's see . . . a circle that is cast by angels fallen past, and . . . something about summoning the power of the Sisters to close the Guardian's Gate, keeping the world safe from the Beast of . . . of Ages." He turns to me, his eyes shining, his voice giving away the excitement he is trying not to betray. "It's difficult to make out the exact translation here and now. The wall is dirty, the words carved long ago, but it does seem to be an incantation of some kind."

"An incantation?" I say. "So it *is* a spell? One that might be used to close the Gate at Avebury?"

Dimitri's nod is slow, and I see the working of his mind. "It sounds that way. Almost any spell could be called a rite as well,

I suppose. And it does say 'with the power of *this* Stone,' which could mean the Stone was here, hidden with the words of the Rite all along."

"Except it wasn't. Or it's not now, in any case," I say, looking around. "Unless..." I look at Maeve. "Did you take something, Maeve? Was there once something here that isn't here now?"

Anger flashes in her eyes. "I didn't take anything! I only come to watch." She turns her head, gazing stubbornly at the wall of the cairn. When she speaks again, it is in a mutter. "'Tis other people who take. I only watch. Watching's all I do."

Her words shake something loose in my mind, and I reach toward the ledge just beneath the carved words of the Rite. The indentation in the rock is smooth and round. I look up, and Dimitri's eyes find mine through the shadows of the cave.

I turn back to Maeve. "I'm sorry, Maeve. I understand now. You only watch. It's the others who take. The others who *have* taken, isn't that right?"

She meets my gaze for only a moment before looking away once more, but it is all the time I need.

I turn back to Dimitri. "Let's go."

We have just closed the horses in the barn and are preparing to make our way to the house when Dimitri puts a hand on my arm.

"They're not part of the Guard, that much we can be sure of."

I nod. "Yes, but that doesn't mean they aren't working on behalf of the Guard, and it doesn't mean they aren't dangerous in their own right."

Dimitri nods. "They're involved somehow, that's for certain. Since we've arrived, they've done everything in their power to ensure that we would not find the cairn."

"Or the Stone," I add. "Besides, they ask too many questions, show too much interest in our comings and goings."

"How do you feel?" I hear the hesitation in his question and know he does not relish asking it.

Gazing up at him as the clear morning light streams into the barn, I am equal parts offended that he thinks me weak and grateful that he senses my waning strength.

"I am... fighting. Fighting to stay strong."

His eyes soften. "You're always fighting, Lia. That is never in question. I need to know how strong you are right now. This moment." His eyes burn more deeply into mine. "And you must be honest."

I swallow hard, looking away and taking a deep breath before speaking. "I'm not as strong as I would like. The adder stone is nearly cold. My power..." I turn to face him, wanting him to see conviction through my doubt. "Well, it is undoubtedly weaker than it was three months ago, when I could count on the full force of Aunt Abigail's authority to augment my own. But I am still more than capable of putting up a fight, if that's your concern."

"I don't know what we face, Lia. I wish..." He rubs a hand over his face, a sigh of frustration escaping his body. "I wish I

had somewhere safe to send you, but I fear there is nowhere safer for you than with me."

I lift my chin. "I wouldn't go anyway. My place is here, bringing the prophecy to its end."

A smile of admiration creeps to his mouth. "And?"

I stand on the tips of my toes, wrapping my arms around his neck and leaning my head back to look in his eyes. "And," I say, "with you. My place is with you."

One of his arms slips around my waist and he pulls my body closer to his. "So you will stay."

His mouth, when it meets mine, is soft and tender. Our kiss lasts only a moment, but I feel somehow stronger when we pull apart, and as we make our way to the house, I tell myself that together we can do anything. I tell myself it doesn't matter if Mr. O'Leary and Brigid work on behalf of the Souls, the Guard, or Samael himself.

Then I tell myself I believe it, despite the voice in the back of my mind that calls me a liar.

I think I am prepared for anything, but upon stepping into the parlor and coming face-to-face with the shotgun, I realize I am not.

"Come in, now, why don't you." Mr. O'Leary is sitting in his chair in the parlor, holding the gun like someone accustomed to holding one. "I do believe we have some talking to do."

Brigid stands behind his chair, her eyes dark and unreadable in the firelight.

Dimitri reaches for my hand, pulling me closer and stepping in front of me so my body is shielded by his. "I don't think there is any need for the gun, Mr. O'Leary. Surely we can be reasonable with one another."

The older man's laugh is wry. "I've seen the way your kind means 'reasonable.' I don't think we agree on its definition."

I cannot see Dimitri's face, but I sense his confusion. "I'm not sure what you mean by 'my kind,' but I do believe you have something we need."

Mr. O'Leary narrows his eyes at Dimitri. "I'm sure I don't have anything that's yours."

Dimitri nods slowly. "It's true that it isn't mine. But it isn't yours, either, is it? And I promise you, our purpose is far more noble than that to which you have aligned yourself."

"How dare you?" Brigid breaks in, her eyes flashing. "Do you think us so simple that we'll believe your lies? That we'll consign the world to the dark fate that awaits it at your hands?"

Confusion lights Dimitri's eyes in the ensuing silence as I grasp about the muddied waters of my own mind. I see Brigid, her too-curious gaze probing mine. Her many questions. Her uncommon knowledge.

Stepping out from behind Dimitri, I try to make my voice calm. "Whatever you believe, I promise you, we're on your side."

Dimitri turns to look at me, shock and confusion on his face. "Lia? What are you doing?"

I make my way toward Brigid, trying not to look at the gun pointed in my direction. "You took it, didn't you? You took the Stone from the cairn?"

To her credit, she does not blink in the face of my approach. Her father, on the other hand, tenses as I near them. "It's time for you to step away from my daughter. Time for you to leave this house altogether, I think."

"I'm sorry, Mr. O'Leary, but I cannot do that." I have to swallow around the lump of fear in my throat in order to get the words out.

Dimitri steps toward us. "Lia, I—"

The sound of the shotgun being cocked causes Dimitri to step back.

"You're not alone, Brigid." I reach for my left wrist, pushing the sleeve of my shirt up just enough so that the mark is visible.

Her eyes drop to my wrist, and I see her bosom rising and falling as her breath comes fast with the proof of my mark.

I reach for her arm. "May I?"

She nods even as her father shouts, "You will do no such thing. Now! Remove your hands from my daughter."

But I cannot. I hear Philip's distant voice: *I've already been told, you see, that the girl no longer resides in the town. Apparently her mother died giving birth to her, and her father took her away some years later.*

I half-expect to hear the roar of the gun, but it is Brigid's voice, softer than I've heard it in the time we've been at Loughcrew, that breaks the tension.

"It is her, Father. Just as Thomas said."

I shake off the shock I feel at the mention of my father and reach for her hand. I now understand why her gowns are too

large, their sleeves too long, for when I push up her sleeve to reveal the soft flesh of her left hand, the mark stares back at me.

Sonia's mark. Luisa's mark. Helene's mark.

The mark of the final key.

"I thought so." Brigid's skin is warm under my fingers, and I rub my thumb over the familiar symbol. The Jorgumand. The snake eating its own tail. The circle.

Turning my own wrist, I cross my arm over hers, aligning our marks. Our eyes meet for a moment before her gaze skips to her father, behind me. Her nod is almost imperceptible, but it seems to be all Mr. O'Leary needs.

He sets the gun aside, pausing for a long moment before speaking. "It seems we have a lot to discuss after all—and not much time in which to do it."

23

"Your father was far more clever than I first thought—and I already thought him very clever, indeed." Dimitri eyes me over the steam rising from his teacup.

It has been less than an hour since the moment when Mr. O'Leary lowered his gun. Dimitri and I have spent the time filling the O'Learys in on the details of the prophecy, the Otherworlds, the Souls, the other keys. I expected Brigid to be incredulous. To deny the things that still sound fantastical when spoken aloud.

But she does no such thing. She simply sits, rapt, as if she knew it to be true all along.

I look at her. "You were born in England like the others, weren't you? How did you come to be at Loughcrew in the very place hiding the Rite?"

It is not Brigid who answers but her father. "My wife died in childbirth, you see. We were in England so her family outside of Newbury could help with the birthing, but it didn't do any good."

Brigid reaches over to pat his hand. "We stayed on there so that my mother's family could help care for me, but when I was a girl of ten years a visitor arrived who changed everything."

"My father." I think of his many trips and wonder which of them made it possible for me to find the final key so many years later. I wonder what I was doing while he was orchestrating the events that would secure my possible future.

Mr. O'Leary nods. "I suppose it was. At first I didn't want the commission to be the caretaker of this desolate place, but Thomas promised me a good house in which to care for Brigid, and a pension for the rest of my days. It seemed a chance for a fresh start, and I thanked God for it even as I feared the things he told me."

"And what did he tell you?" Dimitri asks.

Mr. O'Leary looks down at the scarred tea table. "That the mark my lass carries on her wrist meant something evil would come for her. That our only hope was to disappear." He raises his eyes to mine. "Disappear and wait for you."

I shake my head. "Why didn't you say something? We thought you were . . . that is, we wondered if you might be working on behalf of the other side."

Mr. O'Leary chuckles. "We thought the same of you. Your father didn't give us your name. He thought it would be danger- ous should someone—or something—attempt to . . ." He

squirms uncomfortably in his chair. "Should we be pressured to reveal your identity."

"How did you know we would come at all?" Dimitri asks.

Brigid speaks from the chair next to her father. "We were simply told a woman would come. That she would bear the mark on her wrist and that she would be looking for the Stone. But we were told others might come for it as well. And that they would be people to fear." She looks at Dimitri. "He didn't mention that a gentleman would be in the woman's company, and we've had a number of questionable 'researchers' over the years. Researchers we have turned away to protect the Stone in anticipation of your eventual arrival. We've learned to be wary, and when you didn't return after your trip into Oldcastle, well, we assumed you had found something there to aid you in your search for the Stone, especially since it happened to be the equinox."

I look down at the exposed mark on my wrist before looking at Brigid. "I was so careful to hide my mark from you."

Brigid smiles. "I as well."

I feel a sudden thrill at the realization that we now have the final key and the Rite. That we are two steps closer to ending the prophecy for good.

But this victory is bittersweet without the Stone.

As if reading my mind, Dimitri speaks. "But surely you are aware that the Stone isn't in the cairn? We were there this morning with Maeve McLoughlin during the equinox. It was clear that the Stone is meant to be there, to be illuminated by the sun once each year, but I'm afraid it's not."

Mr. O'Leary does not look surprised. "Maeve is harmless enough, but she has a bad habit of drawing attention to the cairn each spring as she waits for the equinox. We couldn't risk that she might lead the wrong person to the Stone."

"Which is why," Brigid says, reaching into the bodice of her gown, "I have guarded it with my very life for some years now."

Her fingers grasp a silver chain, which she pulls until it reveals a black satin bag at its end. She lifts the chain from around her neck, grabbing hold of the bag and pulling it open. When she turns it upside down, a large rock falls into her other hand.

I expect it to be beautiful. To shine and shimmer with power. But it appears to be a simple gray stone, albeit a perfect oval.

"Are you... Are you certain this is the right one?" I do not want to offend the O'Learys, but it is difficult to believe that such a rock, one that looks like all the others within the cairns at Loughcrew, holds the power to aid us in closing the Gate to Samael.

Brigid smiles, and I realize the smiles we have seen touch her lips until now have been nothing but window dressing compared to the brilliance of this one. "Trust me — when it is lit by the sun, it shines so brightly it puts the other rocks to shame. That's how we found it. How we knew it was the one. But that isn't the only reason." She holds it out to me. "See for yourself."

I feel nothing but nonchalance as I reach for it, but as my hand nears the Stone, I am oddly drawn to it. By the time my hand closes around it, I feel its power. It is not as strong as the

power that was once in Aunt Abigail's adder stone, but I feel the same hum, the same energy, buzzing beneath the smooth, cool surface of the rock.

I look up at Brigid with a smile.

She nods. "It's much, much stronger — and hotter as well — when lit by the sun. I . . ." She ducks her head in embarrassment. "I burned myself, actually, the morning we found it. It was so beautiful." Her voice comes as if from far away as she remembers. "I couldn't stop myself from grasping it, but when I picked it up, when at last I held it in my palm, it shook my body to the core with its power, searing my hand in the moment before I dropped it to the ground."

She turns her hand over to show us the raised white scar in her palm.

I close my fingers around the Stone. "Is it . . . Is it safe to carry?"

She nods. "I've been wearing it beneath my gown for years. It gets hot only when touched by the rising sun, and even that may be only during the equinox. Why?"

"Because we must take it to London." I look at Dimitri before turning back to Brigid, taking a deep breath. "And you must come with us."

For the first time since the mad dash to Chartres, I travel the forest without Dimitri.

I am on horseback, racing through the trees with the Guard close on my heels. I know the wood to be in England, though it is night and so dark I can hardly make out Sargent's neck beneath me.

The Guard is still some distance behind me, yet I hear the beat of their horses' hooves even as I seek to expand the distance between us. Low-lying tree branches whip at my face and ensnarl my hair, grasping at me like greedy fingers seeking to hold me back and feed me to Samael's Guard. Leaning farther over Sargent's neck, I spur him onward with desperate insistence, digging my heels into his flank as I whisper words of encouragement in his ear.

There will be no second chance.

I am beginning to think there is no hope, for the blackness is endless and the horses behind me grow nearer by the second, when I break free of the trees, emerging into a clearing. I sense the fields stretching before me, but it is the fire in the distance that calls to me like a beacon.

Its flames lick toward the sky, the only light amid the bleak desolation of the rolling fields. I know without a doubt that it is my intended destination. I make for it with haste just as the Guard crashes through the trees into the clearing behind me.

As I grow closer to the fire, shadows rise around it, first in a small ring very near the flame and then farther away, in a larger circle beyond it. By the time I approach the first grouping, I understand.

Avebury. I am at Avebury.

Massive stones stand like guardians around the fire, and as I cross them I know that I am in the belly of the serpent. As if in answer to my realization, the fire roars higher. It seems to

reach the sky as a distant hum rises on the wind, across the fields, through my very mind.

Fabric billows around the smaller circle of shadows, and I am nearly upon them, the humming growing louder and louder, by the time I comprehend what they are.

The figures part as I approach, and Sargent makes his way into the center of their fiery circle before I have a chance to instruct him otherwise. Panic closes its fist around my throat as the circle becomes whole once again, trapping me within its center as the chanting of those who surround me continues.

But I do not have time to dwell on their strange ceremony.

The hoofbeats of the Guard's horses are like a whip of thunder to the ground as they spread out, creating yet another ring behind the figures that surround me.

I do not realize the sky is lightening until the robed figures before me reach their hands to the hoods that leave their faces in shadows. As the first one pushes back the fabric, I am stunned nearly breathless to see Helene's dark eyes meet mine. The others continue in quick succession — Brigid, Luisa, and, finally, Sonia, her chill blue eyes burning through mine with white-hot fury.

It is enough to make me gasp aloud. And yet even this does not prepare me for what is next. There is still one. One figure who has not revealed her identity. One figure whose face remains cloaked in mystery.

She reaches with delicate hands for the fabric that folds softly around her face. I can hardly bear to look as she pushes the fabric away from the fine bones of her face. But neither can

I look away. I am transfixed as the fire and the swiftly brightening sky illuminate her features.

It is Alice. Alice stands together with the keys while I remain set apart, surrounded not only by the hated Guard but by the very people with whom I've worked in concert to end the prophecy.

Except even that is not all.

Sonia lifts her arms, reaching for Alice's hand to her right and Brigid's to her left. The others do the same, joining hands and re-creating their circle. Their marks are clearly visible in the dawning sun, and it is this that tells me how very wrong I have been, for as Alice reaches for Sonia's hand, her wrist catches my eye.

It is not the smooth, unblemished wrist of my sister.

No.

It is branded with the mark. And not just any mark. Mine.

Even in the ethereal morning light I see the serpent writhing, curling around the "C" at its center.

I slip from Sargent's back almost without thinking. Stumbling toward the fire, I push up my sleeve, searching desperately for the mark I have always hated but now want to see more than anything, if only to prove I am still myself.

But it is not there. My eyes are greeted only by unmarred skin.

A moment later the sun makes its way a millimeter farther into the sky. As it does, I finally notice the Stone suspended on a tripod of wood above the fire. It is the same plain gray stone Brigid showed me.

Until a small ray of sunlight touches it with gentle fingers.

Then, the Stone sends out a shrill ping and a hum that seems to match that of the robed figures, still chanting, all around me. The vibration from the Stone sends a jolt through my body and I fall to the ground, writhing in pain as everything tips precariously sideways. The hooves of the Guard's horses seem to gallop from within my mind, but it is not this that freezes my heart in terror.

It is my unwelcome knowledge as I finally put it all together.

The mark on my sister's wrist. The smile on her face as she registers my realization.

And my own understanding that even as Alice stands in my place amid the circle, I have taken hers. This time, I am not a savior to the Sisters.

I am their enemy.

I sit up in bed, a scream caught in my throat, my heart beating so fast and so hard that I have trouble catching my breath. I do not know what the dream means. Not really. But I know why I had it even before I lift my hand to my chest.

The adder stone's heat, even as it waned, has been ever present since the moment I awoke on Altus so many months ago. Now I close my fingers around it, trying to squeeze from it every ounce of warmth.

It is cold.

Aunt Abigail's power is nothing but a memory. The Souls know it. Samael and his Guard know it.

And now they will come for me with a vengeance.

Mr. O'Leary does not try to dissuade his daughter from making her way with us to London. It seems Brigid, too, is haunted by dreams in which she is chased by the Souls, the line between her earthly existence and the Otherworlds growing increasingly thin. She knows that which we all now realize: There will be no life of our own until the Gate is closed forever.

After making preparations for the return journey to London, we depart Loughcrew with fresh supplies and one additional person. Brigid settles easily into the routine of rising, clearing camp, riding, and sleeping on the hard ground with only the tents for shelter. She does not complain, yet even as I am grateful for her accommodating manner, I find myself gazing at her with hidden suspicion. I remember her face from the dream of Avebury, her hands linked with those of the other keys, forming a circle with my sister. I remember it and cannot help wondering if Brigid will become my enemy.

If the dream is a portent of things to come.

The prospect that I am going mad seems more possible than ever before. I try to calm myself—to tell myself that it is not possible for everyone and everything to be my enemy. Even Sonia, as much as our friendship has suffered, cannot be called my enemy.

It is only the prophecy, I think. *The Souls. Samael. My own weakness. My own darkness.*

My dreams have only increased in intensity since the night I dreamed of Avebury. I have begun to feel claustrophobic from the darkness pressing in on all sides, as if I am already in the grave and trying to dig free of the soil with my bare hands.

As if it is already hopeless.

Brigid was relieved to unburden herself of the Stone, and I have worn it in the pouch around my neck since the day I discovered it in her possession. I hoped it might give me additional strength in the face of that lost with Aunt Abigail's adder stone, yet it remains nothing but a cold, heavy rock around my neck.

I have become accustomed to holding myself stiffly upright, an expression of calm plastered over the exhaustion and fear eating their way through my skin. Yet, some part of me realizes that my ruse is only a matter of pride. Even as I attempt the show of strength, it is obvious that Dimitri knows my torment. It is he who races to the tent upon hearing my screams. He who holds me until I once again fall into a fitful sleep.

Even so, I dare not allow myself the deep slumber I so desperately need, and my mind remains alert even in the dark of night. My bow and dagger are no comfort in those dark hours, though they are always at the ready. I am increasingly certain that I will wake one morning to find the black velvet of the medallion intertwined around my other wrist, the Jorgumand on its metal disc nestled against the mark on my skin.

It is the afternoon of our fourth day riding when we exit the woods to find ourselves on a road winding through fields that gradually disappear in favor of an occasional pub or inn. The smell of the sea is in the air and it is only a short time later that we come to the rise of a hill and see Dublin and the waterfront in the distance.

I turn to Dimitri. "Will Gareth be our escort across the water again?"

"If all goes well." Dimitri spurs his horse forward.

I do not have to question the uncertainty in his voice. We have both learned that anything can happen when one is dispatched on behalf of the prophecy. I try to push aside my fear that something has happened to Gareth, but I do not breathe easy until we reach the docks and see him standing near a familiar boat in the distance. For the first time in days, a smile rises easily to my mouth.

"Gareth!"

As we bring the horses to Gareth's place on the docks, the welcoming smile recedes from his face. In its place is naked worry. "My Lady ... Are you well? Has something happened?"

I sit straighter in the saddle, embarrassed at his reference to

my appearance. "I'm simply tired, that's all. Sleep does not come easily in this cold."

He nods slowly. "Yes, my Lady. You're lovely as always, of course. Anyone would be tired with such a journey behind them." His words are meant to soothe, but I catch the glance he casts in Dimitri's direction and know they will discuss my health later, when I am not around to be offended.

I work quickly to change the subject, keeping the details of Brigid's presence simple. "I'm sure you remember Miss O'Leary. She will be accompanying us the rest of the way." I realize she has no idea the part Gareth plays in our group, and I turn to her to explain. "Gareth is a childhood friend of Dimitri's and has seen us through more than one perilous journey. He will act as our escort across the water."

Gareth nods his head at Brigid. "It's a pleasure to see you again. But forgive me for saying, you do seem a bit friendlier this time around."

A blush creeps into Brigid's cheeks. "I apologize for my prior rudeness. There was some confusion, you see, about our ability to trust one another."

I give her a smile, grateful for her discretion, and Gareth nods in understanding.

"There are no times more confusing than these." He turns to me. "And speaking of confusion, I find I must correct you."

"Me? Whatever for?"

"I've been given approval to be your escort beyond our landing in England. In fact, I'll be your guide all the way to London." It is obvious from his grin that he is pleased with the development.

"Really?" I do not wait for him to answer. "That is the best news you could have given me!"

Dimitri nods. "I have to agree. There is no guide, or friend, more trusted. And we need all the assistance we can gather."

Gareth waves us down. "Come. Make yourselves comfortable on the boat while I see to your horses."

We dismount, and Gareth gestures toward two men leaning against a sooty building not far from where we stand. They amble over, taking hold of the reins and tipping their hats to Brigid and me before turning to make their way down the dirt walkway.

"Men of few words, are they?" Dimitri chuckles.

Gareth makes his way to the edge of the dock, reaching for Brigid's hand. "The very best men to have in circumstances such as these, wouldn't you agree?"

"There can be no doubt," Dimitri says, holding my hand as I step into the boat after Brigid.

Moments later Gareth and Dimitri untie the boat from the pier. I watch the water warily as we drift away from the pilings, the port and its accompanying noise growing distant behind us.

Brigid leans out over the edge of the boat, gazing into the water as if she expects to find something hidden in its depths. I think I should protect her. Tell her to beware. To stay inside the boat and never, ever put her hands in the water.

But I don't. I simply turn away, slouching farther into the bottom of the boat without putting reason to my traitorous silence.

The ride across the sea is broken by nothing but the rocking of the boat and the occasional distribution of food and water. Our packs have been carefully rationed to sustain us until we reach London, but we are cautious with our supplies nonetheless.

I feel trapped, as if the Souls are shadowing my every move though there is not another vessel in sight. Even with the gentle rocking of the boat, sleep does not come easily. I press my body close to Dimitri's through an impossibly cold night, though I cannot say if it is physical warmth or mental strength that I seek. I drift in and out of consciousness, half-expecting some monstrous beast to rise out of the sea and pull me over the side. I think I would not fight fate should it choose to see my life end beneath the blackness of the water.

By the time the English shoreline comes into view the next morning, I hardly care whether we make landfall or not. The boat, at least, is a reprieve from the burden I feel more fully with each passing minute as we make our way back to London.

I can hardly keep my own thoughts, my own motivations, in order. How, then, will I bring together Sonia, Luisa, Helene, and now Brigid? And how will I do so when my own relationship with Sonia and Luisa is so damaged? How will I get everyone to Avebury to fulfill the Rite as the prophecy says I must?

Most impossible of all, how will I ever bring Alice to our side, for the prophecy is clear in its dictate that Guardian and Gate must work in unity to see the Gate closed forever?

These questions fight for purchase in my mind as Dimitri and Gareth steer the boat closer to shore. Gareth guides the vessel to an empty slip, and soon we are stepping unsteadily out of the boat and onto the dock.

"Will we have horses?" Brigid asks no one in particular.

Gareth scans the waterfront. "We certainly will."

Dimitri takes hold of my hand, and we follow Gareth and Brigid over the splintered wood pilings and onto the road that runs in front of the water.

"Ah, there they are!" Gareth strides toward two young men, each of whom leads two horses.

I recognize Sargent immediately, but the realization does not bring with it the same delight as it has in the past. My pleasure at seeing the horse feels numb and distant, and I can only force a smile as I stroke his neck.

Gareth murmurs softly to the young men. They hand the horses' reins to Gareth and disappear into the teeming streets. The people bump and shove around us, and I have a sudden moment of panic as I try to observe them all, checking their necks for the mark of the Guard.

"It's all right, Lia." Dimitri is at my side, taking Sargent's reins from my hand as he braces a hand against the animal's neck. "Get on your horse, and I will see you clear of the crowd."

I don't know how he senses my panic, but my racing heart slows ever so slightly. I am too relieved to be ashamed that his presence should bring me such comfort, and I grab the saddle and lift myself onto Sargent's back. Being above the masses gives me an immediate sense of security. I take the reins from

Dimitri's hands and inhale deeply, trying to talk myself out of the momentary panic of a few moments ago.

Brigid mounts her horse, a dappled white steed, without difficulty, and soon we are headed away from the waterfront. As we leave behind the odor and rubbish in favor of the open fields and distant woods of the countryside, my panic eases.

But my relief is only temporary, for I know it is short-lived. In little more than a week, I will be back in London, surrounded by unfamiliar people, the keys—and my sister.

25

"What will happen when we get to London?"

It is our third night on English soil, and Brigid and I are sitting by the fire as Dimitri and Gareth settle the horses for the evening. I have not felt like talking and have made a poor traveling companion, but I've grown used to Brigid's quiet presence. She reminds me of Sonia in the days before we came to London, though Brigid's calm seems to come from inner serenity rather than from shyness or fear.

"I'll introduce you to the other keys. Luisa and Sonia were . . . *are* two of my dearest friends. Helene arrived just before I left for Loughcrew, so I'm afraid I cannot tell you much about her other than to say that she is as anxious as we are to be free of the prophecy. Then there are Aunt Virginia and Edmund." I turn to smile at her. The expression feels unfamiliar on my face. "They are wonderful and kind. You'll like them both, I'm sure."

She nods. "And then?"

I take a deep breath. "Then I must speak to my sister, Alice, to see if she will join us at Avebury on the eve of Beltane."

Brigid rests her head on her knees, her eyes shimmering hazel in the light of the fire. "And do you think you can convince her?"

I turn away from her gaze, looking into the flames of the fire. "Alice is . . . Well, I've already told you that she works on behalf of Samael and the Souls. Has always worked on their behalf, if I am to be honest. We are, for all intents and purposes, enemies."

Brigid's eyes cloud over with confusion. "Then how will you get her to help us close the Gate?"

"I don't have that part figured out, but she saved my life once." My voice dims to a murmur as the memory takes hold. I see the rain, the river rushing with furor behind Birchwood Manor, Alice pushing Henry into its swiftly moving current. I see her holding the branch out to me, hanging over the riverbank, placing her own life in peril to pull me to safety.

I turn to back to Brigid. "There are whole stretches of time when she seems a stranger to me, and then, all at once, I think I catch a glimpse of her humanity. I suppose I'm hoping to appeal to her in one of those moments, though I admit it's unlikely."

I do not tell her that Alice and I have already discussed our opposing roles. That she has already refused me, time and

again. Appealing to Alice is my only hope, and telling one of the keys that that hope is already lost will do nothing to aid our shared sense of purpose.

"What will we do then? If she will not stand with us?" I cannot help but admire the calm in Brigid's voice. Though the workings of the prophecy are new to her, she knows what is at stake. Yet, there is no trace of panic in her words.

There is a part of me that would like to allow her innocence, but the time for empty promises has passed. More and more, it seems that the truth is all we have, and I turn to meet her eyes.

"I don't know."

This time, I am not in the woods but amid the icy, barren landscape of the Void.

I am dreaming, but knowing it does nothing to alleviate my terror. I do not dare a glance back as I spur my horse onward, but I know that the Hounds are near from their alarmingly close howl.

And they are not alone.

Behind them, the Souls thunder toward me, their horses' hooves sounding a horrific crack against the thick sheet of ice beneath our feet. I force myself to look forward. To focus on escape. If I dare look down, I will see those trapped, still half-alive, beneath the ice by Samael and his Souls. I will see them and know my fate.

The dream is one in which there is no end. There is no

sanctuary ahead. No place in which I might find refuge. The ice stretches on and on in every direction, its bleak sameness broken only by the blue sky above. Even as I know it is no accident, I cannot help but think it ironic that the azure sky in the Void is always clear. How cruel to force those trapped beneath the ice to view, day after day, the beautiful sky, the golden Otherworldly sun, and to know they will never again feel its warmth.

The futility of my attempt to escape weakens my resolve, and my pace slows even as I will the horse forward. It is no use. The Hounds are closer still, their yelps and howls clearer and more ominous. The Souls are just behind them, their horses gaining ground by the moment.

And the truth is, I am tired. I am tired of fighting the will of the Souls. Tired of fighting fate. Tired of fighting my sister. Perhaps Alice is right, after all. Perhaps it is wiser to salvage what I can of my own life and the lives of those I love.

But then I remember Henry. I remember his death at Alice's hands, and I know the Souls share responsibility for his demise. Wasn't it they who whispered, coaxed, and cajoled Alice to do their bidding? Wasn't it they who worked to turn her to their cause from the time she was a babe in the cradle?

The thought awakens my fury, and I lean farther over the horse.

Dream or not, one thing is certain: The Souls cannot be allowed to catch me. Not in my dream world. Not in the physical world. Not in the Otherworlds.

If they do, I know I will be consigned to the Void forever.

Dimitri stays with me in the hours after my nightmare. I worry about him leaving his post outside the tent, but he assures me that Gareth can manage a night so quiet. As the morning light gradually seeps through the canvas of my tent, Dimitri drops off to sleep. I do not have the heart to wake him, and I listen to the rise and fall of his breath, planning to let him sleep just a while longer.

But he is not allowed the luxury. A moment later we are both startled by a shout from beyond the tent walls. Dimitri jumps up as if he has been awake all along, racing outside without hesitation, clothes askew, as I shove my feet haphazardly into my boots. I do not bother lacing them before following Dimitri into the morning sunlight.

It takes a moment for my eyes to adjust to the brightness, and I shield them by holding a hand to my brow.

"What is it? What's the matter?" Dimitri and Gareth are standing near the horses and packs as I shout from across the camp. But it is only when my eyes scan the area, looking for the source of their concern, that I notice oddly shaped and colored objects strewn across the ground.

Making my way to Dimitri and Gareth, I pass the articles lying about and realize they are our belongings.

Gareth turns to me. The confusion in his face causes me to worry even before his words can. "It's our water. Someone has emptied our water."

I look around, not sure to what he is referring. "Our water? Whatever do you mean?"

Dimitri holds up one of our water skins, turning it upside down. Not even a drop falls from its spout. "Someone came into our camp during the night and emptied all of our canteens and skins of water."

"But who would do such a thing?" Brigid's voice comes from my side. Her hair is still unbound, the copper highlights catching what little light shines from the gray sky above. "And why?"

Dimitri wipes a hand over his face in a familiar gesture of tiredness and frustration. "I don't know, but that's not the thing that bothers me most."

Gareth is on the ground, digging through the remaining packs, as I try to grasp the meaning of Dimitri's words.

"What bothers you most?"

"Whoever it was came into the camp even with Gareth and me on guard. It's true that I was with you during the latter part of the night, but prior to that we took turns attending to personal matters and sleeping. Gareth says he did not leave the camp unguarded for a single second after my departure."

"Someone stole into the camp? They snuck around you even as you stood watch?" I feel new admiration for Brigid as she asks the questions, for there is only curiosity in her voice, and an obvious desire to understand the situation.

Gareth stands up. "The horses and packs were under the trees at the perimeter of the camp. We have not been worried about our supplies, only our physical safety. I suppose it's possible someone stealthy could have managed it." He pauses, looking around. "But I'm afraid that is not the most disturbing thing about the situation."

"What could be more disturbing than someone violating the privacy of our camp and disposing of all of our water while we're only feet away?" Brigid asks.

Even before Dimitri answers, I have an unsettling feeling that I know what he will say.

"Someone violating the privacy of our camp without leaving a trace of their presence." He looks at me before turning back to Brigid. "Gareth and I found nary a footprint or hoof mark. Whoever it was, *whatever* it was, came and left as if it were a ghost."

Replacing our water is not so much difficult as bothersome. It would be nearly impossible to die of thirst in England, but refilling the canteens takes time, and we are all aware of the ticking clock and the many things left to do before we can perform the Rite at Avebury. The mystery of what happened to our water—and more specifically, who is responsible—adds another layer of tension to our small group, and we are silent, all lost in our own thoughts as we bend over a river near the camp before we depart for the day.

"Who do you think it was?" Brigid asks.

Water replenished, we are picking up the clothing and personal items strewn about the camp while Dimitri and Gareth break down the tents.

I shake my head. "I would say it's someone working on behalf of the Souls, or perhaps the Guard, only..."

Her eyes meet mine. "They left no tracks."

I nod. "The Souls are prohibited from using magic in the physical world. The one exception is shifting, but I have thought it through, and any animal that might have made its way into camp unnoticed would not be able to empty the canteens."

Brigid folds one of Gareth's shirts, pushing it into his pack. "Could the intruder have shifted yet again once within the boundaries of the camp?"

I nod. "I know what you mean. If one of the Souls was able to make its way into camp as, say, a hawk, it might not leave tracks. And if it shifted back into a man once here, it would be able to empty our water. Still...Even though the horses and packs were under shelter of the trees, I do believe Dimitri and Gareth would have noticed another man there, even for a short time." I hesitate to voice the other thought at the back of my mind, but Brigid senses my unspoken words.

"There's something else, isn't there?"

I sit back, tying my pack closed and looking at Brigid as I speak. We are in this together now. "I cannot figure the why of it. Why would someone go to the trouble of emptying our water? It's easy enough to replenish. It's not as if we're in the desert. It seems an impractical way to delay our return to England. Almost...childish. Futile. Don't you agree?"

Brigid looks at the ground, mulling over my words. The silence between us confirms what I already believed: Brigid has no more answers than I.

We do not have time to discuss the matter further, for moments later Dimitri signals that the tents are packed and

the horses ready. Brigid and I rise without another word, but all day she is quiet, and I know she has not forgotten our conversation.

She is not alone. I turn the events over and over in my mind, and though I do not fully understand their meaning, I cannot help but believe that, in the game of the prophecy, a substantial move has been made.

And deep down I know it is only the beginning.

26

We travel the next day without incident. Gareth and Dimitri double back repeatedly to look for tracks but find no hint of anyone in pursuit. The sun, at last free of the overbearing clouds, fights its way through the branches and leaves of the trees, tipping everything with gold. The countryside is beautiful and peaceful, the sun bringing with it a welcome warmth. But it does nothing to lift my spirits. I am haunted by the feeling that someone or something is in pursuit.

I know the forces of evil well. They will be back.

Gareth and Brigid keep each other company in front while Dimitri remains close behind. We do not feel the need to speak, and I try to recall if James and I ever spent so much time together, alone but silent. I am surprised to find that I cannot remember, as if everything that has happened since leaving

New York has rendered my past a faded watercolor. I can make out the shapes, but all the details are gone.

Everything but Henry, who remains as vivid as if I saw him only yesterday.

I force the thought from my mind. Like Henry, James is gone, though in another way entirely. Thinking of him will do me no good, except in the context of saving him from Alice's grasp. My time with James has come and gone. It will not return.

And though I love Dimitri, he cannot factor into my plans, either. My future cannot be determined by love alone. There's far too much at stake.

For me. For the people of Altus. For the world itself.

When sleep comes I return to the Void. The Hounds are nearer still, the Souls close on their tails, and I drive my horse across the frigid landscape, catching glimpses of faces, frozen into grimaces and screams, beneath the ice. A moment later I am awakened by my own screams, surprised to find Dimitri bent over my blankets and shaking me awake.

"Wake up, Lia! It's only a dream!" His eyes are black pools in the darkness of the tent, and for one frightening moment, he resembles a corpse.

I sit up, clasping a hand to my chest and trying to calm the rapid beating of my heart, the breath that comes too quickly from my lungs.

"Are you all right?" Dimitri's voice is gentle. "I've been here for some time. I heard you whimpering, but I could not wake you until just this moment."

Running a hand through my tangled hair, I touch my fingers to my temples, noting the dull throb beneath the skin. "How long have you been here?"

"About five minutes, I suppose."

I meet his eyes. "And I...I wouldn't wake up?"

He shakes his head. Even in the darkness of the tent, I see his worry.

"You don't think I was traveling, do you?" I am not sure I want to know the answer, but neither can I allow myself the luxury of not knowing.

He sighs deeply, looking away as if afraid to meet my eyes. "I don't know. It's against the laws of the Otherworlds, the laws of the Grigori, to force someone to the Plane against her will—"

"I didn't will myself to the Plane, if that's what you are insinuating!"

He reaches out, tucking a strand of hair behind my ear. "Of course you didn't. I'm simply trying to consider all the possibilities."

I already regret the bite of my words, and I lean into him, resting my forehead on his shoulder.

"I'm sorry. I'm just so tired, Dimitri. I don't know from one night to the next if I'm dreaming or traveling. I don't know if the Souls are trying to weaken my resolve by toying with my mind, or..." Even now, I am afraid to finish the thought.

"Or what?" he asks softly.

I lift my head to look into his eyes. "Or if it is simply me. If,

after all this time, I'm finally going mad. Or worse, if I'm being lured to their side, little by little, without even realizing it."

There is a long stretch of silence before Dimitri pulls me to him. "You are not going mad, Lia, and you're not being lured to their side. It is —"

But he is interrupted by a shout outside the tent, and he lifts his head, turning toward the noise before rising and making his way to the tent flap.

I follow him with my eyes. "What is it?"

"I don't know." He steps from the tent, looking back at me. "But stay here."

I am unsure how long I stay in the tent, but it is not as long as Dimitri would like. The rising voices are impossible to ignore, and I wrap a blanket around my shoulders before stepping outside to see Dimitri and Gareth, standing amid a flurry of rubbish, our packs once again torn open and emptied on the ground.

"What is this?" I turn in a circle, taking in the damage as Brigid emerges from her tent, rubbing her eyes.

"I told you to remain in the tent." Dimitri's voice is tight.

I fix him with a glare. "I don't often do as I'm told, as you must surely have noticed by now."

He sighs. "I'm only trying to protect you, Lia."

"What has happened? What's going on?" Brigid's voice is an intrusion into my silent war with Dimitri, and I turn to look at her.

She is still clad in her nightdress, a look of shock fixed on her face as she surveys the scene.

I try to keep my voice from shaking as I answer. "Something—or someone—has gotten into our packs again."

Gareth stalks around the camp, finally throwing something into the trees in frustration. "It's worse than that, I'm afraid. This time, they've gone after our food."

Brigid rushes forward. "Our food? Do you mean to say all of our food has been destroyed?"

"Not destroyed, exactly," Dimitri breaks in. "I think we can salvage some of it."

"But who would do such a thing? And how?" Brigid's eyes are wide with fear, and I suddenly wonder if it is feigned.

"That is a good question." I narrow my eyes at her. "Who do you think would do it? There is no one here but us, and I imagine if Dimitri and Gareth search the camp for tracks, they will find none but ours, just as they did the last time."

Her face goes white. "You don't mean to imply that I did this?"

"I'm not implying anything. I'm simply stating the facts."

"Why would I do such a thing?" she asks.

I feel a moment's doubt but press stubbornly forward. "You tell us."

"Lia—" Dimitri's voice is a warning, but he does not have time to finish before Brigid stalks across the camp, stopping right in front of me.

"The answer is, I wouldn't. Of course I wouldn't." Her voice is pleading. "I was asleep in my tent, just as you were."

"Yes, but Dimitri was with me. Who was with you?" I know it is unfair even as I say it.

"Well, no one, of course, but..." She looks from Gareth to Dimitri. "Tell her! You know I wouldn't do such a thing!"

Gareth holds her gaze before turning to look at me. "My Lady, I thought I heard something in the woods. Someone stepping across the ground. I was gone only a few minutes, and when I returned, Dimitri was with you in your tent and things are as you see them now."

I pull the blanket tighter around my body, not wanting to give up my theory. I do not want to acknowledge the fear coursing through my veins. The growing feeling that I am being shadowed by something beyond my control.

"What has that to do with Brigid?" I ask.

"I simply don't think any of us could have created this kind of havoc in so short a time without alerting Dimitri," Gareth says. "The tent walls are not thick enough to muffle the sound of someone creeping through our camp."

I dare a glance at Brigid and feel a flush of shame when I see the hurt and anger in her eyes. Still, I cannot bring myself to give in. "Well, something, or someone, did."

Dimitri moves to pick up a pack from the ground. "Yes. And until we discover who, or what, it is, it seems we will have no peace."

Our ride the following day is quiet and without the easy companionship to which we've grown accustomed.

Tension fills the air as we make our way out of the forest, and I breathe a sigh of relief as the plains come into sight before

us. Ever since the horrifying journey to Altus in which the Hounds gave chase and I was forced to subsist without sleep for nearly three days, I have not been able to rest easy when surrounded by the eerie quiet of any wood.

But there is a price to pay for the openness of the fields, and we spend the day eyeing the surrounding farmland, watching for any hint of trouble or pursuit. Remembering my fevered race to outrun the Guard in Chartres, I know nothing will see me safe from them, truly safe, except the closing of the Gate.

As night falls, we seek what shelter we can find and make camp amid a small grove of trees at the edge of an open plain. I work in tense silence with Brigid to put together a simple dinner while Gareth and Dimitri see to the horses. Finally, she puts down the knife she is using, breathing a heavy sigh. I feel her eyes on my face but I do not turn to meet them.

"I didn't do it, Lia. I swear to you." There is no anger in her voice, something that causes me great shame, though I cannot say why.

I reach for a stale loaf of bread to cut into slices. It was obviously the victim of one of the nighttime raids, and I brush the dirt from it carefully as I speak. "How can you be certain? The Souls are crafty, you know."

"Lia." She touches my arm, and I finally raise my eyes to hers. "It wasn't me."

"I'm not saying it was or that if it were, it would have been intentional. The Souls..." Unable to hold her gaze, I busy myself with the bread once again. "Well, they turned Sonia

against me once. Sonia, who was more a sister to me, in some ways, than Alice."

She drops her hand from my arm. "I am not Sonia. Or Luisa or Helene or Alice."

It is the first time I have heard true anger in her voice. It causes me to pause and soften my voice. "I know. And I'm sorry the past haunts our new friendship. Truly, I am."

She takes a deep breath, turning her body to face mine. "It is not my fault that I came to the prophecy when so much has already happened. I ask only to be given a fair chance to prove myself, as everyone else has been given before me."

Something clear and bright shines in her eyes, and all at once, I believe her.

I reach out to embrace her. "You're right, Brigid. You are owed that much, and an apology besides. I'm sorry my past with the prophecy and the Souls has made me cynical even where your friendship is concerned."

"It's all right," she says. "Just tell me you believe me."

"I believe you. I do." I say it and mean it, leaving out the words that drift unbidden into my mind.

But if it wasn't you, then who was it? And what does he want?

The Hounds are so close I can smell them. I remember the strange scent—wet fur and tangy sweat—from the journey to Altus and know they are at least as close as they were when they came upon us at the river and Dimitri arrived to see us safely to the Isle.

225

But this time, there will be no Dimitri. No Edmund.

Now I ride across the frozen tundra of the Void with nothing save the cape on my back.

Even my pack—and with it my bow—is absent in this dream.

The journey across the ice seems to take forever, like a dream in which one is running down a hallway only to find that it goes on and on. The hooves of the Souls' steeds reach a crescendo as they race behind the Hounds, ready to surround me and consign me to the Void for eternity.

I am almost prepared to fall, to give in to the slow torture of my fate, when a mighty wind begins to blow. It whips the hair around my face, and particles of snow and ice spin wildly through the air, making it hard to see anything beyond my horse's neck. I am filled with terror, but there is something else, too.

It is a euphoria that builds from within, thrilling me with its power. The unbroken expanse of the Void lies beyond my vision, but it is, at last, quiet. The snarl of the Hounds is absent, as is the thundering of the Souls' horses. Everything has gone silent, and for the first time since Father's death, I am at peace.

But it lasts only a moment. Only a moment, before the voice begins to find its way through my sleep-fogged mind.

I try to tune it out. To ignore it. I have labored long for this rare moment of serenity, and I am loath to relinquish it, even in my dream. Yet the voice, too, is stubborn. It does not allow me the luxury of ignorance, and a moment later it breaks through with words that cause the bottom to drop out of my world.

"Lia! What have you done?"

27

"I don't understand."

I am sitting with Dimitri by the dying light of the campfire, my mind still thick and heavy with sleep.

Gareth and Brigid are trying to repair the tents, but I am not yet in possession of enough of the facts to feel bad about what has happened.

Dimitri takes my hand. "You were standing outside the tent with your eyes open and the wind..." He does not continue, and when I look into his eyes they are haunted by images I cannot see.

"The wind?" I prompt softly.

He shakes his head, remembering. "It was...swirling around you, blowing and shredding the tents, destroying everything in its path."

"But I was *asleep*." I hear the insistence in my voice.

"Yes. But it seems to have been something more than sleep."

I am beginning to see where his words are leading, and I stand, turning away from him to face the fire. "It wasn't. I was sleeping. Dreaming."

His voice is tender but firm behind me. "I don't think you were, Lia."

"If it's as you say . . . If I was outside the tent . . . How did I get there?" I demand. "You were on guard. You said that you wouldn't leave."

His answer is simple. "I didn't. You walked right past me. I was surprised at first, and after a moment I called out, thinking perhaps you needed to see to something personal. But you didn't answer. You simply kept walking until you stood in the center of camp, and then you raised your arms and the wind began to howl."

For a moment, I think I see it all in a residue of memory, a nearly forgotten dream. And then the glimpse is gone.

I think back to the previous incidents, trying to remember the sequence of events, and my mind lights on a morsel of hope. I feel a rush of relief in the certainty that I am absolved. "But the other times, you and Gareth were on guard and did not see me leave my tent. And the night our food was disturbed, you were actually in my tent, waking me from a dream, when Gareth called out."

Dimitri lowers his head, his shoulders sagging in an uncharacteristic show of defeat. "You were dreaming, Lia. I think that's the part we must focus on. You told me that your nightmares have become worse, that sometimes you're not even certain you *are* dreaming."

I swallow the lump of foreboding that rises in my throat. "Yes, but whether or not I was dreaming, we can both agree that I was *not* in the middle of the camp destroying our supplies, at least not prior to last night."

He sighs. "But if you *were* on the Plane, isn't it possible the Souls were able to use you? To channel your exhaustion and bitterness into a spiritual rampage of sorts?"

I am still not prepared to face the reality required to answer his question. "You said . . ." My voice catches as my body begins to tremble with unwanted knowledge. "You said the Souls could not force me to the Plane against my will."

I wish I could freeze the pause that follows, for I know I will not like what Dimitri is going to say next.

"They can't."

I turn to face him, lifting my chin defiantly. "Well, they must have. I don't wish to travel the Plane." I laugh aloud at the notion, but it sounds brittle and false. "I avoid it at all costs, as you well know."

He does not rise, but looks up at me from the log on which he sits. "I know that you mean to avoid it, Lia. But I told you before that the Souls are more powerful than you can imagine. That they would find a way to use you without your consent."

I look past him to the tents, leaning and torn, in the middle of our campsite. "I don't have the knowledge to conjure such power."

"Yes," he says, "you do. You're a Spellcaster, like Alice, and

though you've not fully honed the forbidden authority that is yours, you must have known it was lying in wait. All it needed was a good push from a formidable master. Given the proper motivation, you could easily have done it all—the water, the food, the tents."

"You're saying it was me." I turn away again. "All this time."

I do not hear him rise, but a moment later his hands are warm on my shoulders as he comes to stand behind me. "Not you. Not really. Not you any more than it was Sonia on the way to Altus."

The mention of Sonia, instead of soothing my growing alarm, only serves to anger me. "You compare me to Sonia? You compare this…this…unauthorized use of my power to her *betrayal*?"

He makes a noise of frustration. "Why are you being so difficult? Whatever has happened, it will not be changed by your denial, Lia. You must face what is happening if you're to have any hope of fighting it." He throws up his hands and walks away before turning back around. "You want me to stand here and tell you that you didn't sabotage our camp. That it was not your Spellcaster power that ransacked our packs, tried to destroy our food, our shelter. Well, I'm not going to lie to you. And you can unleash your fury and indignation all you want, but it will do you no good. You will not drive me away. I'm still here, Lia. And I always will be, just as I promised."

He stalks off, but he does not get far before my resolve crumbles. Tossing the blanket to the ground, I race toward him, pulling on his arm until he stops and turns to face me.

There are so many things I want to say, but they are too large for words and I am too weak to voice them aloud after all

that has happened. Instead, I speak of the one thing I must confirm, for everything else Dimitri has said now makes sense.

"You said I would need the 'proper motivation' to be so used by the Souls." I raise my palms to the sky. "What motivation could I possibly have?"

He shrugs, his answer simple. "Exhaustion? Resignation? It's no secret, Lia. We all see it in your eyes, and none of us blames you. Anyone would be tired of fighting after all you've been through. All you've lost and been forced to endure."

I look into his eyes, wanting him to believe my next words. "But I haven't stopped fighting! I haven't! Don't you see me, day after day, riding toward London and the possible end of my life?" I hear the desperation in my voice and hate myself for it.

He pulls me to him. "No one doubts that you're fighting as hard as you can. But in your sleeping hours, during the times when you can, at last, let everything go, isn't it possible there is some small part of you that seeks release? That welcomes an end to the fighting, however it may come?"

His words ring of a truth I have not dared consider.

"I don't know." My voice shakes, and I work to calm it before pulling back to look him in the eye. "But what more can I do to protect myself, and everyone else, from the workings of the Souls? I cannot stay awake every moment. Not for long. We have at least four more days until we reach London, and that is if we ride very hard and very fast. Once there, we'll have to put everything in order for the trip to Avebury. What am I to do during all that time?"

He reaches for my hand. "You'll entrust yourself to me."

I begin to protest, but he does not allow me to finish.

"Everyone must trust someone, sometime, Lia. Even you." I am surprised to feel tears sting my eyes as he continues. "Trust in me. I'll stay with you while you sleep and wake you if anything seems untoward." He sighs. "It isn't foolproof. I cannot protect you on the Plane if I'm not there. But I can wait and watch for anything in this world and wake you if it seems I must."

I do not tell him it is a paltry plan. Instead, I swallow my fear of trusting him. Of trusting anyone. I swallow it and step into the protection of his arms.

Because he's right. It's all we have.

❦

We travel through the woods and over the fields of England the next day, and the next, and the next. I lose track of the fields and trees and farms. They blur together as my physical strength, sapped by sleepless, dream-filled nights, weakens.

My apology to Brigid is met with a warm embrace. Her graciousness is my secret shame, for I was not as quick to forgive Sonia, and I suddenly wish I could go back to the moment on Altus when Luisa, Sonia, and I stood on the cliff overlooking the sea. I wish I could go back and do it all again. If I could, I would like to think I would embrace Sonia the way Brigid did me.

Gareth spends each night guarding the camp while Dimitri watches over me as I sleep. I feel bad for forcing the arrangement, but Gareth's smile is as bright as ever, though he can steal only moments of sleep when we break during the day. He and Dimitri treat me just the same, though with more tenderness than before. I search their eyes for hints of the anger and resentment that I think must be there. It was my actions, after all, that cause us to sleep in tents that leak in the rain. My actions that force us to brush dirt from our bread.

Yet there is nothing but affection and worry in their eyes. Their generosity only highlights my own weakness, and I spend much of the little time I'm coherent loathing myself and contemplating my many failings.

As the days wear on, a comforting sense of apathy wraps its arms around me. For the first time since discovering the mark inscribed upon my wrist, there are hours and sometimes days when I cannot find the energy to worry about the prophecy and my place in it. Times when I think I would be just as happy to see it end with Samael ruling our world in darkness as I would to see him banished from it forever.

Now it does not always seem to matter how it ends. So long as it ends.

I believe I manage to hide my growing sense of complacency behind casual conversation and forced smiles, but I cannot be certain. I no longer trust my perception of anything at all. It is entirely possible that Brigid, Dimitri, and Gareth are already aware of my frightening lack of commitment to ending the prophecy. Yet even this leaves me unconcerned. I am resigned to my fate, whatever it may be.

By the eighth night of our travel, I have become accustomed to staying up well after Brigid goes to bed and Gareth has taken up his post at the other side of camp. I will not be able to delay

sleep forever. But every hour spent by the warmth of the camp-fire, a blanket wrapped around my shoulders, is one less I'll spend with the Souls haunting my slumber. I stare into the flames, my mind terrifyingly blank.

"Here. Have some of this." Dimitri approaches from the periphery of my vision, handing me a steaming cup of tea. He lowers himself to the ground beside me. "It will help you sleep."

I take the cup but do not drink from it. "I don't want to sleep."

Dimitri sighs. It is a heavy, tired sigh, and I feel a moment's regret for causing him worry. "Lia, you must. There is still much to do, and you must be strong for what's ahead."

I glance at him sharply. "I *am* strong."

He reaches over, taking my hand in his. When he speaks, his voice is soft and full of sadness. "I'm only trying to care for you at a time when it is difficult for you to care for yourself."

A lump of sadness suddenly blocks my throat, and I squeeze Dimitri's hand. "I'm sorry. It's just..."

I feel his gaze on my face even as I stare into the fire. "What is it?"

I turn to look at him, wanting to lose myself in the depths of his inky eyes. "I'm afraid to sleep. My dreams are...well, they're frightening, Dimitri."

"So, tell me. Tell me about your dreams so I can share your burden."

I hesitate, wondering how much to tell him in the moment before I decide to tell him everything.

"They chase me." It is a whisper, and I wonder if I have even spoken aloud.

"Who chases you?"

I stare down at my cup as if the murky liquid within will make it easier to speak of the demons that hunt me in my dreams. "The Souls. The Hounds. Samael. Everyone."

Dimitri's fingers wrap around my own and remove my hand from the cup. Taking it from me, he sets it on the ground at my feet and pulls me into his arms, tucking my head under his chin.

"Are they dreams? Or *are* the Souls pulling you into the Plane as you sleep?"

I burrow closer to his chest, finding comfort in the scent of him. It is wood and fire smoke and chill spring air. "I don't believe I'm traveling. But they seem to be more than simple dreams as well."

"What do you mean?" His voice is a rumble from his chest under my ear.

"It's difficult to explain. I don't feel as if I am on the Plane, and yet each time I dream of the Souls, they're closer. And somehow I'm certain they'll continue to get closer with each passing day, and that if ever they're allowed to catch me, dream or not, I'll never wake again. I'll be stranded in the Void forever."

There is a moment when he says nothing, and I wonder if I've gone mad after all. If he is contemplating my madness and his response to it. But then he breathes deeply and begins to speak, his voice gentle.

"They cannot take you to the Void unless they capture your Soul on the Plane, and you have already said you don't believe you're traveling."

"Yes."

"Then...what? If you don't believe you're traveling, why do you fear capture and banishment to the Void?"

I hear the dread in his voice. It makes me hesitant to tell him, for what if he no longer trusts me? What if he doubts my commitment to closing the Gate? I think of James, of my unwillingness to share myself with him fully and the consequences of keeping my secrets. Am I willing to lose Dimitri to the same fate? To the wedge that will be driven between us if I cannot be wholly myself in his presence?

I pull away to look at him. "Sometimes I feel as if they're inside my head. As if everything is not as it seems and they're manipulating me to their own cause. As if all the things I believe to be true are only a figment of my imagination, so that I'm never quite sure if my reality is accurate. It makes me think of my father and his fall into the Plane. I understand now why he would be vulnerable to the Souls masked as my mother." I force myself to continue. If I am to be true to Dimitri, to our love, I must say it all. "I may not be traveling while I sleep, but the truth of it is, I don't trust myself enough to be sure."

He pulls me closer, his arms wrapping me tightly. I feel in this moment that nothing could separate us, in this world or any other.

"It doesn't matter." He kisses the top of my head. "I trust you, Lia."

And I know from his fevered embrace that the words he speaks are true.

28

We are still miles from London when we see the smoke from
the city's street lamps rising into the darkening sky. I would
like to say that I'm happy to see the city looming in the distance. It is the closest thing I have had to a home since leaving
Birchwood and New York. But it is impossible to assign so simple an emotion to the feelings that swirl through my heart. I'm
happy that I'll be able to sleep in a proper bed, though sleep is
no longer the release it once was. I'm happy that I'll see Aunt
Virginia, for I crave her unique brand of motherly attention
and quiet strength.

Yet, there are other matters that cause my stomach to tighten
with worry.

I will have to face Sonia and Luisa and my own lack of forgiveness, even as I tell them about my betrayal at the hands of
the Souls. I will have to come to terms with the fact that there

are now four keys instead of three, and it will be necessary to bring Brigid into the already tense fold.

Most worrisome of all, I will have to confront Alice. I will have to attempt to bring her to our side, though at this moment, nothing seems more impossible.

"Are you worried, Lia?" Brigid's voice is soft beside me as we pass a weary young mother and her two small children on the road leaving London.

I nod, both embarrassed and relieved that my emotions now show so easily on my face. I suppose I no longer have the energy to contain them.

She smiles. "There is great kindness in your heart. Your friends must see it, too. I feel sure they'll understand."

I reach down to stroke Sargent's neck as I speak. "I hope so. I'm afraid...Well, I'm afraid I've not been much of a friend."

"We all fall short at times, don't you think?" she asks. "But we forgive others their shortcomings and hope they will do the same for us."

"Perhaps. But that's the thing; I have not forgiven their shortcomings as readily as you forgave mine. Now..." I sigh. "Well, now I suppose it seems unfair to expect them to extend that kindness to me."

She smiles. "The closest I've come to friendship is what I've read in books. That, and this journey with you," she laughs. "But it does seem that it's more about acceptance than fairness. Unless I'm just being naive."

I find a measure of comfort in the simplicity of her ideals.

Perhaps she is right, and we can all find a way to forgive one another after all.

I grin at her. "You're very wise for so sheltered a girl. And brave, too."

She throws her head back and laughs. "Then I am putting a good face on things. I assure you, I'm trembling on the inside."

"Well, you're not alone, Brigid." The lightheartedness of the moment evaporates as I look toward the city. "You're not alone."

I am surprised when Dimitri dismounts, handing his horse off to one of the stable hands at Milthorpe Manor.

"Board him with the others, will you?" he says.

I give Sargent to the same stable boy and turn to Dimitri in surprise. "But . . . don't you have to get back to the Society?"

Dimitri shakes his head. "I told you I was going to stay with you until this is over, and that is what I mean to do."

It takes me a moment to understand. "You plan to stay *here*? At Milthorpe Manor?"

"I plan to stay with you while you sleep, as I promised."

"In my *bedroom*?" I cannot keep the incredulity from my voice.

He raises his eyebrows, and even now I think I see a hint of his wicked charm. "Unless you plan to sleep elsewhere, yes, I imagine that's where I'll have to stay."

Brigid looks on, pressing her lips together in an attempt to hold back the smile.

"But Aunt Virginia will never allow it! People will . . . Well, they'll talk!" It seems a bit late to worry about our impropriety, but staying together on Altus or in the woods of England seems a different matter from allowing a gentleman in my private chamber in the heart of the city.

"I think we have bigger problems than the gossips of London, don't you?" He doesn't wait for my answer. He simply takes my arm and looks up at Gareth, still on horseback. "Do you remember the address?"

Gareth nods. "I'll get settled and come back here tomorrow."

"You're staying in London?" Obviously, plans have been made without my knowledge, but I cannot bring myself to mind when I think of how safe I feel in Gareth's company.

He nods. "I am, my Lady. I cannot see you this far only to turn my back. Dimitri informed me of your, er, trouble, after—"

I turn to Dimitri, my face flushing with shock. "You told him? About our journey, about...everything?"

There is no apology in Dimitri's eyes. Only resolve. "It makes no sense to keep it from him after everything that has happened. Besides, we need every trusted ally we have, and I think we can agree there are few more trusted than Gareth."

Gareth has held me in such high esteem. I wonder how this new knowledge, the prophecy and my dark place in it, will affect his feelings for me. But when I turn to him there are only compassion and affection in his kind blue eyes.

"Of course," I say, trying to smile. "I'm happy to have you with us, Gareth, though it does add to my concern. I wouldn't like for you to be hurt or used."

"No need to worry over me, my Lady. It is those who dare to

threaten you for whom you should pray." He smiles, but there is no pleasure in it. For a moment, I fear for anyone on the other end of that smile. He continues, "I'll stay and make the trip to Avebury with you as an added assurance against trouble along the way. I do believe Lady Abigail, may she rest in peace and harmony, would approve."

"I do believe you're right," I say softly.

He turns his horse with a nod. "I'll see you in the morning then." Looking back, he flashes Dimitri and me a devious grin. "Sleep well."

It is not Sonia and Luisa, standing quietly near Helene, that garner my attention, but Aunt Virginia. Even in the dim glow of the fire and small lamps scattered throughout the parlor, I can see that she does not look well.

"Lia! You're home!" She rises to meet us, with help from Helene.

Hurrying to her side, I cannot help but notice the slight stoop in her posture, or the wrinkles that seem deeper, despite the fact that I have been gone for only a month.

"Aunt Virginia! I'm so happy to be back!" I wrap her in a gentle embrace. "I wanted to send word that we were on our way, but there was no one whom we trusted with the message."

"It's quite all right, my dear. I was worried, but I had a feeling you would appear soon."

I pull back, staring into her face. "Was everything well while we were gone?"

She nods, but I see the hesitation in her eyes and know she has much to tell me in private. "Everything was fine. Sonia and Luisa became better acquainted with Helene, and they all kept me good company." She looks past me to Brigid standing to the side of the parlor doors. "And who is this?"

I step back, taking Brigid's hand and pulling her into the room. "This is Brigid O'Leary." I look from Aunt Virginia to Sonia, Luisa, and Helene. "She is the final key."

There is a moment of utter silence in which I can nearly feel the shock reverberating through the room. Luisa is the first to speak.

"The last key? But..." She shakes her head, looking from me to Brigid and back again. "I thought you were going to Ireland in search of the Stone."

I nod. "I was. And I found it. But it turns out that Father put everything in place before his death. He hid the Stone near the final key so they would be found together. And there's something else."

Sonia's eyes shine bright with unspoken questions. "What is it?"

"The Rite was there, too, written on the wall of a cave where the Stone was supposed to be hidden."

"What do you mean 'supposed to be'?" I am surprised to hear Helene speak. I had forgotten the uniquely low quality of her voice. "Were you not able to locate it?"

I nod, beginning to see how very difficult to understand this must be for anyone who wasn't at Loughcrew. "Eventually. It was in Brigid's hands for safekeeping, you see."

It is not my imagination that the other girls survey Brigid with new suspicion, and I drop my eyes to her wrist, covered by the sleeve of her shirt. "Will you..." Raising my gaze to hers, I hope she knows that I am her friend. "Would you mind showing them?"

She nods, moving to roll the cuff of her sleeve.

Sonia and Luisa lean slightly forward, wanting a better look but trying to be polite. When the mark is finally exposed, I lift Brigid's hand gently in their direction. "See? It's just like yours. Father found her many years ago and installed Brigid's father as caretaker of the cairns. He told Brigid we would come for the Stone, and she kept it hidden while she awaited our arrival."

No one speaks for a long moment. When the silence is broken, it is by the low murmur of Aunt Virginia's voice. "So that is it. The keys. The Stone. The Rite." She looks into my eyes. "Everything is in place."

I shake my head, not wanting to tell them the thing I have known since shortly after Chartres. "Not everything."

"What else is there?" Luisa asks with a shrug.

I look at them, one by one, trying to find the words and wishing I had not been so stubborn about filling them in sooner. There is no gentle way to say it.

"Alice," I say simply, finally ready to banish this last secret from our midst. "The missing page declares that Guardian and Gate must work together to deny Samael entry with the Rite of the Fallen." I pause. "Which means we need Alice."

For a moment, I do not think they've heard me. No one speaks. No one moves. In the end, it is Luisa who breaks the silence.

"Alice? Why," her laugh is harsh and cold, "you may as well expect the Queen Mother to help us. In fact, I'd say you would have a better chance with her!"

Her dismissiveness frightens me. But I cannot stop now. I must tell them everything if we are to begin again. If we are to have any hope of regaining our friendship.

"I'm afraid that's not all."

Sonia steps forward. "What do you mean?"

I take a deep breath. "We must have Alice's help—and we must have it by the eve of May first. The eve of Beltane."

Helene's gaze drifts to the fire. "But that's..." She turns her head back to meet my eyes.

I nod. "Only four weeks away."

I bid Sonia, Luisa, and Helene good night, entrusting Brigid to their care while I wait in the parlor with Aunt Virginia and Dimitri. We have much to discuss, and even as I hope to mend the bridge of my friendship with Sonia and Luisa, there are some things that must be done privately.

We tell Aunt Virginia about Brigid and her father, the back-stone in the cave that held the Rite, and the journey to London and all its challenges. I expect her to be shocked, or at least dismayed, to learn of the Souls' use of my power, but she only nods in understanding.

"I, too, am suffering at their hands. In fact, I believe we all are, though the girls are younger and show the signs less obviously."

"What do you mean, Aunt Virginia?" I try to imagine all the things that could have happened while I have been gone. "What's happened?"

She dismisses the worry in my voice with a wave of her hand. "We are hunted in our dreams, tempted to travel the Plane."

I shake my head. "All of you?"

"Yes, to one degree or another." She hesitates, as if trying to decide whether to continue. "Sonia seems to be bearing the worst of it, but I do believe she is holding her own."

I do not tell my aunt that it looks as if *she* is bearing the worst of it, for she seems to have aged ten years in the last month. I know she will not acknowledge the extent of her struggle, however difficult, and instead turn my thoughts back to Sonia.

"How can you be sure, Aunt Virginia? How can you be sure Sonia is holding her own?" As soon as the words leave my mouth, I feel guilty for my distrust, but to leave the question unasked would be to put us all in even more danger.

Her sigh is not one of exasperation but of sadness. "She is fighting them with every ounce of strength she has. She loves you. You are her dearest friend, even now. She wants only to help you. To make up for her earlier betrayal. I think she would die before turning to the Souls' cause again."

I nod. "All right."

I find I must fight the urge to go to Sonia this very minute. To apologize and beg her forgiveness. To see if there is anything I might do to help her. It will have to wait, for there is one more thing that must be discussed this night.

"We found a way," I begin, looking briefly at Dimitri before turning my attention back to my aunt. "A way to keep the Souls at bay and allow me some measure of rest."

She raises her eyebrows, waiting for me to continue.

"It is . . . Well . . ." I feel myself blushing and reprimand myself silently for behaving like a silly schoolgirl when the fate of the world hangs in the balance. "Dimitri stays with me. During the night. He does so to ensure that I do not do the Souls' bidding while I sleep."

"And I would like to continue staying with her at Milthorpe Manor until this is all over, for her own protection and the protection of everyone else in the house," Dimitri adds. "I know it is unconventional, but you have my word that I will sit in a chair at Lia's bedside through the night. Nothing more."

At first Aunt Virginia does not reply. She simply stares at us as if we were speaking an entirely different language. Finally she shakes her head softly, looking at us both as if we are mad.

"Stay here? In Lia's *chamber*?" She straightens her back. "I am well aware the prophecy has created some unconventional situations, but I can't possibly allow this, Mr. Markov. Lia's virtue is at stake, and while I'm certain you would honor your promise, it would look entirely untoward. Her reputation would never recover!"

I stand for a moment before kneeling in front of her and taking her hands in mine. "Aunt Virginia, you know that I love you as a mother, don't you?"

She hesitates before nodding, and I believe I see the shine of tears in her eyes.

I try to soften my voice. "Then you must know that I say this with the utmost respect, but I'm..." I sigh, surprised at how difficult it is to defy her. "Well, I'm not asking your permission. Milthorpe Manor will always be your home. Always. But I am its mistress, and I'm afraid I must, in this instance, insist. Dimitri has seen to my safety on more than one occasion.

"I cannot fight the battle ahead without rest, and I cannot rest without someone to watch over me. You said yourself that everyone else is under attack as well. Under these circumstances, I think it wise to keep Dimitri in the house, for everyone's sake."

The hurt is visible on Aunt Virginia's face, and I feel a pang of regret at having put it there. But I am no longer a child. I have fought many battles. I have suffered great loss. I have earned the right to speak for myself.

And there is no other way.

She rises with a sigh. "Very well. As you say, you are mistress of Milthorpe Manor." There is no resentment in her voice, only weariness, and regret. "It is your decision to make."

She leaves the room without another word, and I wonder why I am not pleased with my ability to finally choose my own path. To make my own decisions.

But it is not pleasure I feel; it is fear. Fear that I am not as equipped to make the decisions as I would like everyone to believe.

And fear that my making them could lead to the ruin of us all.

29

"Are you comfortable?"

Dimitri surveys me from the chair near my bed, having kissed me chastely on the forehead and tucked me in like a child. There is nothing remotely suggestive in his voice, but even now, with everything that hangs over our heads, his partially unbuttoned shirt and easy slouch are frighteningly appealing.

I nod. "Yes, thank you. Except I feel guilty that you'll spend the night in that chair, though you do make it look rather pleasant."

He grins, patting his knee. "Well, I've plenty of room for you, if you'd like a change of scenery."

I am both pleased and appalled that we can joke so inappropriately at a time when so much hangs in the balance. I find myself returning his smile with one of my own.

"I don't think Aunt Virginia would approve."

He sighs dramatically, settling deeper into the chair. "Very well, then. Suit yourself."

I close my eyes, finding comfort in the knowledge of his presence. The room is warm, my bed infinitely softer than the ground I have slept on for the past ten days. All of it conspires to make me drowsy, and it does not take me long to fall asleep.

And this time, for some reason, I do not dream.

Dimitri is resting in the room arranged for him by Aunt Virginia, and I can only assume Luisa and the others are still preparing for the day. I will have to speak to Luisa eventually, but right now it is Sonia who weighs heavily on my mind, and I stop in front of the door to her room, lifting my hand to knock.

I wonder if she will be able to forgive me. If things will ever be as they were. But these are questions that will not find answers in the hallway, and I force myself to knock before I can change my mind.

"Ruth, I wonder if you can—" The door opens more quickly than I expect, and Sonia stands in its frame, surprise evident on her face and the half-spoken sentence hanging in midair. "Lia! I...Come in!" She stands back, opening the door wider to allow me entry.

I step into the room, feeling shy with her for the first time since we met in the candlelit room where she once held séances long ago. "I'm sorry. Am I disturbing you?"

She laughs softly. "It's quite all right. I simply assumed it was Ruth. Luisa no longer knocks and you…" Her voice trails off.

"I no longer come to visit." I finish for her.

Her nod is slow.

I gesture to one of the chairs in front of the firebox. "May I?"

"Of course." She moves to join me, and I remember when I would rush to her room and sit on her bed without ceremony. Sonia would settle next to me, and we would spend long hours talking, plotting, worrying. I feel a pang of sadness that we must so often lose something before we realize its value. I wish fervently that I could go back and do it all again with more understanding.

I look down at my hands, unsure how to begin. "Sonia…" Lifting my head, I meet her eyes. "I'm sorry."

Her face is impassive, her expression giving nothing away. "You have already apologized, Lia. More than once."

I nod. "Yes, but I think even then, part of me felt entitled not to forgive you."

"It's perfectly understandable. What I did *was* unforgivable." The pain in her voice is still raw and unvarnished.

"It should not have been." I reach out to take her hand. "What *I* did was unforgivable. I didn't honor our friendship and the many sacrifices you've made in its name. I didn't make the same allowances for you that you've so readily made for me. Worst of all," I take a deep breath, realizing all at once how true my next words are, "I wasn't there for you when you needed me most."

"The same could be said of me. Those days traveling through the woods to Altus..." Her voice becomes softer, and her eyes are clear even as she remembers. "Well, I hardly remember them. I was only later told that you were forced to stay awake to ensure the Souls did not use you as their Gate. It was my doing, and I was not even able to stand by your side as you suffered."

We are silent as we remember the terrifying time when we were both at the mercy of the Souls—Sonia through her unwitting alliance with them and me through my fear that they would use me while I slept.

But the past is the past, and there it must stay. There is too much ahead to dwell on it any longer, and I finally look at Sonia and smile. "I'm sorry I wasn't a better friend to you, Sonia. But if you can forgive me, I'd like to start over. To be friends as we once were."

She leans over to embrace me. "I should like nothing more."

❧

It is not my imagination that the maids whisper as I make my way to the dining table. Though Dimitri and I made every effort to keep his presence in my chamber a secret, it was inevitable that someone would notice.

The other girls are already at the table—all except for Sonia, who is still upstairs, dressing. I settle myself next to Brigid, trying to ignore the sidelong glances of the serving girl as she spoons food onto my plate. I will have to explain

Dimitri's presence, but I cannot do so in the company of the household staff, so I sit stoically by, watching them serve and thinking that I like London society less and less the more time I spend in it.

"Did you sleep well, Lia?" Brigid's voice startles me from my private thoughts, and I turn to her with a smile.

"I did. Remarkably well, actually. And you?"

She smiles. "It is wonderful to sleep in a bed again, though I did enjoy the outdoors on the way here."

"I know what you mean."

I hesitate for a moment, trying to think of a way to bring up Dimitri before deciding it is best to be direct. Lifting my teacup, I try to sound casual.

"I'm sure you've all heard that Dimitri will be staying with us."

They meet one another's eyes and it is obvious Dimitri's presence was a topic of discussion even before I came to the table.

"Brigid tells us it is to look after you," Luisa finally says. "To ensure that the Souls don't use you while you sleep."

I nod, grateful to Brigid for paving the way. "Aunt Abigail's adder stone is cold, and it seems that without its power, I'm more vulnerable than I would like to admit. It is for all our sake that Dimitri will be here, though we must accept that there will be talk among the staff."

Luisa laughs and waves of her hand. "Psh! I couldn't care less what the household staff thinks! I would just like us all to sur-

vive to the end of this journey. If Dimitri's presence increases that possibility, I'm all for it."

I have already explained the situation to Sonia, but I look now to Helene and Brigid. "Do you have any objections?"

Brigid smiles. "If I had objections, I would have voiced them before now."

I turn my eyes to Helene. "Helene?"

She furrows her brow as she chooses her words. "I don't think my father would approve."

An abrupt laugh escapes from Luisa's full lips as she regards Helene. "Your *father*? Who plans to tell *him*? By the time you get a letter to Spain and your father gets one back to you, this will all be over!"

Helene straightens her back. She looks suddenly prim, though I have not noticed the quality in her before this moment. "Yes, well, just because I don't have time to tell him doesn't mean I should disobey his wishes."

Luisa sighs. "I think it admirable that you wish to honor your father's values, Helene." She stops suddenly, her eyes surveying the ceiling as she ponders her next words. "Actually, that isn't true. I think it ridiculous and shortsighted. But what I think is beside the point."

I feel an urge to laugh hysterically, inappropriately, as Luisa continues.

"The thing is, there are bigger concerns at hand, don't you think? Things like our survival," she begins ticking them off on her fingers, "the fate of our souls, the future of mankind. Things

such as that. I vote Dimitri stays." She places her palms flat on the table in a gesture of finality as she meets Helene's eyes. "And since we already know the others agree, I'm afraid *you* are outvoted."

I try not to smile as Helene excuses herself from the table, her chin held high the whole time. It is Brigid who bursts into laughter once Helene's footsteps have receded down the hall.

I resist the urge to do the same. "Do you think one of us should go after her?"

Luisa waves away my question as she takes a sip of tea. "She'll be over it in an hour. Trust me, Sonia and I have learned how to deal with Helene."

30

I am somewhat surprised when Aunt Virginia decides to accompany us on a stroll through town, but as she drops behind with Helene, I began to understand. They walk side by side in companionable silence, and I realize that living with Alice has made my aunt uniquely suited to understanding someone like Helene. She may not share Alice's dark nature, but she sets herself apart in much the same manner. It seems natural that my aunt should give her special care, and I find myself grateful for her kind spirit.

The streets of London are bustling with midmorning traffic. Carriages rattle past as all manner of people rush to and fro. Luisa and I walk together, with Sonia and Brigid up ahead, talking easily as Sonia points out the sights.

"It's nice to have you back, Lia." I hear the smile in Luisa's voice and turn to see her smiling. "You *are* back, aren't you?"

Her words fill me with such sadness that I cannot return her smile. "Yes, I do believe I am. But..."

"What is it, Lia?" Her voice is gentle.

I look down at the cobblestones as I walk. "I was so hurt, so scared, by Sonia's betrayal. And after you both returned from Altus, you seemed closer than ever before. Looking back, it seems mad to have worried over your loyalty, but at the time, it felt like I had everything to fear from every person in my midst. Can you forgive me?"

She reaches down, giving my hand a squeeze. "Oh, Lia! You're such a silly thing! You needn't *apologize*. Just tell me you're back, that *we* are back, and everything will be behind us in an instant."

I squeeze her hand in return, smiling in gratitude and wondering at the irony in something as dark as the prophecy bringing with it the rare and beautiful friends I call mine.

"Now," she says, her dark eyes gleaming, "tell me what I've missed."

For the next twenty minutes as we pass dress shops and bakeries, I do. I tell her about Loughcrew and the discovery of the Stone. I tell her about the Rite and how the sun lights it only once a year, during the equinox. I tell her how frightened I am that Alice won't help us and how I think of little else but what to do if her refusal should come to pass.

"But how do all the pieces come together in the actual ceremony?" Luisa finally asks.

I am preparing to answer when Sonia, half a block in front of us, calls back, "We're going into the hat shop!"

I wave her and Brigid forward. "Go ahead. We'll be right along."

They disappear into one of the many storefronts, and I look back at Luisa. "I didn't understand it at first, either. But the more I think about it, the less complicated it seems."

Luisa furrows her brow in concentration. "Well, perhaps I simply need to think about it more, then."

I laugh aloud. "The final page of the prophecy says that we must return to the belly of the serpent. It makes sense that it refers to Avebury. You and all the other keys were born in proximity to it. The prophecy seems to say that's where it all began, and so we should return there to end it. The belly seems to point to its center. If it really is a sacred place, its power may well be concentrated in its center in the same way the cavern under Chartres held special meaning."

We come upon the hat shop, stopping in front of the window. Through it, we watch as Sonia and Brigid laughingly try on several enormous hats. They adjust them for each other, giggling until the shop owner glares their way.

"What of the...how is it phrased? The 'Circle of Fire'?" Luisa asks.

"I've had dreams that speak to it, I think." For a moment, it is not Luisa and me reflected in the glass, but the fire inside the circle from my dreams. The strange chanting. The hooded figures. "There are people chanting around a fire, and the Stone is propped atop a wooden mount, probably to catch the first rays of sun on Beltane." I turn my head to look at her as Aunt Virginia and Helene reach us. "I think that's how it's supposed to go."

Luisa nods somberly as Helene peers through the window at Sonia and Brigid, who replace two hats on their stands before grabbing two new ones.

"What are they doing?" Helene asks.

"They're having fun." There is an undercurrent of annoyance in Luisa's voice.

I turn to Helene. "Would you like to go inside?"

She looks surprised. "I've no need for a new hat."

Though I feel a moment's sadness at her inability to enjoy herself, I cannot help the note of resignation in my sigh. Aunt Virginia comes to the rescue.

"Shall we go back?" she asks with a smile. "I could use a cup of tea."

Dimitri returns from the Society with Gareth in tow, and we share a laughter-filled dinner as they play off each other in comical fashion. I take no notice of the passing hours, but by the time the men push away from the table to take brandy in the parlor, exhaustion has sunk its teeth into my bones. I want nothing save my quiet chamber, my soft bed, and some solitude in which to contemplate my options for bringing Alice around to our cause.

Even the thought of it is ludicrous, and I have to force myself to ignore the voice in my head that tells me it is impossible.

After bidding the others good night, I retire to my room to change and wash for bed. The flames are blazing in the firebox, and I crawl beneath the covers, trying to imagine what I will say to Alice.

And when.

Reason tells me that it must be tomorrow, for the time until Beltane grows shorter by the day. The journey itself—though not as long as the one to Altus or Ireland—will require planning, and with so large a party, we will have to allow for extra time.

I try to imagine the things that motivate Alice. The things that might give her pause in her desire to aid the Souls. But Alice's motivation has always been clear. She seeks to gain as much authority as she can muster. She doesn't care whether that power is wielded under rule of the Good, as it is now, or under rule of the Souls, as it will be if she has her way.

There is no one Alice loves. No one to whom she is loyal.

Unless one counts James.

The thought is but a glimmer in the deepest well of my heart, and I sit up in bed as the implications of such a development, if it were true, begin to click together in my mind.

Can one count James? Is it possible—even remotely possible—that Alice really loves him? The idea brings to mind the first ray of hope I've felt since the moment I figured out that the prophecy required my sister and I to work together.

"What are you thinking about so seriously in your bed?"

The voice is lazy and startles me from my thoughts. I sit up, the embroidered coverlet dropping to my waist as I follow the voice to the figure near the closed door.

"Dimitri! You startled me."

"I'm sorry," he says. "You were deep in thought. I didn't want to interrupt you."

He walks slowly toward me, sitting on the edge of the bed. His weight on the mattress, his proximity, the smell of brandy and fire smoke... It all makes me feel flush and overly warm.

"Did you have a nice visit with Gareth? Is he comfortable in your room at Elspeth's?" It is not a very witty attempt to distract myself from Dimitri's presence, but it's all I have in the moment.

He flashes me the grin of a rogue, lying down next to me atop the coverlet. "He said he's most comfortable, though I'd say not nearly as comfortable as I." His eyes travel to my lips and then to the place where the ribbon of my nightdress ties near my collarbone.

"You," I say, placing two hands on his chest and giving him a gentle shove, "are a very bad influence. You're supposed to be in the chair."

He wraps his arms around me, pulling my body close to his, and though the coverlet is between us it does little to dampen the rush of blood through my veins.

"Do you want me to go?" he asks.

"Yes...No...That is, you should go." My voice weakens as he kisses first my cheek and then the tender skin at the base of my throat. "You must."

"Must I?" A shiver races up my spine as his warm breath moves over my neck.

I sigh, pressing closer to him for a moment despite my best intentions. I do not want him to leave. Not this bed. Not me. Not ever.

"Well..." My breath is a whisper into the room. "Maybe not yet."

And then his mouth his on mine. His tongue slips between my lips, and I am lost in the heat of our kiss as the room tilts beneath me. My hands come up as if they have a mind of their own, stroking his broad back until I wish there was no coverlet, no clothing separating our fevered skin. Everything falls away as we push the boundaries laid before us, those set by Aunt Virginia and society itself. There is nothing but the press of Dimitri's body to mine.

Then he is pulling away with a soft groan, sitting upright. His breath comes hard and fast.

I do not have to ask him why he's pulled away, and I give him a moment to collect himself. I take advantage of the time to will away the fire still burning in my belly, to clear my head of the desire-fueled fog that has settled there.

When the rise and fall of Dimitri's breath seems more regular, I touch his back softly.

"I'm sorry. It is difficult not to be carried away, isn't it?"

He turns to look at me, his eyes unreadable. "Difficult does not begin to describe the discipline I must use when I'm close to you, Lia."

I smile, finding an odd pleasure in the effort it takes for him to maintain his distance.

"I don't want you to go," I say. "Do you think you could find the discipline to lie with me for a while? To lie with me, and nothing more?"

He stretches out beside me, laying his head on the pillow next to mine.

He grins wickedly. "Can you?"

My laughter is soft. "It will be at least as difficult for me, I assure you. But I'm not ready to be alone with my thoughts just yet."

His face grows serious as he reaches up to touch my face. "And what thoughts would those be?"

I take a deep breath. "I keep trying to think of something, anything, that will sway Alice from the path she has chosen. I cannot put it off any longer. I'll have to see her tomorrow."

He lifts his head. "So soon?"

"I must. Beltane is less than a month away, and there is still much to do before we can even think of leaving. Besides, what will change between tomorrow and the next day, or the next? I want to be done with it."

He nods. "I'll come with you."

I look into his eyes and smile. "This I must do alone, Dimitri." I hold up a hand as he begins to protest. "I know you mean to protect me. I do. But she's my *sister*."

His eyes darken as he clenches his jaw. "It's too dangerous."

"It isn't. The next battle to take place will be waged at Avebury and on the Planes of the Otherworlds." I reach out to smooth the worry from his brow. "Don't you see? I finally figured out why the Guard did not give chase as we made our way from Loughcrew."

He waits for me to tell him.

"They know that, finally, I have no enemy greater than myself. Without Aunt Abigail's power in the adder stone, I am as weak as I've ever been. There is no need to send the Guard. Not now, when there is every possibility I will do the work of turning myself to their side."

Anguish shadows his eyes in the moment before he clasps me to him, burying his face in my hair. "You will never turn to their side, Lia. I won't let you."

I don't answer, for there is nothing to be gained by repeating the words that linger like smoke in the back of my mind: *If only it were yours to decide.*

31

I wait for Alice outside the Savoy the next morning. Concerned that she might refuse me, I have not announced my desire to see her, and I stand with my back against the stone wall of the hotel, waiting for her to emerge, as she undoubtedly will. Alice would never stay indoors on a day like this one. Spring has finally come to London, and the day is capped with a crystalline sky.

I plan to rehearse my plea, to memorize exactly the right words to bring Alice to our side. But in the end, I can do nothing but stare at the hotel doors, my heart in my throat as I wait for a glimpse of my sister.

She appears some time later, and I press my back against the wall, not yet ready to be seen. As she nods to the doorman on her way out, I recognize the curt tip of her head. Alice has never been fond of those she views as beneath her, and I wonder if she sees James, a common bookseller's son, that way, too.

She continues down the road, unmindful of those around her, her chin lifted as if in quiet rebellion. It is a strange sensation, to observe my likeness make her way down the street. To see the men offer her admiring glances as the women eye her jealously. I have never thought myself pretty, and I wonder with surprise if perhaps I am, or if it is Alice's brand of confidence and aloofness that makes her the subject of so much attention.

When she is almost half a block in front of me, I step away from the wall and begin to follow her fluttering cape. I tell myself it would be unwise to announce my arrival so soon. That it would be smarter to see where she's going. To wait for a private place in which to speak.

But I am scared. Not of Alice. Well, not entirely. No. I am scared to force this final worldly confrontation. To let go of my hope, however improbable, that she might be willing to help close the Gate to Samael.

Alice makes her way past the many shops lining the street. It is not difficult to follow her without being seen. There are few people who carry themselves with as much assurance as Alice, and fewer still who pay less attention to those around them.

She crosses the street and I speed up, making it to the other side just before a stream of carriage traffic would make it impossible to keep her in view. I follow her for a few more minutes and am not at all surprised when she turns to pass through the gates of a park, largely obscured from the outside world by the many large, leafy trees that form a wall around its perimeter.

The park is a small one, and as I step through the entrance I find myself on a narrow cobblestone path. Alice seems nearer in such a confined space, and I drop back in order to stay out of view. We make our way deeper into the park, winding our way through the sun-dappled shade of the many trees on the grounds. I duck abruptly behind a tree as Alice finally comes to a stop at the edge of a pond, watching as she lowers herself onto an iron bench near the water's edge. A family of ducks paddles in the distance, and I wonder if she is naming them, as we used to do with the ones that lived in Birchwood Manor's pond.

Taking a deep breath, I gather my courage as I step away from the security of the tree. *Say something now,* I think, as I approach her from behind. Being in such close proximity makes me feel off-balance, and I am suddenly flooded with conflicting feelings of loathing, sadness, and, yes, love.

Even now.

I am a few steps behind her, preparing to say her name, when she speaks, her words carrying softly across the water. "Why are you hiding, Lia? Come and sit beside me, will you?"

I am surprised, but not by the fact that she knows I've been following her. It's the quality of her voice, the lack of anger, of *passion,* that startles me.

I don't answer. I simply step forward, taking my place next to her on the bench.

I follow her eyes across the water, observing the ducks as they paddle their way toward us, likely trained to expect bread or food of some kind.

"Do you remember when we used to ride our horses to the pond and feed the ducks old bread?" Alice's voice is wistful, and in my mind's eye I can see the fields surrounding Birchwood, my sister riding fast and strong in front of me, her hair blowing out behind her in the wind.

"Yes." It is difficult to speak around the heaviness in my heart. "You always rode too fast, too far in front of me. I was afraid of being left behind."

A smile plays at the corners of her mouth. "I was never as far away as you imagined. And I would not have allowed us to be separated, whatever you might have thought."

I take a moment to process this new information. Even so small an admission changes the way I view my sister. "Why did you do it when you knew it frightened me?"

She gives a small shrug. "I suppose there was some part of me that relished your dependence. Your fear. But as to the real why of it, I honestly don't know."

I look back out over the water. It ripples, gray and leaden, even in the light of the sun. I suddenly do not know what to say. How to begin. I search the opposite shore, studying the grass at its edge, the trees in the distance, as if they hold the words I need. I am not surprised when Alice speaks first.

"I already know he doesn't love me."

It is obvious she refers to James, but her words give me no sense of victory. "I wasn't going to say such a thing."

She drops her gaze to her hands, folded in her lap. "You don't have to. I see only you when I look in his eyes."

I let the words sit between us. Not to hurt Alice, but because I am trying to think of a way to motivate her to help us when she already believes James doesn't love her.

Finally, I can speak only the truth. "Whatever the situation now, Alice, James will not be able to love you if you refuse to aid us in closing the Gate. If he learns of your role in allowing Samael to rule the world as you desire."

"It seems I have only two futures available to me." Her voice is soft, and without the rebelliousness that has always been characteristic of my sister. "Help you and live as a married woman to a man who loves my sister, or take my place beside Samael and rule the world." She turns to look at me, her eyes a sharper green than I have ever seen them. "What would you do?"

I consider her question, imagining myself in her place. It takes me only a moment to find the answer.

"I would accept neither," I say. "I would find a way to make a future for myself. One in which I might be loved, really loved, and one in which I did not have to trade power for that love."

She holds my gaze for a moment, and I think I see doubt flicker in her eyes. But it is a tiny flame, extinguished before I have time to be certain it is there.

She turns back to the water. "Then you are a better person than I, Lia." Her smile is wry, and when she speaks again, her words are shaded with a subtle sarcasm. "Then again, we did not need to have this conversation to determine that, did we?"

I do not want to revisit Alice's assertions that I was always the favored twin. "We all view things based on our own per-

ceptions, Alice. But whatever you think, Father loved you. He loves you still. We all do."

She lifts her chin, avoiding my gaze. "All except for James."

Standing, I pace to the edge of the water, turning my back to her. "James is... Well, the situation with James is my fault. I didn't—" I choke on the words, for even now the memory of leaving him, of hurting him, causes me sorrow. "I didn't handle it as I should have. I didn't talk to him as I should have. It left many unanswered questions in his mind." I turn to face her. "But don't you see, Alice? Those questions can be laid to rest now. I love Dimitri. James and I, well... Ours was a love for another time. Another place. If you will only stand with me to see the Gate closed, you might have a fresh start with him. You might have a chance at a life in which you can live, happily and in love, real love, without the shadow of the prophecy and your place in it."

She doesn't answer for a moment, but when she does, it is not to speak of James, but of our father. "Did you know I used to watch you and Father in the library? I would stop by the windows outside the house or stand in the doorway to the room, watching the two of you, laughing and discussing books. It seemed so easy, the way you shared everything, but when I tried to take an interest in the library or Father's collection, he would only half-listen, always eager to get back in your company."

I sigh. "I'm sure Father knew that you were not really interested in the library, Alice. He no doubt appreciated your effort but didn't want you to have to make it."

"Of course. It cannot be that he simply wasn't interested in me, can it?" Her voice trembles. "I was alone, Lia. Mother was dead. You had Father and James. Henry had Edmund. Aunt Virginia was always looking after you, even before I understood why she eyed me with suspicion."

Her words fall like lead. She's right. The knowledge is a knife to my heart, for doesn't that make me as culpable as Alice in her choice to deny her role as Guardian? Isn't it possible that, if given the love that she was denied, Alice might have aligned herself with the cause of the Sisters?

I cross the rocky path to resume my place beside her on the bench, turning my body toward her and taking her warm hand in mine. "I suppose I never realized you were lonely. You always seemed so happy. So carefree. Talk of the library appeared to bore you, and after a while I suppose I stopped trying."

"I didn't want you or Father to see how much it hurt. Didn't want you to have that power over me." She shrugs, looking away. "So I pretended not to care."

"I'm sorry, Alice. Sorry to have caused you pain." It is more difficult than I expect to say the words. Not because it isn't true, but because of Henry. Because every injustice, every sorrow inflicted upon Alice seems deserved in light of what she did to Henry.

But I say the words. I say them because Alice needs to hear them, and yes, I say them because I must if I am to have any hope of gaining her support.

"It doesn't matter anymore." Her throat ripples as she swallows the emotion of a moment ago.

"Perhaps not," I say. "Can we put the past behind us, then? Can we work together to close the Gate to Samael so that we might begin again? So that *you* might begin again, with James?"

She pulls her hand slowly from mine, tucking it into her lap and looking back out over the water.

"It isn't my place," she says simply.

It is a strange statement, and I find I must make an effort to hide my annoyance. "But it *is* your place, Alice. As Guardian, it is your place more than any other."

"You must try to understand, Lia." Her voice seems to come from farther and farther away, and I have the distinct impression that I am losing her. That my window of opportunity to bring her to our side is closing. "I have always been one with the Souls. Have always been an aid to their cause. Always."

Her words resonate with a finality I cannot deny.

My heart is once again heavy in my chest as I answer. "So you will not come to our aid? Will not fulfill your role as Guardian, even as you stand to lose James?"

She turns to me. "I'm sorry, Lia. It's too late. I don't know who I am if not the one to aid the Souls in their cause. It is too much a part of me. Too much a part of my purpose. Without it, I think I would cease to *be*." She stands, gazing down at me with something sad and indescribable in her eyes as she prepares to leave. "I'm sorry for you, Lia, and I wish you luck in fulfilling your destiny. I'm afraid you'll need quite a lot of it."

32

I do not respond to the soft rap on the door, but Dimitri enters anyway. He crosses the room in silence, sitting next to me and gently pulling me into his arms. At first I resist, but it does not take long for my body to lean into his.

Smoothing my hair back, he kisses the top of my head. "She said no?"

I do nothing for a long moment, not wanting to acknowledge the truth. But there is no time for pretending, and finally, I nod.

I feel the sigh lift his chest. "I'm sorry."

Sitting up, I pull my knees against my body, wrapping my arms tightly around them. "It was naive of me to think it would be so easy."

He shakes his head. "Not naive—optimistic. It would have been foolish not to try." He shrugs. "Now we know."

I stare into the fire, not wanting to meet his eyes. "For all the good it does us."

In my peripheral vision I see him run a hand through his hair. "We will simply wait, that's all. We'll continue to work on Alice, and we'll wait until next year at Beltane. It doesn't have to be this year."

I lay my head on my knees, turning to look at him. "I cannot wait, Dimitri."

"Yes." He nods. "You can. The prophecy doesn't dictate a specific year. It simply says you must gather on the eve of Beltane. If it takes us another year to convince Alice, so be it. If it takes ten years, so be it."

I smile softly. "I won't last that long, and we both know it. I'm already weakened by the Souls. My alliance with the other keys is fragile, and I have no way of knowing if I can even convince Helene to stay another full year. It has to be now."

"But how? If Alice will not agree to help us, I don't see how we can possibly force her. It's true we might be able to get her to Avebury against her will, but there would be no way to force her to participate in the Rite."

"I don't have the answers, Dimitri. Not now." I close my eyes. "I simply know that I cannot wait, and that I'm very tired."

He stands, bending over me. Before I can protest, he lifts me into his arms and begins walking toward the bed. His arms are strong and unfaltering, and I feel as if he could carry me forever without tiring.

"What are you doing?" I ask softly.

His face is very near mine, his eyes bottomless pools of liquid onyx. "I'm taking you to bed so that you may sleep."

We reach the bed and Dimitri lowers me gently to the mattress, pulling the covers up to my shoulders. He sits carefully on the edge of the bed, bending to kiss me softly on the mouth. His lips are supple on mine.

"Everything will look better in the morning, you'll see. Just sleep, my love."

It seems an impossible task, but soon I am slipping into the darkness.

Dimitri's face is the last thing I see.

I am back in the Void, Samael closer than ever before. The putrid scent of the Souls is overpowering. I feel the hot breath of their horses on my back.

Even in my dream, I am tired. I go through the motions of spurring my horse forward. Of trying to outrun the Beast and his army of fallen angels. But part of me already knows it's futile, and my horse slows a little at a time until a great tug pulls me from his back.

I hit the ice hard, but it is a sensation I only dimly register. I don't feel the pain of it as I would in my world. And there is no time to dwell on it. The army of Souls surrounds me in a circle as I lie on the ice, and I know it's over.

Now I will be consigned beneath the ice for all eternity.

But first, He will come.

I hear the horse, snorting as it makes its way through the

crowd of parting Souls, as if angry I have led it on such a chase. I feel the heartbeat, beginning as a low rumble in my chest, vibrating from within as it grows stronger and nearer. Soon I hear it, too. Not just the heart of Samael, the Beast, but my own heart, beating in time with his.

It is strangely comforting, and if I close my eyes, I can almost believe I am in the womb. I lie back on the ice, giving myself over to the beating heart, the feathers of Samael's wings fluttering like black snow around my body. They touch my face, soft as a kiss, when they fall.

And I think, *Yes. It is this easy after all.*

When I awake I am shaking. My bones are rattling as if loose in my skin, my teeth clanking together.

"What? What is—"

"Lia! Wake up, Lia!" It is Dimitri's face that hovers over mine, and I wonder absently why he does not want me to sleep.

Didn't he say I was supposed to sleep? Or was that a dream?

I am confused, disoriented, and I look around, wondering if I am in the woods on the way to Altus, in Loughcrew, in one of our many camps on the way back to England. But no. I see the richly papered walls of my chamber, the carved wood of my bedposts at Milthorpe Manor.

There is pressure on my shoulders. It is uncomfortable, nearly painful, and when I look I am surprised to find that Dimitri's hands are the source.

"What are you doing?" I try to sit up. "You're hurting me!"

He drops his hands from my body, holding them up in a gesture of surrender. "I'm sorry! God, I'm sorry, Lia. But... You..."

His gaze is dark, haunted, and when I follow it I see why.

Something is in my left hand. Something trailing black velvet. I sit up, my breath catching in my throat as I open my fingers and see the medallion resting there. In my palm, not on my wrist as it should be. As it was when I went to sleep.

I look into Dimitri's eyes, and he moves to take the medallion from my hand.

"You were thrashing about in your sleep, and when I came to wake you, you suddenly stopped." He ceases talking, a look of puzzlement crossing his face as he meets my eyes once again. "And then you just lay back and removed the medallion from your wrist, as calmly as if you were wide awake and aware of what you were doing."

I shake my head. "But I wasn't. I didn't."

"Yet, the fact remains: You removed the medallion yourself, Lia." There is real fear in his eyes as he continues. "And you were trying to use it to bring forth the Souls."

I know from the expression on the other girls' faces that I look as bad as I feel.

I have called them to the parlor, along with Aunt Virginia, after a sleepless night in which Dimitri and I discussed every possibility. I knew from the beginning there was only one thing to do, but he insisted on walking through all of the options. In the end, he agreed to my decision only because he had no choice. I will do what I must with or without his support.

There is simply no other way.

I scan the faces of the keys—Luisa, Sonia, Helene, and Brigid. They are so much more to me than pieces of the prophecy, yet none of us will be free if we don't act now. And whether they realize it or not, our alliance will not suffer another year of waiting—of hoping—to bring Alice to our side.

"Is everything okay, Lia?" Sonia asks. "You don't look well."

She sits next to Luisa on the sofa, with Brigid on her other side. Helene sits on the tall-backed chair. I am already unsurprised to see her so separate from the others.

"I've been up most of the night trying to formulate a plan for moving forward."

It is no accident that I do not answer her question by telling her that I'm all right. That everything is fine. I will not lie. Not to myself, and not to the others whose lives have been altered by the prophecy.

"Alice refused you." It is a statement of fact, though Sonia's voice is gentle. She, more than anyone, knows how my feelings for Alice still twist and turn.

I nod, swallowing against the lump in my throat.

None of the girls looks surprised, but it is Luisa who speaks. "Now what? What do we do next?"

I take a deep breath, studying my hands, not wanting to meet their eyes. "Though the prophecy doesn't technically have to be concluded this year, I will not survive to see another Beltane."

Sonia begins to protest, but I look up, raising my hand to stop her. "It's true, Sonia, however much we wish it were not. I haven't been well. I battle the Souls even in my sleep, and I grow weaker by the day." I bite my lip, for the next will be the hardest thing to admit yet. "Just last night Dimitri stopped me from wearing the medallion over my mark. From bringing forth more Souls."

Sonia's eyes are full of sadness, and something close to pity. It rallies my sense of dignity, and I sit straighter, willing strength into my voice. If I must lead them toward danger, I will at least be worthy of the responsibility.

"I don't know if I have the strength, the authority, to close the Gate without Alice. It may not even be possible. But if I don't try... If I wait..." I look at each of them, wanting to be sure they understand the ramifications of waiting. "I'll be waiting to die. To have my soul entombed in the Void. Then no one will be able to close the Gate until a new Angel is appointed. And that could take centuries."

"We could *all* die this way." There is a note of accusation in Helene's voice when she finally speaks.

I hesitate. "Yes, though I don't believe you would. Without me, you are, forgive me for saying, somewhat useless to Samael and the Souls. It is my belief that whatever happens at Avebury, you would be spared."

"But you cannot be certain," Helene points out.

I shake my head. "No."

"But, Lia..." Brigid's voice is gentle. "If you cannot close the Gate, will you not *certainly* die? What if the Rite calls you to

the Otherworlds? Wouldn't the Souls be able to detain you there, given your weakened condition?"

I cast a glance at Dimitri before answering. My easy acceptance of my possible fate is not as easy for him.

"It's possible, yes. But I cannot…I cannot sit here waiting, day after day, for the Souls to weaken me enough to claim me for the Void. I am—" My voice shakes, and I try to steady it before continuing. "I am tired. I would rather see this end, for all of us, than subject you to an endless wait in which all of your lives are placed on hold."

"So we would travel to Avebury in time for the sunrise on Beltane, fulfill the Rite, and…what? Try to close the Gate without Alice?"

I nod. "I would summon what power remains and ask you to do the same, and we will try to force the Gate closed without her. It's a gamble, but no more than the one we take each and every day we wait." I play with a loose thread on the skirt of my gown.

"And if we are unable to do it without her?" Sonia asks softly.

I shrug. "Then whatever will be will be. I'll likely be detained in the Void, and you will all go on to live the full lives you so deserve. It's a sacrifice I'll make to end my own torment and see to your freedom." I look at Aunt Virginia, taking in her frail frame. "All of you."

Luisa looks at Dimitri. "I assume you've already tried to talk her out of this?"

His arms are folded across his body, his jaw set in a line of barely controlled frustration. "All night long."

Luisa nods, turning back to me. "Then there's nothing to do but help you, Lia. Help you find the peace you need. I, for one, will do everything possible to see that you get it. Even this."

"And I, as well," Brigid says.

We all look at Helene. She straightens her back, heaving a frustrated sigh. "Well, if it will free me of this business and get me back to Spain, I suppose I'll do it."

I wonder if it is my imagination that the rest of us breathe a collective sigh of relief into the room.

My gaze rests on Sonia, and she stands, walking toward me and lowering herself next to Luisa. "I would bear the burden of being a key forever to keep you with us, but if this is what you need, you have it. There's nothing I wouldn't do to help you, Lia."

Tears of gratitude spring to my eyes. I push them back as I give Sonia and Luisa's hands a quick squeeze before rising.

"Let's prepare to leave then, shall we?"

33

A week has passed, and as I prepare for bed in my chamber, I am still surprised that we are packed and ready to go.

Gareth, Dimitri, and Edmund have made most of the arrangements, putting everything quickly in place despite the fact that we have a larger group than ever before. Luisa, Sonia, and I have done everything possible to prepare Helene for the rigors of the journey, for while Brigid held her own on the way back from Loughcrew, Helene has in the past ridden only sidesaddle — and certainly never in breeches.

As I put on my nightdress and brush through my hair, I think about the time Sonia, Luisa, and I have spent trying to increase Helene's confidence with the horses. After two frustrating days at Whitney Grove, we have lost patience with her whining and despair that she will not be able to stay atop her horse should strenuous riding be necessary. To make matters worse, she flatly refuses to wear the breeches that Brigid accepted without question. I couldn't care less about her attire the rest of the time, but in this case, her stubbornness could cost us all our lives should we have to race through the forest as we did on the way to Altus.

I turn toward a knock at the door, knowing it's probably Dimitri. "Come in."

He steps through the door. The worry lines about his eyes tell me that he is unhappy to have agreed to tonight's plan. Crossing the room, he makes his way to me, reaching for my hands and bringing me to my feet. He pulls me toward him, wrapping my body in the arms that never cease to make me feel safe, however false the illusion. It is not my imagination that he has held me tighter, longer, these past few days. As if afraid I'll disappear from his grasp at any moment.

Finally, I pull back just enough to look into his eyes. "Are you ready?"

He nods. "But only because there's no way to change your mind."

I feel the sadness in my smile. "You're right. There isn't."

The decision to visit the Otherworlds one last time was an easy one to make. I don't know what will happen at Avebury, but I must be honest with myself: Without Alice's help, there is every possibility that my soul will be detained in the Void, my body left to die. My parents—and probably Henry with them—have risked their souls to remain in the Otherworlds in case I should need their assistance. It is only right that I should free them to cross into the Final World, in the event

that I don't live to see it done. And though I am at peace with my fate, I want to see my parents and brother one more time. I want to speak to them and embrace them.

More than anything, I want to say goodbye.

I let go of Dimitri's hand, making my way to the bed and climbing into it. He sits next to me, running his fingers across my cheek and all the way to my chin. "If you let me come with you, I'll be able to see that you return safely."

I shake my head. I have already rejected this argument. "I won't have you suffer repercussions — or worse yet, forfeit your place with the Grigori entirely — because of me."

He looks away, clenching his jaw. "You still don't understand, do you?" His voice is petulant.

"What?" I raise myself up on my elbows. "What don't I understand?"

He turns his face to mine. "Do you think I worry over my place with the Grigori? Do you think, after everything that's happened between us, that I care about *repercussions?*" He shakes his head, looking away for a moment before turning back to me with fire in his eyes. "You're everything to me, Lia. I would forfeit my place with the Grigori in an instant if it meant seeing you safely to the other side of the prophecy."

Reaching up, I fasten my arms around his neck, touching my lips to his. It does not take long for the tender kiss to become passionate, urgent, and I press my body to his, knowing that the feelings between us are all the more powerful for the knowledge that we may lose each other in the coming days. A flutter rises from my stomach, becoming urgent as it spreads to

every part of my body. He must feel it as well, for he tips my head to gain better access to my mouth, and I press myself even closer to his body, wanting to melt into him in this one moment.

Wanting to be inside his skin, his body, his soul.

He removes his hands from the tangle of my hair, placing them instead on my shoulders.

"Lia...Lia." He lifts one of my hands, turning it over and kissing my palm before leaving a trail with his lips to the tender skin at the inside of my wrist. He leaves a last kiss on the raised skin of my mark before meeting my eyes. "I had hoped to have a lifetime to hold you. To love you."

I reach out, touching my fingertips to his forehead before letting my hand drop back into my lap. I don't know how I can smile, but somehow his love makes me stronger, and it's not so hard after all.

"I promise I'll fight, Dimitri. I'll fight to stay with you." I shrug. "The rest will be up to fate."

He nods as I scoot farther under the covers, lying back on my pillow. "Do what you must, and come back to me."

He drops another kiss on my lips and leaves my bedside to take his position in the chair. Should we reach toward one another, we could probably touch fingertips. Yet, he already feels a million miles away.

Closing my eyes, I still my mind and slip into the half-sleep that will enable me to travel and still retain some control over my destination. I think of my parents—of my mother's green eyes and my father's booming voice. I think of Henry and the

infectious smile that seemed to light not only his eyes, but the eyes of those around him as well.

I think of them all. I picture their faces in my mind. And then I fall.

I feel sure I will meet them in the fields surrounding Birch-wood. It is the only real place to say goodbye.

This time I walk by the river behind the great stone house. It's just as I remember it. The house my great-grandfather built peeks through the big oaks. There is nothing dark or sinister about it in this world.

I feel a pang of sadness as I spot the large boulder James and I called ours and try not to wonder if he and Alice now call it theirs. The river gurgles happily nearby, and I realize that all rivers sound different. It doesn't make sense, really; they should sound the same. Wherever they may be, they are all water run-ning over rock. But this is *my* river, and it calls to me like a lost friend.

Closing my eyes, I stand on the bank, concentrating on the images of my family in my mind until I hear the sound of boots making their way through the dry leaves on the wooded ground.

I should be prepared. I know they're coming, for I've sum-moned them with every ounce of my now considerable power, but it still takes me by surprise to turn and see my parents and Henry walking—*walking*—toward me.

The sadness lasts only a moment, for when he smiles his big

Henry smile, I can do nothing but run toward him. I see my parents as well, but it is my brother I long to embrace.

He rushes me with a strength he didn't have when he was alive, and I realize that I have never seen or felt him strong. He spent his life as a prisoner to his steel chair. He lived and died with it. The tears flow freely down my cheeks as I hold him, knowing that now he is finally free.

"Henry! Oh, Henry!" It is all I can say. I'm overflowing with something that is altogether too much and too powerful to name.

"Lia! I can walk, Lia! Do you see? I can walk?" His voice is just as I remember it, the still-high voice of a child with all the excitement and enthusiasm that were his gifts.

I pull back and look at him. "I *do* see, Henry. I do. You walk beautifully."

His grin is as wide as the blue sky above. "Then why are you crying?"

I laugh, wiping the tears from my cheeks with the back of my hand. "I'm simply too full of happiness, Henry. There isn't enough room for it all inside me."

Next to Henry, my father chuckles softly, and I turn my attention to my parents.

I reach out and embrace my father, holding him close and breathing in the scent of pipe smoke and cedar. "Father. I've missed you so much."

"And I you, Daughter."

I turn to my mother and repeat the embrace, feeling a new kinship to her since my time on Altus.

"Lia," she says, breathing into my hair. "You're all right."

We pull apart and look at one another.

She smiles and shakes her head in wonder. "You've grown into a beautiful young woman."

My pleasure at the compliment is fleeting. A moment later, my father looks around, a cloud of worry passing over his strong features.

"You are safe here for now, Lia, but we shouldn't risk it for long."

He is telling me to hurry, though neither of us wishes to rush our visit. It's all the harder for me, knowing it will be our last.

I take his hands. "Father, I've come to ask you to cross into the Final World with Mother and Henry."

I expect him to be surprised, but his shoulders drop, and I see resignation in his eyes. "You don't need us anymore?"

I shake my head. "I'll always need you." I look from him to Mother and Henry. "Always. But it's not safe for you here. It hasn't been safe for some time. I should have asked you to cross long ago, for your own protection. Allowing you to remain in this in-between place was selfish."

"Lia." My mother's voice is soft, and I turn to look at her. There can be no secrets between us. The inherent connection shared between mother and daughter is ever-strong, despite the fact that we have seen each other only once in the Other-worlds since her death. "There's something else. Something you're not telling us."

I brace myself, wanting to sound strong and unafraid. "It's time for me to convene with the keys at Avebury, and though the prophecy says Alice and I must stand together, she refuses to come to our side."

My mother furrows her brow. "But if the prophecy says you must have Alice's aid, why would you travel to Avebury now?"

"I cannot..." I look into her eyes, knowing that if anyone will understand the torture of the Souls, it's my mother. "I cannot sustain my strength against the Souls for much longer. I must try to use the power I still have, for I grow weaker by the day."

"Such a course is dangerous," my father says. "You must wait until you have everything you require so that you might come out of it alive."

I shake my head. "It's not just me, Father. The keys, too, are fragile. They are suffering as I suffer at the hands of the Souls."

"You've found the keys?" he asks. "All four?"

I nod. "All four. But I don't think I can get all of them to remain in London for another year." I try to smile. "It's simply time, that's all. I'm prepared to fight. To use what power I have together with that of the keys. To try. And if I must die trying, if I must consign my soul to the Void to ensure Samael cannot use me as his Gate, well, I would prefer that to the alternative."

Their faces are somber as they contemplate my words. My mother speaks first.

"This is your decision to make, Lia. I know well the havoc the Souls can wreak. You must do what you think is right."

I smile into her eyes, so like mine. "Thank you, Mother. I knew you would understand. I only wish..."

She reaches out to touch my face. "What do you wish, darling?"

I sigh, finding a sad smile. "I only wish we had more time together. That our time in the physical world hadn't been cut short."

She nods. "And I only wish that I had had your courage, Lia. Your strength."

I lean in to embrace her. "Goodbye, Mother. I pray you find peace in the Final World and remember that I love you always."

Her voice is hoarse, her eyes shining with unshed tears. "I love you, too, Lia. No mother was ever as proud as I."

I look into her eyes as we pull away. "And no daughter as proud as I."

The tears finally overflow onto her cheeks, and I know she is thinking of the choice she made to end her life rather than face her role in the prophecy. Perhaps now she'll let go of her private shame, forgive herself as I have forgiven her.

I turn to my father, trying to memorize his face. The kind eyes and gentle smile that have always made me feel safe in any world. Their memory will bring me comfort, whatever my fate.

"Thank you for staying as long as you did. For looking after me and for seeing that I was able to find everything I needed."

He pulls me into his arms, and I breathe in the scent of him as he speaks. "I'm only sorry it wasn't enough."

Releasing him, I pull back and look into his face, needing to give him the peace of knowing he has done all he can. "Not everything was in your power to give, Father." I think of Alice.

Of her decision to stand with the Souls, against her sister. Her twin. Her blood. "If it were, I have no doubt it would have been provided."

He grabs hold of my shoulders and his eyes take on a new intensity. "Don't give up, Lia. You have great power. If anyone can bring this to an end, it is you."

"I won't give up, Father. I promise." I smile, wanting to offer him reassurance. "You may see me yet in the Final World."

He touches my forehead. "May it be so, my dear girl. And may it not be for many more years."

I take a step back, swallowing the emotion that's already rising in my throat. I don't want to look at Henry. I don't want to stare into his eyes, dark like my father's. Saying goodbye once nearly killed me.

I shall have to be stronger this time.

As if reading my mind, he says, "Don't be sad, Lia. We'll be together again."

Something dark within me lifts, and a smile blossoms on my lips. "Yes, Henry. We will." I bend down and wrap him in my arms.

"I knew you weren't the bad one, Lia. I knew it."

And now, I *do* look into his dark eyes. I see love there. Love and truth and light.

All the things for which I am fighting.

"No, you were right all along. I'm not bad, Henry." I hesitate, looking into his eyes. "Maybe no one is. Maybe it's not that simple."

It is only as I say it that I think it might be true.

Henry nods somberly.

"I'll miss you." He smiles. "But I'll see you again."

I nod. "Yes." Leaning forward, I kiss his cheek. It is as smooth and soft as I remember.

For once, I don't regret that he won't grow to have a man's rough cheeks. For once, I think I believe that Henry is meant to be in the Final World with Mother and Father, and I am meant to be in my world, at least for now. I am meant to end the prophecy for myself and all the Sisters to come.

I rise and smile. "Go, now. Be quick. Seek the shelter of the Final World, and know that you are always in my heart."

My father takes my mother's hand, and she takes Henry's. They turn to go, and my mother looks over her shoulder one last time. I think she will say something meaningful, and in a way, she does. In a way, it is the most meaningful thing she could say, and it causes me to break into a wide smile.

"I don't envy the Souls right now, Daughter. I don't envy them at all."

I am still smiling as I watch them disappear into the trees, and in this moment, I don't envy the Souls, either. In this moment, I believe I can do anything.

34

We leave London without pretense of secrecy. Our party is too large to go entirely unnoticed, and we're too weary and rushed to make the plans necessary to travel with less fanfare. None of us says aloud the thing we all know: It can be no secret that we're on our way to Avebury.

Alice knows, and that means that the Souls, and likely Samael himself, know as well.

The second day dawns with an eerie shine. I peer at the sky as we begin the day's ride, trying to place the odd cast to the light.

"Solar eclipse." Edmund's voice startles me. He has been riding in the front but must have dropped back while I studied the sun. "Doesn't happen often, but it will be almost entirely dark within a few hours."

I can only nod, the strange light suddenly making sense. It will get stranger still as the moon comes closer and closer to blocking out the light of the sun, and it seems somehow fitting that we are riding to Avebury to close the Gate amid so rare an occurrence. It's unsettling. A portent of the promised darkness should I fail.

Such weighty thoughts remind me of Henry and my parents. I turn to Edmund as we ride.

"Edmund?"

His eyes don't move from the field in front of us. "Yes?"

"I . . ." It is still difficult to say Henry's name in Edmund's company. I've no wish to remind him anew of the pain he felt upon Henry's death, but in this one instance, it will do him good. "I wanted to let you know that I've seen Henry on the Plane. With Mother and Father."

Edmund turns his head to look at me, a wall of blankness dropping over his eyes. "Have you now?"

I hear in his voice the strain of keeping himself in check. "Yes. I wanted to say goodbye. To ensure that they had moved on to the Final World before the Rite at Avebury."

"And have they?"

"They have now." I give him a small smile. "I wanted you to know that they're well. Henry is well. He is safe and happy, and can even walk with the use of his very own legs."

Wonder touches his eyes. "He can walk?"

I nod, my smile growing as I remember Henry running toward me in the Plane. "Yes. Quite well, in fact."

He stares at a point in the distance somewhere over my shoulder. When he speaks, his voice is wistful. "I wish I could see it."

"Edmund."

He brings his gaze back to my face.

"You will. You will see it. That's what I'm telling you. Henry is safe and well in the Final World." I look into his eyes. "And you will see him again someday."

Hope lights his eyes in the moment before he turns his gaze back to the fields. "I'll see him again."

I smile, turning my own gaze forward. "Yes."

We ride in silence for a while before I turn my attention to the other person for whom we share affection.

"How is she holding up?" I nod toward Aunt Virginia, slumped atop one of the horses making its way through the field in front of us.

"She's doing well, under the circumstances. I think she's stronger than any of us realize, and she's too stubborn to stay behind anyway. Much like someone else I know," he adds without looking at me.

I shake my head. "It's not the same thing, Edmund."

It has been painful to watch Aunt Virginia struggle to maintain a facade of strength since we left London, but I cannot bring myself to wound her pride by asking after her health. Her intentions were obvious the moment she emerged from Milthorpe Manor on the day of our departure, valise in hand. And though I argued and refused, she walked calmly toward the horse Edmund had provided for her, insisting that she was still my elder and would accompany me whether I wished it or not.

But my own insistence on going is different. She has played her part in the prophecy. Has done her duty. Mine will not be

done until the Gate is closed to Samael or until I am rendered unable to assist him.

"Besides," I say, "if you were so against my going to Avebury, why didn't you try to talk me out of it, like everyone else?"

He lifts his shoulders in a quick shrug. "Wouldn't have done a bit of good, and we both know it."

I sit a little straighter, feeling an odd sense of satisfaction despite the exhaustion that permeates every bone in my body. "Well, *that* is true enough."

We ride for a few more moments in silence, Gareth in the lead followed by the keys and Aunt Virginia. Dimitri, as always, rides at my back. I try not to think about the reason. About his fear that the Guard might give chase or, even more sinister, might creep upon us slowly and simply snatch me away from the group before anyone notices. I am stalked by nightmares through every night's sleep, and though I go through the motions of carrying my bow, I don't have the energy to worry about the things that might come for me in the harsh light of day. I do my best to leave those worries to him.

Edmund breaks the silence between us. "Even as I acknowledge the strength of your will," he says, "I feel I must ask if you are certain, absolutely certain, that this is the course you wish to take."

I don't defend my position right away. Instead, I take a moment to think about his question. To think about the other options available to me. Or the other option, really, since there is only one: Wait until we can bring Alice to our side. Wait and hope.

I wonder if he can see the reluctance in my nod, for even I wish there were another way. "I'm certain. I don't…" I look out over the rolling gray-green hills that stretch before us to another wood in the distance. "I don't want to end up like my mother."

For a long moment, Edmund doesn't reply. His words are halting when he finally speaks. "Your mother was a wonderful woman. Bright and vibrant when the Souls didn't have her in their grasp. I don't wish to speak ill of her. There are very few who would be able to resist the call of the Souls. But I do believe you're one of them. I'd bet my life you wouldn't fall to the same fate as your mother, however long it takes to gain Alice's cooperation." He nods to the keys, Aunt Virginia, and Gareth in front of us. "And it does seem you have some help, to say nothing of Mr. Markov."

"Yes, but I don't feel strong on the inside, however it may appear. Even now, Samael tries to use me as I sleep. It is Dimitri's presence, not my own strength of character, that prevents me from doing something terrible."

Edmund meets my eyes. "Your willingness to keep Dimitri with you speaks to your commitment. Your mother, and most of the Gates before her, as I've heard it told, sought solitude. Traveling the Plane with the Souls' blessing, allowing themselves to be used by Samael… Well, it is a pleasure for most of the Gates. A calling. Yet, you don't feel it quite that way, do you?"

I shake my head. "I *do* want to deny them. To deny him." I sigh. "But my will grows weaker—*I* grow weaker—with each passing day. With each night's torment.

"A year is a very long time. Once this Beltane has passed, I would be forced to wait twelve months for another. It's a risk I cannot take. I would rather sacrifice myself to the Void and force Samael to wait for another Angel. At least then you and the others will be safe."

"I thought as much." He turns away, focusing on something in front of him. "It would be difficult to find meaning in this world should something happen to you, but I understand the need to protect the ones you love. I can't find fault or try to dissuade you when I've spent my life doing just that."

His back remains straight, his face impassive, and affection rises in my chest, filling my heart until I can hardly speak around it. "Thank you, Edmund. I know I can count on you to look after Aunt Virginia, whatever happens."

His nod is so slight that I hardly register it. We ride on and do not speak of it again.

❧

The journey that would take Dimitri and me three days of hard riding takes longer with so large a group. Helene's riding is an impediment to speed, as is Aunt Virginia's failing health. Still, I do not begrudge them. Whatever happens, I am relieved to be riding toward my destiny instead of waiting passively for Alice to change her mind.

By the third day, we're just over halfway to Avebury. Aunt Virginia is tired, and we make camp while the sun is still high, thinking it wiser to allow everyone the extra rest and begin again in the morning. I try not to think about the fact that

Beltane is only four days away, but it is a reality that is impossible to ignore. My mind tells me that it is only wise to consider other alternatives. To entertain the possibility that we won't make it in time.

No. I banish the idea from my mind. *We will make it. We must.*

With the camp set up and the horses settled, Helene retires to her tent for a rest while Sonia, Luisa, and Brigid congregate beneath a freshly blossoming tree, studying three pieces of parchment. I know without asking that they are memorizing the words of the Rite, given to them before our departure from London. It will not be easy for them to recite in Latin, but it seems safer than trying to produce an accurate translation in English.

I don't need to study. The Rite is already as familiar to me as my own name. I resolve instead to take advantage of their focus on the unfamiliar words by convincing Dimitri to keep watch while I bathe in a slow-moving creek not far from camp.

After quietly alerting Gareth to our intentions, Dimitri and I slip from camp and make our way to the water. The forest is quiet save for the skittering of small animals and the movement of birds from tree to tree. Dimitri and I do not speak as we make our way through a pathway cluttered with overhanging tree branches, and I'm grateful for our comfort in one another's presence. For the first time in days, I feel a measure of peace.

A few moments later we finally break through the trees, coming to a sloping bank at the edge of the water. Even the

river's meandering current causes my heart to beat faster in my chest, but I ignore my fear and turn to Dimitri with a smile.

"Thank you," I say, looking into the infinite brown of his eyes.

"You're welcome." He grins lazily at me, unmoving.

"You, sir," I raise my eyebrows playfully, "may wait over there." I tip my head in the direction of the woods.

"What if I promise not to look?"

I sigh, trying to suppress a smile. "I give you high marks for effort, Dimitri Markov, but I'm afraid you'll have to go. Having you keep watch in my chamber while we are both fully clothed is scandalous enough, but having you in close proximity while I'm naked would cause Aunt Virginia to have a conniption."

He leans in until he is only inches from my face. "So, were it not for Virginia, you'd let me stay, then?"

I give him a gentle shove. "Well, you'll never know, now will you?"

"Oh, I'll know, Lia." He holds my gaze a moment longer, his eyes alight with desire before he turns, walking back the way we came. "I won't be far."

His words echo in my mind, causing my face to flush even as I stand alone in the forest. I wait until he disappears from view before removing my riding breeches and shirt and placing them on a large boulder near the water. I am not sure where he is waiting, exactly, but I'm certain it is close enough that he'll hear me should I need assistance. I cannot help but think how much things have changed, how much *I* have changed, that I am more concerned with my physical safety than with the fact that I'm stepping naked into the crystal waters of a river, in plain view of anyone who should happen by. Of course, it's unlikely anyone will, but I still feel bold.

The frigid water is a shock and I almost cry aloud in the moment before I submerge my head, deciding it will get no easier. Swimming toward the center of the river, I'm careful to stay close enough to shore that I can reach it without difficulty. I'm relieved that the current moves so slowly. It trickles lazily past with a small, happy gurgle, and I tilt my head back, letting my hair flow out behind me.

The water is delicious against my bare skin, even as cold as it is. I wonder that a simple bath has never felt this good. That I have never noticed the slide of water against my nakedness. I think of Dimitri and his promise that he will remain close. It would be easy to call for him, and goose bumps rise on my arms and thighs as I imagine his bare skin against mine in the water, his arms encircling my naked body.

Standing up on the rocky river bottom, I shake the image from my mind. I'm feeling reckless. As if I have nothing to lose. I don't want to give myself to Dimitri in such a manner. Don't want to demean myself and our love by going to him with anything but a clear head.

I'm running my hands across the surface of the water, smoothing it against my palms in an effort to clear my mind, when I see it.

At first I think I am imagining the peculiar shimmer of the water, the strange distortion.

But no.

As I watch the water's surface, the figure comes into view,

riding through a forest not unlike the one in which I am bathing. The man's golden hair shimmers in sunlight so bright I can almost feel it, and I sense rather than see that there are many behind him.

And one in front of him, trying to escape.

It is Samael's Guard in pursuit, the terrifying man who almost captured me at Chartres leading the charge. The mark of the serpent is coiled around his neck, just visible beneath the fabric of his open collar. His face is a mask of fiery vengeance, and I remember his guttural howl outside the cathedral when I slashed his throat with my mother's dagger before taking refuge inside the church.

My heart begins to hammer, and I push down my panic, trying to determine if the vision is from the past, present, or future. From the bright sunlight, it could be another day entirely or simply another forest, for the sky above me is dimmed with large spring clouds and not nearly as clear as the one in my vision must be to allow for so much light.

But that is all I can decipher. I know he's not alone, and I know that he and the rest of the Guard are in pursuit of someone on horseback. Following this knowledge to its logical conclusion, there is only one person I can imagine them pursuing, and that is me.

I wade to the bank of the river, stepping from the water and grabbing the blanket I brought to dry off. Wrapping it around my body, I pick up my clothes and make my way toward the tree line.

"Dimitri? Are you there?" I speak more softly than I would

have even fifteen minutes ago. It is difficult not to be paranoid knowing that the Guard may be close behind us.

It takes only a moment for Dimitri to appear beneath the trees in the distance. Something in my expression must alarm him, for he sprints the rest of the way and is standing before me only seconds later.

He takes hold of my shoulders, pulling me to him for a moment before speaking. "Are you all right?" He leans back, alarm in his face. "What's wrong? What happened?"

Water drips from my hairline onto my face. I feel it make tracks down my skin as I try to find the words. I don't want to say them, but in the end, it is all I can do.

"It's the Guard," I say. "They're coming."

35

"What are our options?" Brigid asks as we sit around the fire.

I sit next to Dimitri, my hair still damp and dripping water onto my shirt. I have told them everything I saw in my vision, avoiding Aunt Virginia's eyes the whole time. It is no secret that she blames herself for our slow pace.

"There aren't many." Edmund paces, his brow pulled forward in consternation.

"But what if they're not even after us?" Helene asks from across the fire.

Luisa shoots her a look of annoyance, and I answer before Luisa can do so with bite. "They may not be, but when you see a vision in the scrying waters..." I try to think of the simplest way to describe it to someone who has never cultivated the ability. "Well, you can either summon a vision about a particular thing, or one can be given to you, in a manner of speaking.

That's how this was; it just appeared. And usually when that's the case, it means the vision has something to do with you."

Helene's eyes do not waver from my face. "Yes, but how do we *know*?"

Luisa, standing across from Helene, places her hands on her hips. "Who else would they be following, especially since they've come after Lia before?"

I break in, trying to keep my voice calm, before Luisa can become truly rude. "It is probably wisest to assume they're after us, Helene."

She is still for a moment before nodding her head.

"What do we do?" Sonia asks.

"We can ride fast and hard," Gareth says. "Try to beat them to Avebury."

I avoid Aunt Virginia's eyes. She cannot manage such a ride.

"It won't work," Dimitri says.

Gareth opens his mouth to argue, but Dimitri continues before Gareth can speak again. "We must get to the site before they do, to set up the Rite. We cannot just ride in and begin. We need to secure lodging and make sure the perimeter is safe, and we must ensure that we have access to the center of the circle so the Stone will catch the first rays of the sunrise on Beltane."

"He's right," Edmund agrees. "We have to lose them before we get to Avebury, and we have to put enough distance between us that we have at least a few hours on them."

The silence grows heavy as we contemplate our options. I could call on my ability to scry and bring forth the vision once

304

again, hoping for more detail, but I do not wish to anger the Grigori with the use of forbidden magic. Having the vision appear unbidden is one thing. Calling it forth would be an unsanctioned use of my power, and though I am the rightful heir to the title of Lady of Altus, the Grigori is still cloaked in a mysterious power that I am hesitant to test.

I look around the fire at my companions, stopping at Brigid as my mind grasps at the ghost of an idea. I remember the care-taker's cottage at the otherwise abandoned site of Loughcrew. Her father's cottage.

I look up at Dimitri. "Where will we stay at Avebury?"

"What?" He shakes off his confusion at my sudden question. "Elspeth told me there's an inn. She said it's small, but it will still afford us more shelter than camping outside. I had planned to secure rooms there."

I stand, pacing as the idea takes root, gathering shape in my mind. "Gareth?"

He nods. "Yes, my Lady?"

"Could you find your way to Avebury alone?"

He answers without hesitation. "I know this country like the back of my hand."

I turn to Dimitri. "Gareth will be able to reach Avebury faster without us. What if we send him ahead to secure the inn and the area around it? It will give us safe haven once we reach the site, at least. Once there, he can make arrangements for our lodging and determine the ideal location to perform the Rite."

"That assumes that we can outrun the Souls," Helene says.

I fight my irritation that she is always the one to voice the negative. "Yes. But if we cannot, they'll catch us anyway. Sending Gareth ahead will give us the best chance of safety, and the time to set up the Rite." I let my hands fall to my sides, resignation threatening to take over the slim measure of hope I felt only a moment ago. "It isn't much, but I cannot think of anything else."

Gareth rises. "I'll leave immediately."

"I'll go with you." Brigid stands beside him, surprising us all.

Gareth shakes his head, and I wonder if the others see the regret in his eyes. "I cannot allow it."

Brigid lifts her chin. "It's not for you to allow or disallow. It's my choice. I can ride every bit as fast as you can, and I can help you ready the inn once we arrive. Besides, it's one less woman for Dimitri and Edmund to worry over."

I don't know if it is the rebellious glint in her eyes or the logic of her argument, but a moment later, Gareth nods slightly in her direction. "Pack your things, then. We'll leave immediately and put as many miles behind as possible before nightfall."

I watch them both make for the tents, stifling an almost overwhelming frustration. I do not wish to be left behind to lumber through the forest. I want to fly toward Avebury atop Sargent's back, not wait and hope for others to make it safe.

But I won't leave Aunt Virginia. Her weakness makes her a target for the Guard. I could not live with myself if anything should happen to her while I rode ahead to safety. And as we help Gareth and Brigid mount their horses and say our goodbyes, I begin to understand that sacrifice has many faces. Wait-

ing when I wish to act is one. I will make it in the name of the prophecy, as I have made so many others before.

Less than an hour after my vision, Gareth and Brigid are gone. I turn away from the sound of their horses' retreating hoof-beats, trying not to imagine the fair-haired Guard from Avebury making his way, closer and closer, motivated by both revenge for my actions in Chartres and loyalty to the Beast that is Samael.

"Are you frightened?"

I'm startled by Sonia's voice, soft as it is, as she lowers herself next to me on the log by the fire. "What are you doing awake?" I ask her. "I thought everyone had gone to bed."

She smiles. "You are changing the subject."

I return her smile in spite of myself. "Not really. I'm only surprised to see you up so late, that's all."

"Well, the others are fast asleep, and I couldn't settle my thoughts long enough to do the same. Since Dimitri is on guard, I thought I'd keep you company. Do you mind?" she asks.

I shake my head. "Of course not."

"So are you?" she asks again. "Frightened?"

I don't have to ask her what she means. We are only two days from Avebury and the end of our journey. It will all be over soon, one way or another.

I gaze into the fire, watching as a blackened piece of wood crumbles under the heat, sending sparks up into the night sky. "A little, though not as much as I expected to be. I suppose I'm ready to see it done, whatever happens."

I see her nod out of the corner of my eye but do not dare look her way as a strange melancholy grabs hold of me. We have traveled a very long road together, indeed.

She reaches for my hand. "I need to tell you something, Lia. Will you look at me?"

I turn to meet her eyes, grateful for the warm pressure of her hand on mine.

"You are the dearest friend I've ever had. The dearest friend I *will* ever have." Her eyes shine as she continues. "I believe you are strong enough to come through the Rite at Avebury, but I simply . . . I simply could not leave to chance that you wouldn't know how very much you mean to me. How very dear you are to me."

I nod, squeezing her hand as the emotion threatens to spill over the confines of my heart. "I feel the same way. There is no one with whom I'd rather have shared these past months." I lean toward her until our foreheads are touching, and we remain that way for a few moments before I rise. "We should try to sleep. We'll have to keep our wits about us with the Guard in pursuit."

She nods, rising to stand next to me. And as we make our way to the tents, I cannot help but feel relieved.

It is only wise to begin saying goodbye.

❦

I do not consciously will myself to the Otherworlds. Doing so would be foolish so close to Beltane and the moment when I will have to summon the Beast in order to banish him.

Yet, I find myself on the barren Plane of the Otherworld I most closely associate with Alice. Though it is not intentional, I'm not surprised. Alice has weighed heavily on my mind as we have made our way toward Avebury. I cannot help remembering our last conversation, in the park. Recalling the flicker of doubt in Alice's eyes, however brief, I wonder if I've done all I can. If perhaps Alice is closer to switching sides than I imagined.

I know the rules of the Otherworlds well. One either wills oneself to the Plane or is summoned there by another. But as I stand amid the fields—touched with only black, gray, and an undertone of angry violet—I'm not sure what has led me to the bleakness of this Otherworldly Plane. It is true that I was thinking of Alice. That she alone could have led me to seek her out. Of course, she could have summoned me as well, but then, too, she should be here to meet me.

I turn in a small circle, gazing across the empty expanse of tall grass, toward the charcoal trees in the distance. This is a silent world. The birds do not chirp. There is no rustle of small animals in the grass. Even the trees, blowing in a wind I cannot quite feel, do not make a sound.

I wait for what seems a long time, a knot tightening in my stomach. Regardless of my reason for being here, Alice is nowhere in sight, and I cannot afford to wait long. It is not easy to avoid detection by the Souls in the Otherworlds, and I don't intend to let them take me to the Void. Not yet. Not this way. If I am banished there, it will be during the Rite at Avebury.

And I will not go without a fight.

I scan the fields one last time, hoping to see my sister approaching from any direction. It is the first time I've been disappointed by her lack of presence on the Plane, but I don't have time to ponder this strange turn of events. My disappointment is too shaded with uneasiness, and I close my eyes, willing myself back to the physical world, all the while wondering about Alice. Wondering where she is—and what could keep her from the Plane that was her domain long before I was aware it even existed.

36

We ride as fast as we're able the next day, though it's not as fast as I would like. Edmund rides at the front, pushing us as hard as he dares given Helene's inexperience atop a horse and Aunt Virginia's obvious fatigue.

Beltane is only three days away, and I have fallen into a state of hyperawareness. My nerves crackle with anticipation, yet I lack the sense of urgency that I felt while fleeing the Guard in France. It's difficult to push my body so hard when I am allowed only snippets of sleep between nightmares in which the Souls — and increasingly, Samael himself — give chase. They haunt me long after I wake, for they are not mere glimpses into my eventual capture. These are different. These nightmares are ones in which Samael welcomes me.

Ones in which I welcome him.

They play to my darkest fear: that I will not be strong enough.

That I will allow myself to be used as a weapon to usher in the chaos of the ages.

I don't want the others to feel they have cast their lot with someone who already doubts her will to fight. So I keep the fear secret and close, in the bleakest parts of my heart.

We have slowed our pace in an effort to find a spot to camp for the night when Aunt Virginia drops back to ride by my side. She obviously has something to say, but we ride for a moment in silence before she finally opens her mouth to speak.

"I'm sorry, Lia."

I look at her in surprise. "Sorry? Whatever for?"

I hear the weariness in her sigh. "For insisting that I come along. For slowing your pace at a time when you cannot afford it."

"Don't be silly. Helene is ten times slower. It wouldn't have mattered if you'd stayed in London. We would be traveling at this pace anyway." I smile at her. "Besides, it brings me comfort to have you here."

And these may be our last days together, I think. *I'm grateful for every moment.*

Nodding, she turns her gaze to the woods around us. "It may not be possible to close the Gate without Alice, but as a Sister and former Guardian, I would like to stand with you in the Circle of Fire. I would like to lend my power—what little I have left—to closing the Gate. It is why I insisted on coming."

I don't answer right away. It's impossible to forget the feeling I've had in my dreams of the Rite at Avebury. The feeling of

being torn in two. Of being split down the middle by Samael as he attempts to use me as his entrance to this world. Darkness settles over my soul at the memory. I don't wish to subject Aunt Virginia to such a thing.

"It is dangerous," I tell her. "Samael's power is . . . Well, I have felt it in my nightmares these past weeks, and I don't think it would be good for your health."

A smile lights her eyes. For a moment, I see the shadow of my mother. "Lia, do you think I don't know the risks? It is true that the stakes were not quite as high for your mother and me. We were simply Guardian and Gate, as were hundreds of sisters before us. You are Angel of the Gate, and that brings with it—has brought with it—much difficulty. Far more than I can imagine." Her eyes, as green as my own, grow serious. "But there is no greater purpose than this, and though I have bequeathed my title as Guardian to Alice, I still have a measure of strength. I don't wish to live with the knowledge that I stood by and let you fight this alone." She smiles once more. "We are more than aunt and niece, child. We are Sisters of the prophecy. It is my duty to stand by your side."

There is an unfamiliar light in her eyes—one that speaks of hidden strength and conviction—and I know that I will not deny her. That I will not be responsible for the loss of that light.

"Very well," I say. "I welcome your power, Aunt Virginia."

She bows her head slightly, and I recognize it as a sign of deference to my position as potential Lady of Altus. "Thank you."

I dip my head in return, keeping quiet the prayer that rings through my mind: *May the Gods, the Grigori, and the Sisters be with us.*

That night, it is more difficult to let Dimitri leave my tent. I pull him toward me when he tries to sit up, pressing myself against him atop the blankets. Tucking my head under his chin, I try to push from my mind everything but his breath in my hair, his heart beating under my ear.

Though there has been no sign of the Guard, I know they're near. I cannot tell if they are simply drawing closer or if they have actually infiltrated my consciousness, but they lurk in the shadows of my innermost thoughts.

I feel the weight of their persuasion even in my waking hours. It's insidious, for it doesn't come in the form of obvious coercion. Rather, I begin to feel that I have been wrong all this time. That I have tempted fate and thrown everything out of balance by fighting my destined role as Gate.

"What is it?" he asks after a moment.

"Nothing," I lie.

His chest rises as he takes a deep breath. "I don't believe you, but I'll be here if you change your mind and want to speak of it."

I hold fast to him as he begins to move. "Don't go."

"I'm not going anywhere, Lia. I'll be right here." He bends his head, touching his mouth to mine. "But you must take what sleep you can. Tomorrow we arrive in Avebury. You will need all your strength."

I am relieved when he seems to settle deeper into the blankets, obviously not intending to move. We are both beyond worrying what anyone thinks. He pulls me closer with newfound gentleness, and I think I understand that he's beginning to say goodbye, too.

I lie in the dark for a long time, my head resting on his chest as his breathing slowly becomes softer and more regular. He has not slept deeply since his insistence on watching over me during the night, and I don't have the heart to wake him. I am here, in his arms. It is preferable to his being awake and alert across the tent while I try to sleep alone, and I rub my face against the soft fabric of his shirt, relishing the sensation. The rise and fall of his chest is soothing, and it is not long before my eyelids become heavy. It's lovely, lying in the dark with Dimitri, knowing he's close. And in the moment before I finally slip into the nothingness of sleep, I am not afraid.

Even in my dreams I am in Dimitri's arms. In the state of half-consciousness that is the closest I come to sleep, I am grateful for the gift of his presence. His heartbeat, under my ear as I drifted into slumber in the darkness of the tent, is still there.

Thump-thump. Thump-thump. Thump-thump.

It is a lullaby, and I allow myself to float through the darkness. To think of nothing but Dimitri's arms around me, the comforting solidity of his chest under my ear. We are no longer on the hard ground beneath the tent's canvas roof, but surrounded by scarlet silk and plush velvet cushions. I breathe a sigh of contentment as my own heartbeat amplifies, beating in time with his as a hand begins to stroke my hair.

"Yes," he whispers. "Yes."

His hand travels from my head to my neck, stopping at the tender divot where my pulse throbs just beneath my skin. His fingers linger there as if relishing the heat of the blood moving through my veins, then continue their journey to the curve of my shoulder, the skin of my upper arms.

I stretch my arm the length of his, our hands coming to rest palm-to-palm. We intertwine our fingers and I have never felt so content. So safe. So certain of my place.

Even when his fingers leave mine, trailing lightly across my palm until they come to rest on my wrist, I do not want to move. It is only his skin that sounds an alarm somewhere in the recesses of my mind. It is not soft and warm, as it usually is, calloused by many hours with the reins, the lead, the rifle.

It is... different.

Dry and cold.

It is only now that I notice the flutter. It is a small noise, a rustling, but when I lift my head to search for its source, my vision is blocked. In my dream, Dimitri has suddenly grown so tall that his body blocks my view. I try to push him away, to see his face, but the harder I push, the tighter he holds. A vise of panic grabs hold of my heart as I begin to understand.

The flutter grows, sounding at first like a small gathering of birds rising into the air, and then an entire flock. I give a giant push, stumbling backward as he releases his hold on my body.

My eyes travel upward, past the massive, chiseled form, to his face.

Such a beautiful face. The face of a god.

But no.

It is the face of a god, but only for a moment. Only until it shimmers, warping into something vile. Something hideous. His jaws are massive, his jagged teeth glinting like a mirage in the faint memory of the beautiful man's face.

But it is the wings that captivate me. Only hinted at the one time I saw Samael by the river in a dream, he now unfurls them with a great flutter. They spread, tall and wide, on either side of his strangely morphing form.

I cannot look away. Do not *want* to look away. In them lies the promise of comfort. Of release. Giving myself over to their safety is hardly a decision at all. I don't even contemplate it. I simply step forward, sighing with relief as the silken wings enfold me.

I experience a moment of distant panic. A moment when I feel the weakening of the astral cord as the remnants of my worldly consciousness fight for purchase on the Plane. My physical form seems very far away, and I strain against the echo of knowledge that I'm being detained. Samael has me in his grip. I will not be able to return to my body, and when Dimitri awakes in the morning, my sleeping form will be an empty shell.

My struggle does not last long. The relief pledged by Samael's silken wings, his heart still beating in time to mine, is too great

for my apathetic spirit to fight. I feel another tug on the astral cord, the call of my place in the world that has always been mine.

I pull against it as I step toward the Beast. Toward the only peace I can claim as mine.

Then, I let everything go.

I do not think it possible for my sense of shame to grow. Yet, the day after Dimitri wakes me from the travel in which I was fully prepared to give myself to Samael, I feel more disgraced than ever. It doesn't matter that the others aren't aware of the details. I am wicked. And as we ride toward Avebury, my self-loathing rises to new heights until I begin to believe that I don't deserve the opportunity to close the Gate at all.

All that morning, I look to Dimitri, expecting to see pity in his eyes. I brace myself, knowing I will hate it more than any amount of his judgment.

But it never comes.

His eyes, filled only with love and determination, are as clear as the azure sky above us.

It does nothing for the confusion that has permeated my soul since the moment I awoke, for while it is obvious that Dimitri is the same man he has always been, it takes most of the day to banish the memory of his familiar face turning into the terrifying countenance of the Beast.

Shortly after we break for lunch, I feel our proximity to Avebury. The knowledge begins as a slight vibration in my bones and grows to a faint hum when the somber gray stones, standing like soldiers in concentric circles, finally come into view. The mark on my wrist aches with a dull throb, and I glance down at the medallion, feeling the pull of the sacred site from the center of the Jorgumand.

We stop several times among the trees, scanning for signs that the Guard has arrived before us. All the while, the pull of my body to Avebury grows stronger. It is only through sheer force of will that I resist the urge to rush forward.

Finally we make our way toward a small house near the center of the site.

The belly of the serpent.

And though all is quiet, I do not recognize it as the peace of impending closure, but the knowledge that this is the beginning of the end.

37

We are not quite to the front of the house when the door opens.
My heart lifts when I see Gareth step onto the porch. A
moment later Brigid appears behind him, wiping her hands on
the apron tied around her waist. She waves vigorously, a brilliant smile breaking out across her face.

"Lia!" She is off the porch before we have come to a full
stop. "I've been so worried!"

"I take it everything is secure?" Dimitri asks Gareth.

Gareth nods. "It's just us. Come inside. Let us get you some
food and we'll tell you everything."

Dimitri swings out of the saddle, toward me. I know he is keeping himself near in case I should require help, but I'm grateful he
doesn't offer. For all my weariness, I need to feel capable of man-
aging the small things that are required to get through the day.

Dismounting, I turn my gaze back to Brigid, noting her look

of alarm as she takes in my appearance. I try to stand a little straighter, to smile a little brighter, as I meet her eyes.

"Food would be lovely. And some water for washing, if you have it."

The others dismount behind me, Edmund assisting Aunt Virginia, and Brigid leads us into the house as the men see to the horses.

The interior of the house is small and dark, but not at all unwelcoming. We make our way past a room that looks to be a parlor, and Brigid leads us toward a simple, narrow staircase at the center of the house. At the top of the stairs Aunt Virginia and I are shown to private rooms. Luisa chooses one to share with Sonia while Brigid graciously shows Helene to the room they will share. We agree to wash and change before meeting Brigid back downstairs in the small kitchen.

Half an hour later I find the keys seated around a simple, rough-hewn table as Brigid pours tea.

"Where is Aunt Virginia?" I ask, taking the seat nearest to Sonia.

"She said she wanted to rest and will see us at dinner." Luisa's voice is kind, and I realize that I must not be doing a very good job of hiding my worry. "She'll be fine, Lia, you'll see. A few hours' rest will do her wonders."

I nod, taking a chipped teacup from Brigid's capable hands and sipping the hot tea to avoid answering.

"So," Luisa takes a drink from her cup, eyeing Brigid over the rim with a sly grin. "Was it just you and Gareth, all alone in this big house?"

Brigid's cheeks flush the palest rose as she pours tea. "It's not that big."

Luisa raises her eyebrows. "I don't give a whit about this silly house, Brigid. Really! I would much rather hear how you've been keeping yourselves busy these past two days."

Sonia rolls her eyes. "Luisa! Don't be so brash."

Luisa takes an enthusiastic bite out of one of the biscuits on the table. "Don't pretend to be innocent. You want to know as much as I do."

I resist the urge to laugh. Perhaps it's better that Aunt Virginia isn't here after all.

Brigid finally sits, busying herself with the tea towel in her lap. "We haven't been here very long. We only arrived yesterday morning. By the time we negotiated our stay with the innkeepers and saw them packed and gone, it was evening.

"We've spent the time since keeping watch for the Guard and preparing for your arrival. The house doesn't get many guests, it seems. It needed a good cleaning."

I wonder if she is thinking about her own well-kept inn at Loughcrew, for I see a spark of pride in her eyes.

"What did you tell the innkeepers?" Helene's voice comes softly from across the table, and I realize that I cannot remember the last time I heard her speak. I feel a moment's pity as I realize how easily Brigid has become one of us, while Helene still holds herself on the outskirts of our alliance.

Brigid shrugs, two spots of color working their way back onto her cheeks. "Gareth told him we were newlyweds who wanted privacy. He paid them well to vacate quickly."

Luisa's laugh is bawdy. "I'm quite sure he did!"

Sonia smacks at her arm. "Luisa! Goodness!" She levels her gaze at Brigid, fighting a smile. "I'm very sorry, Brigid. I don't know what comes over her sometimes."

Brigid nods, a smile blossoming on her lips. "It was rather nice, having the house to ourselves."

"I knew it!" Luisa practically screams. "And I demand details!"

We erupt into laughter around the table, all except for Helene, who favors us with a simple smile. But Brigid is prevented from continuing, as we hear the thud of footsteps approaching the kitchen. A moment later Gareth appears in the doorway.

"The horses are—" He breaks off, looking at our faces, turned in unison to his as we all think about him and Brigid alone together in the inn. "What?"

Brigid blushes, rising to remove the teacups and plates as the rest of us break into peals of laughter. Even Helene giggles quietly behind her hand, and for a moment I forget that this is Avebury.

I forget the humming in my veins. The whisper of the medallion on my wrist. The call of Samael.

For a moment, I almost forget that these may be the final days in which I'm in possession of my own soul.

Almost.

❦

I am not the only one who seeks to forget, and we pass the evening in pleasant companionship as if we have agreed not to

speak of the prophecy for just this night. Sonia and I help
Brigid prepare a meal while Helene and Luisa play cribbage at
the worn table in the kitchen. Gareth and Dimitri light a fire
and hunt for wine, emerging victorious from the cellar almost
an hour later, holding aloft four dusty bottles of ruby-colored
liquid.

Edmund's worry is the only reminder of our mission. He
takes the rifle to make a sweep of the area at regular intervals
while Aunt Virginia sits on the porch with a blanket wrapped
around her shoulders against the coming chill of night.

Soon enough the table is set. The food is steaming on plat-
ters, the wine poured, and we sit, joined in our shared purpose.
I watch with pleasure as Helene begins to laugh with Sonia
and Luisa and Gareth favors Brigid with affection that brings a
smile to her lips and a flush to her cheeks.

A deep peace settles over my heart as I watch them — these
people for whom I have such love. These people who have
become so dear to me. I am suddenly certain they will be all
right, whatever happens to me. They will survive and be happy.
They will go on, laughing and loving.

It is all I want to know. All I need to know. I feel new
strength in my decision to come to Avebury without Alice,
and as I look around the table I am secure in the knowledge
that my sacrifice, should I be called to make it, will mean the
continuation of everything good.

It is only when I glance at Dimitri that I feel a thread of
doubt, for though he smiles and attempts to laugh, I see the
shadows in his eyes. It's vain to think that he won't go on with-

out me. That he won't find happiness elsewhere. Yet the tight set of his jaw and the sadness in his eyes cause me great disquiet. I don't wish to leave him alone.

Reaching out, I brush his hair away from his brow, not caring if Aunt Virginia or anyone else thinks me bold. Dimitri's eyes meet mine, desire and love licking like fire from their depths. I know if there were anything in the world that could make me change my mind, it would be him.

❧

I sink farther into the hot water, grateful all over again that Brigid came across the old metal tub in the back room of the house. Boiling the water pot by pot and carrying it to my small chamber was a luxury I managed to convince myself I deserved.

At this time tomorrow night we will be preparing for the Rite. Assuming, that is, that the Guard doesn't catch up to us first. Either way, this may be my last night among the living.

I try to empty my mind. To concentrate on the slide of water against my skin, the feel of the cool metal against my back, the slight draft on my face from the colder air outside the tub. It works for only a moment before Dimitri's face fills the darkness in my mind. I see him as he was at dinner, his eyes overflowing with the same need that has steadily grown in my own soul, my own body. Something gentle and promising flutters in my belly at the thought of him.

"Do you wish me to leave until you're finished?" His voice comes from the door, and I turn my head to look at him, standing against the wall inside my room, the door closed behind him. I'm not surprised to see him there. I have grown used to his stealth. His unexpected appearances.

A voice inside my head tells me I should ask him to leave. Reminds me that it is beyond improper to allow a gentleman in the room while I am naked in the bath. But that voice is so small. It is but a whisper now. It's the voice of the Lia I was, and I will never be that Lia again.

Without giving it another thought, I rise, water dripping off my body as I stand in the tub, utterly exposed to Dimitri. His eyes darken further, turning into black pools of desire, as his gaze drops to my breasts, the flat of my stomach, my thighs.

I hold out a hand, oddly unembarrassed. "Would you get that blanket there, please?"

It takes him a moment to follow my arm to the blanket lying across the end of the bed, but finally he retrieves it. Stepping toward me, he holds it out from a distance, as if not trusting himself to get too close.

"Open it, please."

Surprise shades his eyes, but he opens the blanket wide, waiting as I step from the tub, still wet, and walk toward him. His arms close around me, the blanket soft and warm as it drapes over my skin. We stand, unmoving, for a moment. It is impossible not to think about the fact that Dimitri's muscled arms are separated from my naked skin only by the thin material of an old blanket.

"Will you help me dry off?" I ask into his shoulder.

He steps back, opening the blanket slowly. I hear the intake

of his breath as he gazes upon my naked body. It is surprisingly easy to stand unabashedly before him.

His eyes do not leave mine as he gently rubs my shoulders with the ends of the blanket. He works his way from my arms to my breasts, the gentle pressure of his hands sending a powerful ripple of longing through my body. Pulling his eyes away from my face, he drops to his knees before me, moving the blanket across my stomach, over the curve of my hips, to the soft skin on the inside of my thigh. I find myself glad that he moves so slowly. I am in no hurry to shield myself from Dimitri's eyes. My body suddenly seems the deepest of the secrets I have kept, and I do not wish to have secrets from Dimitri anymore.

His hands are patient and careful. His longing, as powerful as my own, is a presence in the room. When he's finished he rises, still holding the blanket. I see the question in his eyes and answer him by reaching for his hand.

"Come." I pull him toward the bed. "Come and lie with me."

He does not speak as I settle into the crook of his arm, touching my hands to the warm flesh exposed between the open ties of his shirt. My fingers travel downward, untying the laces as I go, until they are all undone. Pushing back the fabric, I bare his chest, flattening myself against him and kissing the muscles that ripple beneath his surprisingly soft skin.

I rest my chin on my hands and look up into his eyes. "I love you, you know. You must remember that."

He pulls me up to his mouth so suddenly that it takes my breath away. In an instant I am beneath him, my head sinking

into the down pillow as his body presses against mine. He touches my face, staring into my eyes with a ferocity that nearly frightens me.

"Come away with me, Lia. Come away with me tonight. I'll protect you from the Souls, as long as it takes. We'll work together to bring Alice to our side."

I twine my arms around his neck, pulling him toward me until our lips meet again. Our passion presses at the barriers of the gentle kiss until I finally pull away.

"I must do this, Dimitri. I don't want to live in a world where I have to hide, even in sleep, from the Souls. More important, I don't wish to live in a world where the other keys, my friends, must do the same. A world where you must compromise your loyalty to the Grigori to protect me." He begins to protest, but I hold my fingers gently against his mouth to stop him. Then I look into his eyes so he will know that I mean what I say next. "This is how it must be, Dimitri. Please don't waste our time together speaking of it again. Just be with me here, now. Be with me and know that whatever happens tomorrow, tonight and forever, I am yours."

I lean up to press my lips against his. Then I open myself to him, relishing the feel of his bare skin moving against mine. And I have no regrets.

38

We spend the day in morose silence. Sonia, Luisa, Helene,
Brigid, Aunt Virginia, and I play halfhearted games of cribbage
and attempt to read passages from the few dusty books that line
the shelves while the men take turns riding out to check the
perimeter. By dinner there is still no sign of the Guard, and
while I am relieved, I have no doubt they are out there. I don't
know when they'll arrive, but I know they're coming.

As evening approaches, I retire to my room with Dimitri to
prepare for the Rite. I am folding my things in silence, packing
them for whoever will have to take them back to London
should I not survive the night, when I hear Dimitri's voice
behind me.

"I've been waiting for the right time to give this to you." I
turn to face him. He holds out a package, wrapped in plain
brown paper. "More likely, I was hoping the occasion would

not arise after all. But it's impossible to lie to myself any longer."

I do not take the package right away. I simply look at it, afraid to touch it, as if doing so will set in motion a string of events that cannot be undone. But of course that is pure foolishness. Those events were set in motion long ago. There is nothing I can do to stop them now.

I reach for the package and am surprised by its heft. "What is it?"

He sits next to me on the bed, his weight causing the mattress to dip ever so slightly, so that I slide toward him until our bodies are just touching.

"Something to bring you comfort this night. Open it."

I pull the simple string on the package, turning it over until I find the seam. When I remove the paper, it reveals a thick pile of deep violet silk. When I touch it, a wisp of memory, powerful but barely formed, winds its way into my mind like the remnant of a beautiful dream.

"I ... I don't understand."

A low chuckle erupts from his throat, an undercurrent of melancholy in it. "You are a terrible receiver of gifts. Open it and you'll find out."

I set the package on the bed, plucking at the fabric on top. It reveals more beneath it, but I leave the rest where it is and shake the pile of silk in my hands until it unfurls, a shimmering purple sea that spills in folds onto the floor. Standing, I hold it away from my body to get a better look at it, and then I understand.

"Oh! But ..." I turn to Dimitri, emotion welling in my throat

until I am forced to push it down in order to speak. "How did you get this?"

He nods his head to the package on the bed. "I believe there's a note that explains."

I set the garment on the bed, searching through the pile of fabric and brown paper until I see a thick piece of parchment. I do not recognize the handwriting, and I walk toward the firebox so that I can read it with some measure of privacy. Whatever it says, whomever it is from, it is for me alone.

It takes my eyes a moment to adjust to the elegant slant of the handwriting, but as soon as I begin reading, my breath catches in my throat.

Dearest Lia,

It is strange how something so small can change everything, isn't it? Your presence here on Altus was like that for me. Though you were here but a few days, your friendship was a blessing. I think of you often.

I know the time is drawing near for you to face Samael and his Souls, and I know that you do so on behalf of the Sisters ~ those who have gone before you and all those who would go after you. It seems only right, then, that we are with you in some way, and though I cannot be at Avebury to stand with you in the Rite, I hope you will find comfort and strength in the cloak of our Sisterhood. I hope it will remind you of Altus, and of me. I hope it will remind you that we do stand with you, if only in spirit.

Your people and island need you, my Lady. My friend.
We eagerly await your return.

Una

I stare at the words long after I finish reading them. They take me to another place, and for a moment I can feel the breeze rushing upward from the sea, carrying with it the scent of oranges from the groves on Altus.

"She would be here if she could," Dimitri says from the bed behind me.

I nod, turning to face him with a small smile. "I know."

I cross the room to the package, lifting the first floor-length robe from it before counting the others.

"There are six of them. One for me, one for each of the keys, and one for Aunt Virginia." I am still stunned by Una's thoughtfulness.

Dimitri nods. "They are the robes used by the Sisters on Altus in the ancient festivals and rites."

"They're lovely." I clutch the violet silk to my chest as if doing so will connect me with the strength of the Sisters on Altus. "You must thank Una for me."

Dimitri rises, pulling me into his arms, the robe crushed between us. "You may tell her yourself, when this is all over."

His voice is husky with emotion, and I say nothing. I simply stand there in the protective circle of his arms, letting him pretend for the moment that my survival is a forgone conclusion rather than the leap of faith we both know it is.

I expect the night to pass quickly, as time so often does when one wishes it wouldn't. Instead, the hours seem to crawl past. Dimitri and Edmund rise at regular intervals to scout the field on which Avebury's stones lay, but there is still no sign of the Guard. It does nothing to ease my mind.

If anything, the knowledge that they have not yet arrived causes me even more disquiet. I long to sit astride Sargent and patrol with the men, but I do not bother asking. They will only tell me it's too dangerous, that I must remain cloistered until the ceremony. Even still, I cannot help but think I would rather die atop my horse, in the open fields of Avebury and at the hands of the Guard, than alone in my consignment to the Void.

But that would mean I did not try to close the Gate. And that is not an option.

By the time the small clock on the mantel strikes three in the morning, I want only to see it done. I'm tired of waiting, of wondering.

I am sitting on the small sofa with Dimitri, leaning against him and nestled in the crook of his arm, when he leans down to whisper in my ear.

"I think it's time I take the Stone now."

I nod, lifting myself off him. There is no need to speak. He will arrange the Stone for the Rite and the rising sun while I wait inside with the keys and Aunt Virginia until the time draws nearer to sunrise. It has all been arranged.

I feel the eyes of the others as I lift the chain, heavy with the Stone at its end, from my neck. I hand it to Dimitri without ceremony, holding his gaze in the moment before he stands, nodding to Edmund and Gareth. They make their way from the house in silence. Those of us who remain do not speak in the emptiness left by their absence.

It is difficult not to feel that I am on the way to my own execution. We stand — the keys, Aunt Virginia, and I — near the door of the cottage, waiting for word that it is time to convene around the fire. I see the flames from the window, large and licking at the sky.

I am almost out of time.

Lifting my right hand, I remove the medallion from my right wrist, securing it instead on my left. I have known since the dream of myself at Avebury, the medallion searing my skin, that this would be the final requirement of the prophecy. The final test. I must wear the medallion over my mark to close the Gate.

Which means I may instead open it if I fail.

But it doesn't matter. It is the only way, and I position the tarnished gold disc over the Jorgumand on my skin. My soul seems to expand, nearly sighing aloud as the etched symbol on the medallion nestles against its twin on my wrist. For a moment it seems foolish to have fought so hard when, all along, peace was so close.

Shaking my head against the thought, I let my hand drop

back to my side. Someone's fingers close around mine, and when I turn, tipping my head to see around the hood of my robe, I see Luisa's elegant nose and full lips peeking from beneath the silk of her own.

She turns to me, speaking in a voice so low I wonder if anyone can hear but me. "Lia...I..." She meets my eyes with a sad smile. "Well, you are very brave. Whatever happens, I know you will prevail. In this world or the next. I hope you'll carry me with you, whichever it may be."

"Thank you, Luisa. I hope you'll do the same." I am grateful for her honesty. It is the only time my probable death has been openly acknowledged, and it is somehow a relief not to have to pretend. Even still, I haven't the heart to return her smile, for I know I'm a fraud. I am not brave. In fact, I'm practically shaking from fear, actively resisting the urge to flee atop Sargent's back as we speak.

To run and hide from the Guard and the Souls and Samael for as long as I can.

It is only the truth that prevents it. And the truth is this: I am already dead living this way. There is nowhere to run. As long as the Gate remains open, Samael and his Souls will find me.

Luisa squeezes my hand and we both turn to the door as it opens. Edmund stands, backlit by the distant fire.

He nods. "It's time. We have less than an hour until sunrise, and while I don't like to have you exposed, I don't dare cut it any closer."

A lump of fresh fear rises in my throat, but I nod and step

through the open door. The others fall into step behind me. I hear their footfalls on the rocks of the small road leading from the cottage until we reach the wild grass of the fields. Then all is silent as we follow Edmund to the fire, ringed by the smaller flame of torches encircling it. I lift my head to the indigo sky, noting the faint lightening in the east. It is the clock by which the Rite, and my future, will unfold, and I wonder how long it will be before the sun breaks through the inky darkness to illuminate the Stone.

Turning my attention back to Dimitri's dark figure silhouetted before the fire, I note with relief the shadow of the rifle in his hand. I have asked him not to intervene except to keep the Guard from my body once I am in the Otherworlds, for I've no doubt that is where I am going. But I am only one person, and I will not be able to maintain my faculties in both places at once. Should a battle rage here while I am there, it will fall to the others to fight it.

My senses are heightened as I near the fire. The grass is cool underfoot, and I feel renewed satisfaction at my decision to go without shoes. I feel Avebury's energy in the current that runs beneath my skin, stronger still as I come closer to the stones that stand in the distance. It seems important to be connected to the sacred ground, and I am soothed by the vibration tingling the bottoms of my feet. I will draw strength from whatever source is available — even the now cold adder stone still around my neck. It may not hold spiritual power, but it is a part of Aunt Abigail. Her presence, however faint, is a comfort.

Dimitri's eyes lock onto mine as I cross the ring of torches,

coming to a stop before him. I wish more than anything for the power to banish the sorrow and resignation in his eyes.

In the end, all I can do is let him hear strength in my voice. "I'm ready."

He nods, pulling his eyes from mine to gesture to the fire a few feet away. "Everything is in order. The Rite doesn't require fire, but it will aid Edmund and me in keeping an eye on the fields should anyone approach. We've—"

"Isn't it a risk to use fire when it's not called for?" Helene interrupts.

Dimitri's sigh is full of weariness. "Fire is a sacred part of many ancient rituals, but it's also used for simple illumination. As long as everything else is in place, Lia will have the power to summon Samael."

But everything is not in place, I think. *We don't have Alice.*

I wonder if the others are thinking the same thing, but there is no use voicing the obvious. There is no turning back now.

Dimitri looks back at the fire, his eyes lifting to a raised wooden tripod. "We've positioned the Stone on a wooden mount of sorts to give it the best chance of catching the light of the rising sun. Now you must form a circle, join hands, and recite the Rite as you wait for the sun to hit the Stone."

It will not be as simple as it sounds, but the dim light in the distance is already sweeping the sky, the darkness above us becoming slightly less dense.

I turn to the others, looking at each of them in turn— Helene, Brigid, Luisa, Sonia, and Aunt Virginia. "Thank you for being here with me. Shall we begin?"

39

At first I feel self-conscious. The words of the Rite are stranger on my tongue than they were in my mind. The keys and I do not always recite them in synch, but stumble over them in the circle we form around the fire and the Stone raised above it. I register with perfect clarity Aunt Virginia's cool hand in mine on one side and Sonia's, slightly damp, on the other.

Across from me, through the flames of the fire, Brigid is intent on the words, Helene and Luisa on either side of her. I look to the sky only once, noting with detachment the gathering light as the sun continues its ascent. After that I close my eyes, concentrating on the words of the Rite. On saying them in time with the keys and my aunt. On calling forth the Beast.

The words begin to come more rhythmically. Our timing improves as we repeat the mantra of the Rite, over and over again. The physical world begins to feel more distant until my only connection to it is my feet on the ground at Avebury, its ancient energy pulsing upward through my legs, stomach, and arms until my whole body seems to vibrate with it. I think of Altus, wanting to ground myself in something as ancient as the prophecy itself, and smell the heady scent of oranges mixed with the briny air rising from the sea. I am certain I hear waves crashing below, so near that I feel as if I am standing on one of Altus's rocky cliffs.

Opening my eyes is no longer a thought. I am floating in the ether that lies between the physical world and the Otherworlds. I give myself over to it. To the primeval words rising from our lips. To the heat of the fire on my face. To the sacred ground beneath my feet.

And then my eyes are torn open as if by force, a blinding light illuminating the space behind my lids in the moment before I see the Stone, lit by a single ray of sunlight, now peeking just above the horizon in the distance.

A hum emanates from the center of the circle, rippling outward as the Stone, seemingly lit from within, changes color. It is no longer a dull gray rock, but a glowing green sphere. I cannot take my eyes from it, though my mouth continues moving, as if in near silent prayer, with the words of the Rite. The Stone reaches for me, calling to me until I am lulled into a strangely pleasant state almost like desire. It is a letting loose of the ties that bind me, and I revel in the freedom.

But it lasts only a moment, for seconds later there is a burst of blinding light from the Stone. It rushes toward us, hungrily devouring the ground between the Stone and our circle. I close my eyes to it, but the light is still there, illuminating the darkness behind my eyelids in the moment before I see flashes of other things.

James and me by the river at Birchwood, both looking impossibly young and unconcerned.

Henry, his smiling face turned to mine as we laugh over a book in the parlor.

Luisa, Sonia, and me, our wrists thrust together, our smooth skin punctuated by our nearly identical marks.

Myself on the cliff overlooking the lake where my mother sacrificed her life in the name of the prophecy.

And finally, Dimitri's face, his body moving over mine and lit by firelight in my small chamber at Avebury.

Then there is only blackness, and relief washes over me as I float through it, wondering if I am, at last, dead. But of course it is not that easy, and a moment later I open my eyes to find myself standing on the same beach where I first learned about the strangeness of the Otherworlds and the power of thought. The ocean ebbs and flows at my feet, the same line of rocky caves blocking everything but the beach from view on my left.

Looking around, I feel a moment's uncertainty. Now that I'm here, I am not at all certain how to go about ending the prophecy. It seems strange, after everything that's happened, after all the times I have sought to avoid detection by the Souls in the Otherworlds, to seek them out, but I believe that is what I must do. If it were as simple as wishing the Gate closed, it would be done by now. Yet I am here in the Otherworlds through the workings of the Stone, the Rite, and the keys. I

can only assume that the others still cling to my hands in the physical world. That they continue to chant the words of the Rite. It is their part of our bargain, and I realize with renewed clarity that mine is to summon the Beast, though every moment of the last two years has been devoted to denying him.

I know immediately that the beach is not a good place to do so, with the water on one side and the caves on the other. Neither do I wish to meet the Souls in the Void, for while it is true that entombment there may be my fate, I don't wish to make it easier for Samael to see it done.

No, I should like to meet them, to meet *him*, on familiar ground, and the moment I think it, I know exactly where I'll go. I remember Sonia's words from long ago, from the time when traveling the Plane was strange and foreign to me.

Thoughts have power on the Plane, Lia.

I think of Birchwood. Of the rolling hills that stretch in every direction. Of the forests that carpet the fields and the river that flows behind the great stone house. Of the graveyard where Henry's body lies next to those of my father and mother.

It is both comforting and painful. A fitting end to the burden of the prophecy.

A moment later I am in the air, flying over the caves near the beach, sand dunes and sea grass giving way to gray-green plains that soon become extravagant green meadows. There are creatures beneath me, many of them, all running from the direction in which I fly, as if from a fire. Not even the animals want to be where I'm going. Only I fly toward the Beast, while everything else moves away from him.

But there is no time to dwell on the thought. I begin to drop to the ground, marveling once again at the power of the Plane. That one can simply think about the person one wishes to see or the task one wishes to accomplish, and one is carried there by nothing but the energy of thought.

Touching down, I expect to feel the softness of spring grass against my skin. Instead, something coarse scratches at the soft undersides of my feet. When I look down, I am surprised to see that the grass is brown and dead. I understand when I raise my gaze to the gray and black landscape around me. It mimics the fields surrounding Birchwood, but I recognize it as the dead field where I was once summoned to meet Alice.

It is more than the grass and trees that are devoid of life. The very air seems lacking in oxygen. As if this world has been abandoned. As if everyone in the Otherworlds knows no good can come of being here, and they've all sought their escape. I turn in a small circle, looking for any sign of the Souls.

I hear them — no, *feel* them — first.

It begins as a rumble in the ground beneath my feet, as if a large animal is barreling toward me and will burst through the trees at any moment. My heartbeat speeds up, and I wait and listen, unsurprised to finally realize the sound is the beating of horses' hooves in the distance. It is clear from the noise that there are a great many of them. Far more than ever before. The Beast has no doubt sent every one of his minions to join in this, the final capture and banishment of the one who might usher him into the world that is mine.

Their horses approach with a swiftness that makes the speed

of the Hellhounds seem sluggish by comparison, and I turn toward the line of trees that harbors the greatest noise, bracing myself for the appearance of the Souls and their steeds. It is obvious from the sound of them that they approach from every direction, but it is possible to fix my sights on only one area at a time. A moment later, I'm glad I chose the one I did.

The Souls stream out of the forest, their arms raised, fiery swords glowing red. I had forgotten the enormity of them, for even a member of the Guard is no bigger than a regular man in the physical world. The Souls are the size of two mortal men, and all sitting atop mounts that would dwarf Sargent. They do not slow or hesitate upon seeing me standing in the field but surge forward with renewed vigor as if trying to apprehend me before I flee.

But I do nothing. I did not bother to bring my bow or any sort of physical defense. The time for that has passed. Now it is my calling to *will* them toward me.

And to fight with the strength bequeathed to me by my ancestors in the Sisterhood.

By Aunt Abigail. By Aunt Virginia. And by my mother.

It's no matter now, for they are upon me in short order, streaming out on every side, encircling me until I am but a small animal in their sights. When I am completely surrounded, the Lost Souls, so many on every side that I cannot see the end of them, raise their swords in unison, a guttural howl erupting from their throats. Even without words, I recognize it as the victory cry that it is.

I begin to shake, unable to hide my fear. They are enormous,

their bodies hulking forms of muscle rippling beneath tattered clothing, their victorious grimaces terrifying and hideous behind matted beards.

Closing in on me, they move their horses nearer, the giant animals baring their teeth, snapping at me as the Souls look on with obvious pleasure. I begin to think I'll be spared the Void. That I will die here, trampled to death beneath the horses' hooves before I get the chance to even attempt to close the Gate.

But then I feel as if the beat of my own heart has suddenly multiplied. It is at first distant, so that I'm not sure it's even there, but a moment later it grows stronger. I feel its approach both outside and inside my body until it surrounds me, body and soul. The crowd of Lost Souls begins to shuffle to one side, raising their swords and bowing their heads. The heartbeat grows stronger still, only a half-beat off my own, as the Souls step apart, making way for the Beast.

He rises before me, clad in black. As with the Souls, his size is terrifying. But his countenance is that of a handsome man, and I have a brief memory of the moment on the Plane when his face morphed from this one to that of the fearsome beast who chased me through the woods of my travel, swatting at me with razor-sharp claws. I must not forget it. Must not be lulled by this false and captivating face. By the heartbeat still trying to beat in time with my own.

He looms before me. If he were to charge, I'd be nothing but rubble at his feet. Yet he does not approach on horseback. Instead, he surprises me by dropping to the ground in one swift motion, more graceful than any mortal, despite his size.

"Mistress. You honor me with your presence." His voice is twisted and warped, the sound of one animal trying to coax sound from the body of another.

I swallow, willing my voice to be strong. "I do you no such honor. I come in the name of the Sisterhood to close the Gate and banish you from the physical world forevermore." I sound like a child, even to myself, but it is all I can think of to say.

He approaches me in large strides. His boot steps rattle the ground beneath my feet and seem to reverberate far beyond the world in which we stand.

"You do not have the Guardian."

I lift my chin. "Perhaps not, but I seek to close the Gate, as the prophecy says is my right."

His eyes narrow as he comes closer, and I see that they are nearly gold at their center, and ringed with red. "You are a stubborn mistress." His voice seems to enter through my pores, winding its way through my body. I hear the rustle of wings at his back. "You will find peace only if you let go of your false notions."

He steps closer still, stopping a foot in front of me, his eyes boring into mine. I begin to lose focus on the world around me. The dead field, the Souls... they all fade away as his eerie voice worms its way into my veins, the words expanding in a repulsive hiss. "Your place is with me, Mistress, as you knowww. As you feeeel."

His wings unfold with a tremendous shake, unfurling on either side until they block out even the Souls standing behind him. The wings call to me, the lush feathers shining like

polished onyx, speaking to me of peace and safety. From Samael and, most important of all, from myself.

I shake my head, clinging to a remnant of my earlier purpose. "No. It's not true." But the heartbeat in my head has grown louder. It no longer beats just out of time with my own. Now our hearts pulse in perfect unison, and I feel my resolve begin to slip away.

"Yesss," he says, taking a last step toward me, touching my cheek with the back of his gloved hand. "It is only natural that you would feel our affinity for one another. There is no shame in it. You were born to usher me into the physical world. To reign at my side."

I shake my head to deny it yet again, but apathy seeps like fog from my mind until everything he says makes a curious sort of sense. A comforting sense of rightness settles over my shoulders as his wings fold around me, encircling me in warmth and softness. The heartbeat grows louder. It is one heart now— *ours*—beating together.

And now it is all so simple.

We are one, as the prophecy dictates. It is not my calling to refuse him. Doing so has only brought sadness and loss and darkness. The very things I sought to avoid by denying him entry.

I settle into the sensuous wings, rubbing the skin of my cheek against the feathers, allowing my own heartbeat to settle more solidly into synch with his in the moment before my soul seems to rip in half.

Crying out, I lift my head from the downy chest of the Beast.

A tug on the astral cord connecting me to my body wrenches me from his embrace until I am tumbling once again through silent darkness. My fall seems endless, my first awareness afterward the sound of distant voices, chanting in unison words that are at once strange and familiar. It is the feel of something solid at my back that tells me I am no longer falling, and I open my eyes with effort, as if waking from a long sleep.

The figures standing around me are warped and distorted, the place where their faces should be black and empty. It takes me a moment to make sense of the robed and hooded figures, but soon I remember: the keys. They are still reciting the words of the Rite, but I am lying on the ground near the fire, having somehow broken free of their circle. I remember the Beast with longing as another painful tear rips through my body, causing me to cry out into the night. My wrist burns as if on fire, and I lift my arm with effort, wondering if I am imagining the mark melding with the medallion, searing my skin as the two become one.

I fling my arms out at my sides in a gesture of surrender as I realize that the Beast is coming. He is coming through me at last, and I give myself over to the pain, releasing myself from the burden of fighting. Grasping for the fleeting peace and sense of purpose I felt while encircled by his wings.

I am just beginning to sink into the relief of it when the sound of hoofbeats reaches my ears. I think it is the Souls, coming to aid Samael. Coming to usher me toward the serenity I have earned by being his Gate.

But the sound does not come from that distant part of me still in the Otherworlds. No. These horses are here, just outside the circle of robed figures, and I turn my gaze toward them, too weak to lift my head.

I hear the rise of masculine voices beyond the faceless figures that encircle me. The men's voices are punctuated by one more feminine, beyond the circle.

It is this voice that wins out over the others.

"Let me through! I need to help my sister."

And suddenly Alice is here, kneeling by my side, clutching my hand in hers. I see other figures on horseback beyond the safety of our circle. The face of the fair-haired Guard comes to me through the night, distorted by my own pain and the flicker of the fire, his expression wrathful as he watches Alice.

Now I know. The Guard *was* in pursuit. They *were* giving chase all this time. But it was not me they were trying to stop. Not this time.

It was my sister.

"Are you with me, Lia? Are you here or there?" I try to open my mouth to speak, but I cannot force the words from my throat. She continues without waiting for my answer. "It doesn't matter. Wherever you are, don't listen to him. It is all lies." She drops to the ground beside me, stretching out and taking my hand in hers. Her eyes are overflowing with sadness, and with something else I have not seen in their depths for a very long time. Love.

"Do you think this will make me good again?"

I do not have time to answer. As soon as her hand meets mine, there is another great tug, and this time I am spinning through the blackness with my sister.

40

"You!" Samael spits the word from his mouth. His dark wings flutter, stirring up an angry wind. He is back on his mount, some feet from where Alice and I now stand in the dead field.

She doesn't look at me when she speaks. "We must repeat the Rite together now, Lia."

She begins chanting the words, just as the keys and I did in the moments before I was transported to the Otherworlds: *"Sacro orbe ab angelis occidentibus effecto potestatem sororem societatis convocamus Custos Portaque ut Diabole saeculorum te negaramus in aeternum. Porta se praecludat et totus mundus tutus a tua iracundia fiat."*

It takes a moment for her instructions to make their way through my addled consciousness, but soon I begin repeating the Rite with her. Our voices rise above Samael and his Souls, winding their way through the strange silence of the dead fields. The Souls shuffle on their mounts as our words grow bolder, louder. Their horses begin to back away, despite the urging and whipping of the Souls who are their masters.

Samael's golden eyes find mine, the red rings glowing around them. "You are making a grave mistake, Mistressss."

Strength gathers behind my words as I raise my voice with my sister's. I have always known that we would be stronger together. I wonder if Alice knows it now, too.

The wind grows in strength, and now I both hear and feel it. It rises like a cloud around us, encircling the Beast, Alice, and me until we are cocooned in our own cyclone. My hair whips around my face, and I have to fight to keep my body upright against the force of it.

Samael turns his gaze to Alice. "You will pay dearly for your betrayal." He doesn't shout over the wind, yet I hear him perfectly.

Alice meets his eyes, never flinching, ceaseless in her repeating of the Rite.

A moment later a terrific crack sounds above us. I raise my eyes to it and am somehow unsurprised to see a huge tear in the sky of the Otherworlds. Samael's eyes follow mine, his countenance beginning to change from that of a man to something else entirely.

A monster.

A Beast.

He levels his evil eyes, now almost entirely red, at Alice. "If I go, you go as well."

For a moment I feel as if I'm gazing into water for scrying. His figure shimmers, his clothes tearing with an audible rip as his body grows taller and larger still, wrenching itself free of

the fabric that encased his manly form. The figure that emerges is not the smoothly muscled shape of a man. It is twisted, deformed, and just when I think I cannot take my eyes off the terrifying transformation, his face shimmers, expanding along the jawline to reveal impossibly sharp teeth. They rise to points as sharp and fine as a sword, snapping at us with an explosive roar, his gaze, full of vengeance, on Alice.

But she does not so much as pause in her recitation of the Rite, and I feel the first whisper of fear for my sister. Even now, after all that has happened, after all she has done, I do not want to see her consigned to the Void.

Seeing her determination in the strong set of her jaw, I continue speaking the Rite in time to her words. With another horrifying crash, the crack in the sky grows larger, and the whole world seems to tilt beneath my feet. Samael casts a glance upward before gathering the reins of his horse. The animal rears on its hind legs, casting a long shadow over everything around it in the moment before Samael fixes his gaze on us and charges.

"Do not stop reciting the Rite, whatever happens, until you are back safely in our world, Lia. Promise me, or it will all be for nothing."

I pause just long enough to shout over the howling wind. "I promise."

We continue our chant in perfect unison as Samael gallops toward us, his eyes on Alice alone. I no longer feel his heartbeat in time with mine, but my own heartbeat more than makes up for it as he draws closer. I don't know which is louder, the shrieking wind or the thunderous sound of Samael's approach, but I remember my promise and do not cease my chanting even when he is directly in front of us. Even when he bends lower, reaching for my sister as he passes. He wrenches her away from me, and I grip her hand as tightly as I gripped it in the moment she pulled me from my death in the river behind Birchwood.

But it is no use. My strength is no match for Samael's, and Alice is tugged from my hands. He flings her onto the front of his horse, his great wings drawing around her until she completely disappears from sight. Turning the horse from me, he starts toward the forest.

He does not get far.

A moment later his horse seems to slow before stopping altogether. I see the animal struggling to keep its footing against some invisible force. It rears and whinnies in the instant before it is lifted upward, the Beast and my sister still on its back, toward the ripped seam in the sky above.

Even from my position on the ground, I see the Beast and his steed fight against the power pulling them toward the crack in the sky. But whatever force takes hold, whatever force my sister and I conjured together, is more powerful than even Samael.

And then they are gone.

"Alice!" My voice carries across the fields, now as silent as death.

Looking back toward the Souls, I am surprised to find them gone. The wind is still, the crack in the sky sealed shut as if it were never there at all. I hear the clink of metal on the ground near my feet, and when I bend to look I see the medallion lying

in the grass. Picking it up, I turn it over in my hands, expecting to see the mark etched into its surface.

It is blank.

When I turn my wrist upward, I half-expect to see the mark gone from my skin as well, but it's there, just as it has been since Father's death.

Touching the smooth surface of the medallion, I ponder taking it with me. It has been part of me through things wondrous and terrifying, and I am loath to leave it.

Yet, I am also eager to relinquish its hold over me. I let it fall back to the ground, looking around and thinking of my sister, waiting for the power of the Plane to take me to her as it always has. I imagine her in the Void, on the beach, in any of the seven Otherworlds I have seen, but none of it propels me to her. Instead, I am plunged into blackness once again, falling and falling until my soul drops into my body and I find myself lying next to my sister's lifeless form on the fields at Avebury.

My back arches with the pain of drawing breath, and I gasp for air. I lie there for a moment before gathering the strength to rise to my sister's side. Slipping my arm under her neck, I lift her upper body onto my lap.

"Alice! Come back, Alice. You did it. *We* did it." The words feel strange coming out of my mouth, my throat screaming in protest, as if I have not spoken for a very long time. I am surprised to see tears dropping onto my sister's face. Surprised that I can cry for her. "Come back now. James is waiting." My voice grows harsh, as if I can force her back into her body with my anger. "You did this for him, didn't you? Didn't you?"

"Lia." Dimitri bends down next to me, placing a hand on my arm. "She's gone, Lia. She did what she came to do."

"No." I shake my head, the tears coming faster as I clutch my sister's body more tightly. "It's not fair. She cannot be gone. Not after she fulfilled her role as Guardian. Not after she saved me. After she saved us all."

"Lia." His voice is gentle.

I shake my head. I will not meet his eyes. If I do, it will all be true.

I look instead at Luisa, Sonia, Aunt Virginia... everyone standing around me. "She'll be all right, won't she? It takes time to recover from travel. She's simply sleeping."

Luisa kneels in the grass beside me, her voice soft. I do not want to see the relief on her face. "It's over, Lia. You did it. You closed the Gate to Samael."

I shake my head, rocking back and forth with Alice in my arms. Trying to block out Luisa's words.

But Dimitri will not allow me to hide from the truth.

"Look at me, Lia." His voice is commanding, and I lift my face to his, still not letting go of Alice's limp body. "She knew what she was doing. She outran the Guard all the way here. They only left when you closed the Gate. Alice understood the sacrifice she was making. She knew she wouldn't make it out alive. It was what she wanted."

"She wanted to be good again." The words are choked out in a sob.

"Yes." He nods. "She wanted to be good again."

41

The sun is a warrior, fighting valiantly against the steely clouds
that surround it. I think it fitting that the day is neither gloomy
nor bright, as if even the heavens are unsure how to feel about
Alice's death.

James is a silent presence on my left. We stand in the small
family graveyard on the hill, the freshly turned earth piled into
a mound at our feet, the granite tombstone standing rigidly at
the head of the grave. Dimitri and the others have gone back
to the house, allowing James and me time alone to say goodbye
to my sister.

And to each other.

I am not sure how to begin. I want James to understand the
depth of Alice's love and sacrifice, but I'm still not entirely certain he grasps the truth of the prophecy. I tried to explain everything upon our return from Avebury, but my account of Alice's

death seemed only to bounce off the surface of his impenetrable expression. He has not asked a single question since.

I suppose things are simpler for James; the details don't matter. Only that Alice is gone, and I may as well be.

Finally I turn to gaze upon his dear face and say the only thing he really needs to know. "She loved you, and she wanted to be worthy of your love in return."

I hear the intake of his breath.

He turns to look at me, his hat in hand. "Is it my fault?"

I shake my head. "Of course not. Alice did what she wanted to do, as she always has. You couldn't have stopped her, even if you'd known to try. None of us could have."

He sighs, turning back to the gravestone with a half-hearted nod.

"What will you do now?" I ask.

He shrugs. "What I've always done. Work in the store with Father. Catalogue books. Try to make sense of everything that has happened." He tilts his head to look at me once more. "What about you? Will you ever come back?"

"I don't know. This place..." I scan the rolling hills surrounding the graveyard, the fields covered with wildflowers. "It holds such memories for me." I turn back to look at him. "I suppose only time will tell if I can bear them."

He nods, understanding in his eyes. "If you ever decide that you can, I hope you'll come to call. Let us know how you're faring."

I manage a smile. "Thank you, James. I will."

Setting his hat back on his head, he leans forward, bending

to kiss my cheek. I catch the unique blend of scent that has always been James—books and dust and ink—and am instantly fifteen again.

"Goodbye, Lia."

I blink away the tears stinging my eyes. "Goodbye, James."

And then he's walking away, his retreating figure growing smaller as he makes his way down the hill. I watch him until he is gone.

Turning my head, I allow my gaze to sweep over the other graves. There are the graves of Mother and Father, the wild grass growing in a lush carpet beneath the white lilies I laid there only this morning. There are the dirty, slightly leaning markers of my father's parents.

But it is Henry's grave that draws my eyes. I make my way to it, unsurprised to see that violet wildflowers have overtaken the grass that covers his final resting place. I think of his kind heart and quiet strength and believe it no accident that the flowers adorning his grave are the color of the Sisterhood.

Of Altus.

I picture Henry running under a brilliant sky in the Final World, free at last, like any other boy. He, above all others, is deserving of that peace. I bring my hand to my lips before reaching forward to touch my fingers to the place where his name is carved into the marker.

"Goodbye, Henry. You were better than all of us."

The past is a reminder of the winding road leading me to this time and place. It is a road that continues into the future, for today is more than a day of goodbyes.

It is a new beginning.

I recall the day Dimitri and I stood on the deck of the ship carrying us from England to New York, the sea churning before us as far as the eye could see. I didn't look at him right away. I simply stared out over the water and told him as calmly as I could that I would accept the role of Lady of Altus, and yes, as his partner in all things. He leaned over, smiling in the moment before he kissed my lips with the tender ferocity I have grown used to since our time at Avebury. When he pulled away, I saw in his eyes all the love and certainty in the world, as if there had never been a doubt in his mind that I would make such a decision — or that I would live to do so.

But thoughts of the future are for another day. I turn back to Alice's grave, knowing this may be the last time I stand before it. My eyes are drawn to the epitaph carved into the head-stone's smooth surface:

Alice Elizabeth Milthorpe

Sister, Daughter, Guardian

1874–1892

She has earned all three titles, but I feel a momentary pang of regret for the inscription's lack of emotion. Even now, I don't know what to make of my sister. How to feel about her race to Avebury. Her final sacrifice to aid me in closing the Gate. I thought my feelings would clarify with time, but my emotions are still clouded by too many things for me to distill them into something simple. Something I can name.

I see flashes of us as we were before the prophecy, racing across the fields surrounding Birchwood, Alice always too fast for me to catch and never caring to let me try. I see us lying next to each other in our childhood nursery, our curls mingling atop the pillows as we drifted into sleep. I see us floating, hand in hand, in the sea as we learned to swim, our childish bodies mirror images of each other. I see it all and know that, whatever else I may come to understand in this world, Alice will always be a beautiful mystery.

It is one I am content not to solve. I can love her now in all her lovely darkness.

I run my hands along the top of the granite marker one more time before turning to go, making my way down the grassy slope toward Birchwood Manor and knowing, at last, the only thing that matters.

Alice was my sister.

And we were not so different after all.

ACKNOWLEDGMENTS

Telling this story in its entirety has been five years and innumerable amazing people in the making. It's impossible to thank everyone, but it's only right to keep trying.

First to my agent, Steven Malk. Your initial belief in this story made everything possible. More important, your continued faith in me and the many stories I still have to tell is a gift of immeasurable value. Thank you for being on my side when I was right, telling it to me straight when I was wrong, and putting your faith and considerable skill behind my every endeavor.

Thank you to my brilliant editor, Nancy Conescu, for being the one person who loves this story as much as I do. Your incredible talent has given me a wealth of knoweldge that continues to make me a better writer. It is your firm and compassionate voice I hear in my head as I tell stories at the keyboard. I can never thank you enough for sharing this journey with me.

Thank you to Alison Impey for never giving up on my cover—and for giving me numerous amazing ones.

Thank you to Kate Sullivan, Megan Tingley, Andrew Smith, Melanie Chang, Lisa Sabater, Jessica Bromberg, Lauren Hodge, and everyone at Little, Brown Books for Young Readers for working so hard to bring Prophecy to the world in such an elegant way.

Thank you to Lisa Mantchev, Jenny Draeger, Tonya Hurley, and Georgia McBride, dear friends who have supported me through late nights and angsty interludes. Thank you also to the passionate readers and writers who frequent my website and keep me company online, especially Devyn Burton, Catherine Haines, Adele Walsh, Kaiden Blake, and Sophie and Katie of the Mundie Moms.

A special thank-you to Dan Russo for ensuring that my Latin was correct; to Jenny and her mum, Janet, for helping me navigate the landscape of rural England; and to Gail Yates and Laura McCarthy for giving me the lowdown on historical Ireland.

Thank you to Morgan and Anthony, lifelong members of the Zink posse. And to Layla, the perfect writing partner.

There are never enough words to thank my mother, Claudia Baker, for her support and persistence in the difficult task of understanding and accepting me. When I think of the things for which I am most grateful in this life, you are right at the top.

Last, to the loves and lights of my life, Kenneth, Rebekah, Andrew, and Caroline. Everything is for and because of you.

And to you, dear readers, who make everything possible through the continued reading of my stories. I do not take your faith in me for granted.

Mount Laurel Library
100 Walt Whitman Avenue
Mount Laurel, NJ 08054-9539
856-234-7319
www.mtlaurel.lib.nj.us